ALFRED H. MENDES

I0740276

ALFRED H. MENDES

Short Stories, Articles and Letters

EDITED BY **MICHÈLE LEVY**

THE UNIVERSITY OF THE WEST INDIES PRESS
Jamaica • Barbados • Trinidad and Tobago

The University of the West Indies Press
7A Gibraltar Hall Road, Mona
Kingston 7, Jamaica
www.uwipress.com

© Michèle Levy, 2016

All rights reserved. Published 2016

A catalogue record of this book is available
from the National Library of Jamaica.

ISBN: 978-976-640-609-7 (print)
978-976-640-610-3 (Kindle)
978-976-640-611-0 (ePub)

Cover illustration: M.P. Alladin (Trinidad, 1919–1980), *Limbo Dancers* (oil on canvas, 1958). Image courtesy of 101 Art Gallery, Port of Spain, Trinidad and Tobago, 101artgallery.com. The publisher has tried unsuccessfully to contact the Alladin Estate copyright holder. Any corrections necessary will be made in future editions.

Cover and book design by Robert Harris
Set in Scala 10.25/15
Printed in the United States of America

To the memory of Alfred Hubert Mendes,
West Indian writer, 1897–1991

So long as men can breathe or eyes can see,
So long lives this, and this gives life to thee.
—*William Shakespeare, Sonnet 18*

CONTENTS

LETTERS

INTRODUCTION

ALFRED HUBERT MENDES (1897–1991) WAS BORN in Port of Spain, Trinidad, the eldest of six children. His forebears were Portuguese from the island of Madeira, followers of the Presbyterian minister Dr Robert Reid Kalley, who migrated to the West Indies in the nineteenth century to escape persecution for their faith by the Catholic Church in Madeira. His father, Alfred, was born in Trinidad, but his mother, Isabella Jardine, came from Grenada and was herself a devout Catholic. Alfred Mendes senior was deeply committed to the "Portuguese Church", St Ann's United Free Church of Scotland, and rose to positions of responsibility within its secular hierarchy. His parents' conflicting religious beliefs caused stresses within their marriage and within young Alfred's childhood, which later repeated themselves in his second, unhappy marriage to a Catholic, Juanita Gouveia. A strong vein of anti-Catholicism runs through many of his short stories and comes to the fore most prominently in his writings during the Divorce Debate which raged in Trinidad around 1931–1933. His third wife, Ellen Perachini, was also Catholic, and the opposition between these warring religious forces in Mendes's psyche was finally laid to rest when, at the age of sixty-nine, he remarried Ellen (for the third time) in the Catholic Church of the Assumption, Maraval.

Young Alfred Mendes was schooled in Trinidad at Queen's Royal College in Port of Spain until 1912, when he was sent to Hitchin Grammar School in Hertfordshire, England. His mother had died in 1911 and his father remarried a year later. His son appears to have been deeply affected by this remarriage, and it may have been for his own sake as much as for domestic harmony that his father sent him abroad.

Mendes enjoyed his time at Hitchin. He was gregarious and made many friends there, and participated fully in his school's activities, especially those of a literary nature. He would almost certainly have continued on to university after finishing his schooling, but this ended abruptly with the outbreak of the Great War in 1914.

Mendes's father brought him back to Trinidad in 1915, but Mendes had briefly come in contact with the First World War during a visit to France with his tutor which coincided with the outbreak of hostilities, and he seems to have been infected then with the desire to play a part in it. No sooner was he back home than he enlisted in the Merchants' and Planters' Contingent of Trinidad and sailed back to Europe, where he joined up as an infantryman in the King's Royal Rifles. He was sent to the Belgian front, where he had first-hand experience of the horrors of trench warfare. He fought bravely but was invalided out of the conflict shortly before the end of the war, when he accidentally inhaled poisonous mustard gas. He was awarded the Military Medal for courage in the field in 1918.

Mendes fought alongside working-class British soldiers, "Tommies". He developed an enormous respect for their bravery and cheerful endurance of the most appalling conditions, and the camaraderie he experienced with them stayed with him all his life and coloured his political thinking. Contemporary with the Great War and also highly important as a formative influence, not just in his political thinking but also in his creative development, was the great social upheaval in Russia resulting from the Bolshevik Revolution of October 1917. Mendes's view of the Russian Revolution tended to be idealistic, but even after, much later, he rejected the excesses of hard-line Marxism, he remained socialist in sympathy until the end of his days.

Mendes returned to Trinidad in 1919 and went to work with his father. Alfred Mendes senior had a head for business. From the family grocery shop at 52 South Quay, he expanded into agriculture, acquiring properties both in Trinidad and Tobago that grew cocoa, coconuts, citrus and tonka beans, and investing in a factory that made alpargatas, a kind of sandal made of cloth. Mendes did not enjoy the world of commerce, but it enabled him to meet and interact with Trinidadians from all walks of life and from different racial backgrounds. His interest in people generally found a focal point in the rural and urban working classes whom he encountered on a daily basis as he toured the island on his father's business affairs. He had started to write as soon as he returned to the island, and poured his experiences into short stories which he wrote at night after the working day had ended.

In 1919 Mendes met and married his first wife, Jessie Rodriguez. They had a son, Alfred John, the following year. The marriage was a happy one, but Jessie died tragically of pneumonia in 1921, while pregnant with their second child. Mendes remarried a year later, but this second marriage was a failure. Juanita Mendes, "Nita", was a devout Catholic. She seems to have tried to bring Mendes's young son Alfred John into her own church, and was in addition unsympathetic towards his writing ambitions and friendships with other aspiring writers of different races and social classes. Mendes at this time was involved in the activities of the Portuguese Church, although he later rejected organized religion and professed agnosticism. The struggle ended with the little boy being sent to school in England at the age of eight. Mendes and Nita remained together for some years, but they were basically incompatible, and by the time Mendes left for New York City in October 1933 they had both gone their separate ways.

Mendes's interest in writing dated from his schooldays at Hitchin Grammar School. He had edited the school magazine there, and written articles and poems for it, and realized at that young age that what he really wanted to do was to write for a living. During his years in Trinidad from 1919 to 1933 he produced a huge volume of short stories, wrote poems and articles for the *Trinidad Guardian*, and wrote three and a quarter novels. One of these was *Pitch Lake*, and the quarter was to become *Black Fauns*, which he finished after moving to New York. Early in the 1920s he met C.L.R. James, who was then a schoolmaster at Queen's Royal College, and they attracted a group of like-minded aspiring writers and intellectuals who met regularly, often at Mendes's home on Richmond Street, to exchange ideas, read their works to each other, and listen to music. Prominent among them was Ralph de Boissière.

Between 1926 and 1927 Mendes helped the Reverend Gilbert Earle to edit the *Trinidad Presbyterian*. He published stories of his own in it, as well as poems and a series of critical pieces on past and contemporary poets, the "Pen

Portraits". Two other journals, the *Quarterly Magazine of the Richmond Street Literary and Debating Association*, edited by W.H. Dolly, and the *Quarterly Magazine*, edited by Austin M. Nolte, enabled the young writers to publish their work locally. In 1927 they had their first foreign publication when the English *Saturday Review* published James's short story "La Divina Pastora". Mendes and his friend Algernon "Pope" Wharton followed with their joint effort "Lai John", which was published by the *London Mercury* in January 1929, and in 1930 by Edward J. O'Brien in *Best Short Stories of 1929*. Mendes and James together edited *Trinidad* 1, no. 1, in December 1929, a collection of stories intended to raise money to help James to meet certain obligations, and *Trinidad* 1, no. 2, in April 1930. Then from March 1931 until November 1933, all intellectual activity and writing centred on the *Beacon*, edited by Albert Gomes. Mendes continued to send his stories to foreign journals, and between 1930 and 1934 a number of his shorter stories (called by the English editors "short shorts") appeared in the *Manchester Guardian*.

During the *Beacon* years Mendes became involved in two issues that made him for a time notorious, one of which was to have a lasting effect on him. The colonial government introduced a bill that would permit divorce, and a young man who worked in Mendes senior's alpargata factory brought an action for libel against Mendes. The divorce bill met with fierce opposition from Trinidad's Catholics, and during the years leading up to its becoming law, 1931–1933, the entire society was polarized with factions for and against. Mendes, who had been brought up in the Presbyterian Church and was unhappily married to a Catholic, was actively pro-divorce, bombarding the newspapers with articles and letters, and putting up posters all over Port of Spain in the early morning hours with like-minded friends. He caused considerable offence to Trinidad's Catholics with one article, "Revolt", and the governor, Sir Alfred Claud Hollis, indicated to Mendes's father that he would be well advised to send his son out of the country as the Catholic faction was considering bringing a suit for blasphemy against him. Mendes took the advice and went to Grenada, where he had relatives, and stayed there until the bill was passed, on 1 January 1933.[1]

He was certainly encouraged to do so by the "Sweetman" libel case. He had encountered an attractive but irresponsible young man named Septimus Louhar who worked in his father's alpargata factory, and had put him in a story, "Sweetman", which was published in the *Beacon*. Unfortunately, he kept the name "Seppy" for the protagonist. The *Beacon* enjoyed wide distribution across the social spectrum, and Louhar heard about the story and brought a case of libel against the *Beacon*'s editor, Albert Gomes, the writer, Mendes, and the printer, Lloyd Smith. He won.[2] Mendes was ever afterwards nervous of courts of law. He changed the name of his protagonist to "Maxie" for future publications of the story, and subsequently avoided using names that could be traced to "real" people.

C.L.R. James left for the United Kingdom in February 1932, and Mendes went to the United States in October 1933, a month before the *Beacon* folded, apart from a single issue in 1939, from chronic lack of funding. In leaving Trinidad, both men were motivated by their desire for an environment more conducive to intellectual activity and with greater opportunities for publishing their writings.

Mendes had made over his house on Richmond Street with all its contents, including an extensive library of first editions, to Nita, before he left. He therefore had very little money of his own during the years of the Great Depression in the United States. He lived initially with his brother Frank in Baldwin, Long Island, and found work with the Federal Writers' Project of the Roosevelt Works Progress Administration (WPA). This included a travel book about Long Island, which he co-wrote with other WPA authors, and a guide to the World's Fair of 1939, for which he was solely responsible. He met several other writers at the WPA and socialized among all the leading intellectual groups and literary salons of the day. His particular friends were Benjamin Appel, Malcolm Lowry, William Saroyan and Dorothy McLeary, for whom he wrote "Lulu Gets Married" and to whom he dedicated *Black Fauns* after completing it. Among the writers of the Harlem Renaissance his closest friends were Countee Cullen, Dorothy West, Harold Jackman, and the Jamaican writer Claude McKay.

During the seven years that he lived in New York, Mendes published two novels, *Pitch Lake* (1934) and *Black Fauns* (1935) with Gerald Duckworth, and a number of short stories with "little" magazines such as the *Magazine* and *Story*, and Dorothy West's *Challenge*. He had written three complete novels before he left Trinidad. He wrote another five novels while in New York, including a sequel to *Black Fauns*, but he burned the seven unpublished manuscripts in the course of an emotional crisis before his return to Trinidad in 1940.

In 1935 Mendes had met Ellen Perachini. She became his third wife in 1938 after he had obtained a Mexican divorce from Nita, and their son Peter was born in 1939. Mendes's finances were at a low ebb at this stage. His job with the WPA had come to an end, and he had worked at anything that came his way, including lecturing on literature to women's reading groups and selling vacuum cleaners from door to door for Electrolux. He was eventually forced to go on welfare. His application for American citizenship was turned down because the federal government did not recognize his Mexican divorce. The disappointment, coupled with constant worry over finances and the pressure of a young family, brought on a nervous breakdown, which is as close as one can get to understanding why Mendes burned his novels. He never fully explained his reasons.

Mendes obtained a divorce from Nita in Trinidad in 1940, remarried Ellen, and returned to Trinidad with his family in August of that year. Once home, he again worked in his father's many businesses. He did not, however, abandon writing. He wrote some more stories and published them, along with others which he had written earlier, in the *Trinidad Sunday Guardian*, and he began writing articles consistently for the *Guardian*. He had written several pieces on a variety of subjects before leaving for New York, and he now became particularly interested in the arts of his country, in the painters, sculptors, dancers, actors and playwrights, all making names for themselves as Trinidad moved towards independence from the United Kingdom. In the latter part of the decade of the 1940s he became arts critic for the *Guardian*.

In 1946 Mendes joined the colonial civil service as accountant, Harbour and Wharves. He did well in the position, and in 1949 he was appointed deputy general manager of the Port Services Department, and in 1950 was sent on a nine-month tour of ports in the United States and the United Kingdom. In 1955 he was appointed general manager of the Port Services Department, but disliked the political pressures placed on him by the high-profile position, and retired from the Port Services in 1957.[3]

Mendes had briefly involved himself in politics, first with the West Indian National Party, and then by helping Jack Kelshall to found the left-wing United Front Party[4] in 1946 and travelling around the island with his party on the hustings. He does not seem to have played an active role in politics beyond the defeat of the United Front in the general election of 1 July 1946, although he was always keenly interested in the government of his country and the people who represented it.

After retiring from the civil service, Mendes worked again with his father. In 1966 he joined the Singer Sewing Machine Company as personnel and industrial relations manager. He was with Singer until 1972, during which time he travelled extensively throughout the West Indies on business for the company, and edited the in-house magazine, the *Trinidad Singer*. He wrote editorials for the little magazine, and published some stories and poems of his own in it. During this period he met a young woman of nineteen, Rowena Scott. She became his muse for a short time, and he wrote nine sonnets out of a projected twenty in the Shakespearean manner for her.[5]

In 1972 the University of the West Indies awarded Alfred Mendes an honorary doctor of letters degree for his contribution to West Indian literature. In the same year he retired from Singer. In 1974 he moved with Ellen to Barbados, where they were to live happily for the rest of their lives. Mendes began writing his autobiography in 1975. He persevered with it for two years, but found the effort involved taxing and abandoned the manuscript at the point of his return to Trinidad from New York in 1940. In 1978, in response to requests from scholars interested in his life and times, he produced another draft covering his life in Trinidad until his retirement in Barbados, so there is a complete record of his memories until 1978.[6]

The decade of the 1970s saw the republication of Mendes's novels *Pitch Lake* and *Black Fauns*, and the publication of the collected issues of the *Beacon*. *Pitch Lake* and *Black Fauns* were later republished by New Beacon Books in 1980 and 1984 respectively, and John La Rose of New Beacon Books convinced Mendes to compile a collection of his short stories for publication. The manuscript, called by Mendes *A Pattern of People*, with an introduction by himself, was sent to La Rose in 1983, but was never published. By this time, Mendes's memory was failing. He wrote nothing more apart from letters to family and friends. On 3 February 1991 Ellen Mendes died, and Alfred Mendes followed on 21 August of the same year. They are buried together in Christ Church Cemetery in Christ Church, Barbados.

THE STORIES

Alfred Mendes came to recognize that his true strengths as a writer were to be found in fiction. Since only the two published novels *Pitch Lake* and *Black Fauns* survive of the nine that he wrote, his short stories remain the yardstick by which his creative abilities may most readily be judged. And the title for the collection of stories which he put together for John La Rose in 1983, *A Pattern of People*, reveals where his chief interests are to be found.

The inscription on Mendes's headstone reads, "Alfred Hubert Mendes, West Indian Writer, 1897–1991". The first four collections of his works which I have edited were designed to illustrate his "West Indianness", and in fact most of his short stories and his novels do have a West Indian setting. This latest selection, however, includes one story set on a farm in a cold climate ("The Cat") and two autobiographical stories set in New York City ("The Larsons at Home" and "Cold Turkey"). In keeping with my usual practice, I have mixed stories that have never been published with stories that have previously appeared, chiefly in "little" magazines and journals that are now difficult to locate, if indeed they have survived. The exceptions are the two *Beacon* stories: "Without Snow" and "Ursula's Morals".

Both published and unpublished stories cover a wide range of Mendes's interests and experiences. In keeping with his vision of Trinidad as a multiracial "melting-pot" society, the West Indian stories include characters of Chinese, Syrian, East Indian, Spanish and Portuguese origins, as well as African-Trinidadians and English expatriates. Interestingly, in the New York story "Cold Turkey", many of the vacuum-cleaner salesmen are recent immigrants to the United States.

The earliest of the published stories, "The Cat", was one of a group which Mendes wrote especially for the *Trinidad Presbyterian*. The other stories are "The Cowardly Spider", "The Little Grey Mouse", "Roses", "The Sport of the Gods" and "A Thing of Beauty". They appear to have been intended as a counterblast to certain stories for children published in the magazine, which offered a too-complacent view of a world in which cruelty and death had no place.

In "The Cat" Mendes writes in the persona of a girl of nine or ten years. A retrospective, like "My Mother Was Left Alone" and "Scapular", it shows his ability to evoke the period of childhood as a time set completely apart from adulthood, with its own pains, its uncertainties, its fleeting pleasures and its despairs. A time of isolation, and possibly of loneliness.

The story is set on a farm in an unspecified foreign country. Events take place against a background of farm life and the changing seasons, with the final, inevitable tragedy occurring appropriately in winter. The protagonist, who is never named – she is "Child" to her Aunt Eliza – is an orphan whose only sibling, Susie, has died some time ago. She lives with her spinster aunt, Eliza. The relationship between the protagonist and the cat, which she names "Susie" after her sister, perhaps in an attempt to recreate her own family, is the normal loving relationship that often exists between animals and small children. No explanation is given for the aunt's paranoid dislike and fear of the cat. Maybe it is an intended contrast to the love and trust between her niece and Susie. There is certainly a strong element of the supernatural in Susie's demonic pursuit of Aunt Eliza after the drowning of her kittens, but as in the best ghost stories, the real terror lies in "horrible imaginings".

"Lai John", co-authored with Mendes's friend and fellow *Beacon* writer Algernon "Pope" Wharton, was the first of Mendes's stories to be published abroad. It is a brilliant story which deserves to be better known. Additionally, it is the first in a series of stories which Mendes wrote about relationships between working-class Chinese men and beautiful, often treacherous, creole women of mixed race, usually, as in this story, set against the background of the illegal opium trade. Two such are "Her Chinaman's Way" (*Pablo's Fandango*) and "A Little Cargo" (*Selected Writings*). "Damp" (*Beacon* 2, no. 4) is about a Chinese restaurant owner and a beautiful waitress who is, unbeknown to the customer who tries to win her for himself, the owner's mistress. An unpublished story, "For Ways That Are Dark", relates the adventure at sea which follows Maria's betrayal of Hong Wing in "Her Chinaman's Way", and ends with Hong Wing the sole survivor. The opium connection is sustained in "Bête Rouge" with Bête Rouge's Chinese customer Lee Sang and in "Profit on Opium" in which a Chinese shopkeeper named Wing Sang is used to set up a scam to cheat a young Portuguese man out of one hundred dollars. Wing Sang appears only in name in this story.

The successful Chinese shopkeeper, unconnected with the opium trade, appears as Chin Lee in "Gold Beans" (*Selected Writings*) and as "Sing Lee and Co.", rich Chinese shopkeepers with a string of shops, in "Pablo's Fandango"

(*Pablo's Fandango*). Mendes would have encountered their like on a regular basis as he rode around the island on his father's business affairs. There were Chinese restaurants in Trinidad at the time, and the opium trade remained a thorn in the side of the colonial police. Like Maria in "Her Chinaman's Way" Felicia in "One Day for John Small" (*The Man Who Ran Away*) has a baby for her keeper, Lee Sing, and Mrs Kai Chin in "The Man Who Ran Away" (*The Man Who Ran Away*) has a mixed-race daughter, Philomen.

Mendes was friendly with two gifted middle-class Chinese women: the artist Amy Leong Pang, one of the original members of the Trinidad Society of Independents, and the journalist and painter Ivy Achoy. Both women were *Beacon* contributors and both served respectively as models for the Chinese characters in "Not a Love Story" and "Three Rebels" (*The Man Who Ran Away*). "Lai John", however, establishes Mendes as an interpreter of relations between working-class Chinese immigrants and working-class Trinidadians of other races. The characterization is superb: scrawny, fearful Lai John with his tiny, blackened "mouse teeth"; greedy, voluptuous, treacherous Lucia; and the scornful, racist black and Venezuelan sailors. In this story, as in its successors, the Chinese man emerges as the survivor. The timid, seasick, peace-loving Lai John evolves with brutal suddenness into a calculating and cold-blooded murderer when his own life and future are at stake.

With the publication of "My Mother Was Left Alone" and "The Larsons at Home", the only story remaining to be republished in the manuscript of *A Pattern of People* is "On the Seventh Day", which is a shorter version of "The Good Sloop *Grenville Lass*" (*Pablo's Fandango*). Mendes clearly thought highly of these stories, as he selected them for an anthology which he considered representative of his interests and strengths. "My Mother Was Left Alone" and "Caribbean Scare" seem to belong to a period later than "Lai John" but slightly earlier than the *Beacon*. "Caribbean Scare" may have been written early in the period 1930–1933, when Mendes wrote a number of very short stories about different aspects of West Indian life for a number of English journals, especially the *Manchester Guardian*.

"Tropic Town", also co-authored with "Pope" Wharton, was written no earlier than March 1931, when the first issue of the *Beacon* appeared, based on an internal reference to the journal. I have not found any record of its being offered for publication, strangely, because it is a brilliant study of middle-

and upper-class social mores within a colonial community, called for some reason "Tenessa", but instantly recognizable as Trinidad. Mendes himself wrote another version of it, "Bert and Betty Briggs – English" (*Pablo's Fandango*), which he sent to England at some stage, in the hope that it could be published there.[7]

Where there is no internal evidence to point to the timing of unpublished stories, I have sometimes had to depend on "feel", which may not always be a reliable indicator. I do strongly feel, though, that "My Mother Was Left Alone" belongs to a period earlier than the *Beacon*, when Mendes may still have been trying to come to terms with the death of his mother when he was fourteen, projecting his own jealousy and resentment of his stepmother onto the young girl, Elizabeth. Like "The Cat", it is a reminiscence of childhood seen through the eyes of a child of nine or ten years, but narrated by that child grown older.

Elizabeth lives with her widowed mother Tessie Lou. They are poor but contented, with a predictable but secure existence. Well-meaning friends invite them for a week's holiday at their beach house with the intention of reuniting Tessie Lou with an old flame. Elizabeth is sensitive and artistic. She contemplates one day becoming a writer. Forbidden to play the piano, or to play with the black caretaker's children, and feeling herself shunted aside by her mother's growing interest in the old flame, Elizabeth experiences corrosive jealousy, turning into a savage little animal and biting her mother on the thigh when her mother, for the first time ever, slaps her across her face.

Some mystery precedes the events in the story concerning the earlier rejection of the mother's current suitor and the death of the father, but as in "The Cat" it is merely hinted at, to avoid distraction from the build-up of psychological tensions which, in each case, lead to a violent climax.

"Caribbean Scare" is a war story of sorts. It is a short, humorous study of the speed with which rumours take hold in a small island community. The year is 1915, the same year in which Mendes joined the Merchants' and Planters' Contingent and went off to war in Europe, and Fernando's nightmare of broken young bodies on the field of battle is what Mendes himself experienced, the reality behind the humour. Fernando, a timid barber of Spanish extraction, has eight daughters and a wife exhausted by the birth of the last. A rumour reaches his shop that a German warship has entered the Gulf of Paria, and the humour builds with the growing apprehension of Fernando, the nervousness which causes him to nick his client's ear, his drenching of his own head with bay rum in an effort to calm his nerves, and his gullible acceptance of Mr Hamel-Levitt's teasing assertion that an attacking German force is unlikely to pursue him into the hills to his house in Cascade. The frantic haste with which Fernando hustles his wife and daughters into a taxi which speeds off to Cascade sweeps the reader along with it, only to collapse into anticlimax when the family realize that in all the panic they have forgotten the baby at home.

"Tropic Town" is a story of Trinidad's colonial middle class. It follows the career of Cockney expatriates who emigrate to "Tenessa" when the husband loses his job, and ruthlessly climb the social ladder there. They are poorly educated, but because they are "English" they are able to cross class barriers that would have been insurmountable in their own country and end up being written up in the social column of the *Beacon* along with the cream of colonial society. In the process they are befriended and assisted by the exquisite Portuguese creole Antonia and her friends. Antonia, educated in England and Paris, is a talented musician, actress and artist, and the means by which the Smiths are introduced into theatrical circles. They do not hesitate to "drop" her when the English Dramatic Society invites the husband to become a member, and the final rueful commentary on their social success is written by Antonia in a letter to her friend and supporter, Freddie, at a much later date.

An excellent study of the tensions within the upper echelons of colonial society, the story is fraught with ironies, and with a satirical inflexion which may owe something to Mendes's own status as a third-generation Portuguese creole in a country governed by a foreign power.

"Jacob Ayoub" is the only complete story in which Mendes treats the small Syrian population in Trinidad at the time. The itinerant Syrian pedlar was well known throughout the West Indies in the early part of the twentieth century, and there were many success stories associated with him. There is a Syrian pedlar in "Lulu Gets Married", Habib, and in *Black Fauns* a Syrian pedlar and moneylender, also named Habib.[8] In both cases the pedlar is regarded as an alien by the women of the barrack-yards, humiliated and dismissed by Josephine in "Lulu Gets Married" as "Syrian bitch", and also referred to as "the Syrian bitch" by Ethelrida in *Black Fauns*, although she has been his customer for some time. Jacob Ayoub, however, does not interact with working-class characters apart from members of his own family, his hard-working father and brothers. He is better educated than they, has been to school, and is entrusted with buying goods for their business. However, he is a spendthrift, con artist and "sweetman", kept by various wealthy women. He has married well, the daughter of a wealthy Portuguese merchant, and had children with her. But after he has reduced his family to bankruptcy by his personal extravagance, he relies on a wealthy Englishwoman whom he meets on board ship to bail him out. She takes him to London, where there is every indication that he will abandon her for other, wealthier "keepers". A success story, perhaps, but not in the conventional sense.

"Without Snow", alternatively titled "Richard", is set in Port of Spain. The action takes place on Christmas Eve against a backcloth of seasonal gaiety. The characters are Portuguese creole, and members of the middle class. The story is a study of obsession. The narrator, Albert, like Mendes recently returned from the war, is married to Isabella. Richard, married to Albert's sister Inez, is obsessively in love with Isabella. He has hypnotic powers, and like Svengali in George du Maurier's novel *Trilby*, influences Isabella into playing on the piano a Rachmaninov prelude which she has never learned. There is an element of the demon lover in Richard. He has previously tried to strangle his own wife, but she continues to love him although she realizes he is demented. Tension builds in the household among the Christmas guests. When only the four family members are left, Albert succumbs to a hypnotic trance, from which he is only roused by the screams of his wife. Bursting into their bedroom, he finds Richard in the act of strangling a naked Isabella, apparently to make her finally his own. Albert then brains him with a chair and puts an end to him, hypnotic powers and all.

Mendes was interested in mental disorders. While in New York he wrote a long story, "Another Passion" (unpublished), a study of religious mania which ends in self-mutilation. "Without Snow" works especially through the power of suggestion of some darker influence behind Richard's obsession. His sinister, black-clad figure moves through all the Christmas festivity like an emblem of evil, while the clock which strikes from the Sacred Heart tower reminds of the Nativity, light and life. His powers, however, can be explained by his obsession which borders on madness, and his ability to hypnotize his victims. It is due to Mendes's own powers of description and command of narrative that this story grips, holds the attention, and entertains.

"Young Da Costa" is openly autobiographical. Mendes refers to himself as "Alfred", and he is clearly older than Joe da Costa, who comes to talk to him, not about literature, as he expects, but about a love interest. The name Joe da Costa connects the story with *Pitch Lake*, the protagonist of which is also Joe da Costa. But although this story may owe something to Joe in the novel's womanizing, that is as far as it goes. This Joe is educated, an aspiring writer, and the young lady he fancies himself in love with is also educated, unlike Joe a Catholic, and of mixed race. She is also a young lady of spirit, for when she hears of his mother and sister's disapproval of their friendship, she tells Joe that if she is not good enough for them, she is not good enough for him. Perhaps Mendes projects something of himself onto Joe's flitting from one girl to the next. The anti-Catholic passage on pages 71–72, certainly; his wife at the time would have been Nita.

This is an interesting little story. It suggests that racial tensions existed among Mendes's own people, the Portuguese creoles of Trinidad. It also shows Mendes in his role of mentor to young writers, seated in his study against a background of "about a thousand books".

A relationship between a Portuguese man and a girl of mixed race is also the subject of "Ursula's Morals" (or "The Visit"), but with a significant difference. Ursula and Tony are already lovers, and Ursula, a modern, realistic young woman, accepts that Tony's family and friends would not countenance a marriage between them, and she has in any case no desire to get married. As in "Water Piece" (*Beacon* 1, no. 8) Mendes provides sexy details of the relationship, in keeping with his intention, put forward in "A Commentary", to write openly about human sexuality. Ironically, the lover, Tony, is a timid fellow (Mendes is not above making fun of his own compatriots), terrified of Ursula's overly protective mother and not altogether comfortable with Ursula's open enjoyment of their love-making. The mother herself, in a double irony returning home unexpectedly through concern over her daughter's "headache", will probably drive him away permanently through her plans to entice him into marriage with Ursula. Though working-class herself, she has ambitions for her daughter to rise in the world through marriage into the middle class. As in "Ramjit Das" parents' plans for their children clash with those of their children, born with expectations of greater freedom in directing the courses of their own lives.

"The Larsons at Home" takes place over a single afternoon stretching into evening and including supper and after. It is autobiographical, about a family named Sagar with whom Mendes boarded for a time in New York.[9] The Sagars were a gifted family reduced to poverty by the Depression, and Mendes himself, whose finances were constantly at a low ebb, could sympathize with them and appreciate their gallant fight against adversity. He thought well enough of this story to include it in *A Pattern of People*, and wrote a sad follow-up in his (unpublished) introduction to the collection:

> I lodged and boarded with a family during the Great Depression of the '30s and I could not resist the temptation of portraying them as I saw them. Their plenitude of life, their amazing vitality, their startling dissimilarities in looks, in temperaments, in ideas, in ambitions, their courage, their stoical acceptance of the loss of their prosperity – I was held in thrall to them. After my return to Trinidad I wondered how they would survive. They didn't, for two years later a letter informed me that the younger son, on his return from war, shot himself in the head, and a little later the mother and daughter died of cancer in the breast – a tragic end to a noble family.

The story is heavily dependent on dialogue, and the differentiation of character is brilliantly achieved through tricks of speech as well as the exchange of ideas. The Larson family represents a microcosm of American society during the Depression, with the father a diehard Republican, a kind man who makes unfortunate remarks about Hitler and the Jewish people, and the elder son, Malcolm, a Marxist in sympathy, open and tolerant of all peoples and with sensible ideas, but selfish, dodging his fair share of the household work. The mother, a human dynamo and workaholic, keeps the family together with an iron hand and tries to bridge the gap between father and older son, occasionally overlooking the younger son, who is helpful and more sensitive than his brother. The rapid, unflagging exchanges of ideas and opinions, the political debates and arguments that carry family and boarder/observer through the evening until all the stresses come to a head, make this an unforgettable as well as an unusual story.

Both "The Larsons at Home" and "Cold Turkey" belong to a period when

Mendes, then living in New York City, found himself chronically short of funds. His assignment with the WPA had ended in 1937, and he worked at whatever came his way, including selling vacuum cleaners from door to door for Electrolux. "Cold Turkey" was written by December 1937. In a letter to Ellen, who was then living in Long Beach, California, Mendes mentions sending the story to *Esquire* magazine. *Esquire* rejected it because of its similarity to a story which they had published the month before. Mendes subsequently published it in a slightly altered version in the *Trinidad Singer*, which he edited from 1966 to 1972. Unfortunately, though a copy of the printed story was sent to Mendes's family in the late 1990s by a friend, there is no date given for the issue in which it appeared. And when, some years ago, I contacted Singer in Trinidad, to enquire whether they had archived the publications, I was told that all their copies of the magazine had been destroyed. Despite its late publication, I have kept the story in the chronological sequence in which it was written, to give some idea of Mendes's interests and activities at a particular time in his writing career.

The story is about Mendes's going to Electrolux to find work, and the training which he undergoes before being unleashed on the streets of New York. There is a gulf between the educated, cosmopolitan and committed writer and the working-class Americans, most of them immigrants, who work as salesmen, but they share a common bond – fighting for survival in a time of soul-destroying hardship. It is an acutely observed, funny study, again with Mendes's sharp ear for peculiarities of speech, but behind the humour lies the grim reality of their common poverty.

"Yellow Legs" is a later story, written after Mendes's return to Trinidad from New York. References to the Second World War and Oswald Mosley's Blackshirts place it after 1940, but before the end of the war in 1945. It is also autobiographical, and like "Gold Beans" and "Orinoco Interlude" (*Pablo's Fandango*) a hybrid, part-story, part-journalism and part-travel piece. It refers to an interesting slice of West Indian history, the transportation of men and women of south-west England who had fought in the Duke of Monmouth's rebellion against King James II to Barbados to work as labourers, from where many of them later moved to Grenada. Mendes himself went to Grenada to view the settlement there and his story, though fascinating, paints a bleak picture of poverty, inbreeding and malnutrition. He captures the peculiarities of the

"Yellow Legs'" speech very well, the original dialect of south-west England in the late seventeenth century overlaid by patterns of West Indian Creole.

Mendes loved Grenada. His preoccupation is with the people, the "Yellow Legs" and the stories which they have to tell, but he cannot avoid slipping in the occasional, lyrical description of the lush beauties of the island, in particular the magnificent sunset which has, ironically, no meaning for the underfed and demoralized "Yellow Legs".

Mendes wrote several stories about East Indians in Trinidad. His interest in their culture may well have been stimulated by an affair which he had had with a young Indian woman after his second marriage broke down. According to Ralph de Boissière, he spent many nights with her in a barrack-yard.[10] His stories about East Indians in Trinidad include "Boodhoo" and "Béti" (*The Man Who Ran Away*), "And Then the Hurricane Came" (*Pablo's Fandango*), "A Life" (*Selected Writings*), "Gold Beans", and the three (unpublished) versions of "Old East in New West". "Ramjit Das", the latest of the stories to be published here, owes much to the details of an East Indian wedding described in "Old East in New West". The story is simple: an Indian father arranges a traditional marriage for his son with a young girl, still a child, from a neighbouring village. The young man, however, is in love with a girl of his own age, from his own village. He rejects the customs of his people and elopes with her during the wedding festivities. He is later discovered, poor but happy, in Port of Spain, having married his Rampatia in a registry office. His father curses him, but his mother, who had herself been subjected to an arranged marriage, is sympathetic. She loves her son and wishes for his happiness, and in herself represents a bridge between old and new worlds.

Like "Ursula's Morals", "Ramjit Das" presents a conflict between traditional cultural expectations and lifestyles and new ideas of love and marriage. Without discounting the humiliation of the old father, it suggests that accommodation with new world perspectives may be both possible and desirable. A story of youth and age, it ends on a cautious note of hope for the future.

ARTICLES AND LETTERS

Mendes's lifelong interest in people, and especially the people of his native Trinidad, informs all of his writing. It is especially evident in his journalism, where there is always the possibility of being challenged by readers who take exception to his views. There are some lively exchanges in letters during his years as arts critic for the *Trinidad Guardian*, and in the wake of the late critical piece "Two Cromwells", a controversy that ran for three weeks in print.

Most of Mendes's journalism was written during the 1940s, especially from 1947 to 1949, when as arts critic for the *Guardian* he was writing a column for the newspaper every week, on paintings, sculpture, the dance and the theatre. However, he did write a number of articles before he left for New York City in October 1933 on a range of topics, including the "Pen Portraits" for the *Trinidad Presbyterian*; some arts reviews, political commentaries and letters for the *Guardian*; an editorial and "A Commentary" for *Trinidad* 1, no. 2; and articles and letters for the *Beacon* on various topics, including an (undistinguished) contribution to the *Beacon*'s notorious debate on whether people of European extraction were more intelligent than people of colour. He also wrote the occasional editorial for the *Beacon*, but as its editorials were not signed it would be difficult to determine which ones were written by Mendes or "Pope" Wharton in the absence of Albert Gomes. He is known to have written the editorial for *Trinidad* 1, no. 2, though, as C.L.R. James had not been as involved in its production as he had been in *Trinidad* 1, no. 1. The *Trinidad* editorial is the first piece of this selection of Mendes's journalism. I have reproduced it with its original subheadings, to preserve a sense of the publication as it appeared, as well as the concerns of Mendes and his group.

For the pieces from the *Guardian* I have removed the highlightings, which are not always to the point and tend to distract from the flow of the argument. In some cases where a typescript has survived I have preferred it to the printed piece if the reproduction of the latter is poor. I have worked with photocopies from the University of Florida microfilm of the *Guardian*, and in many cases the print has become blurred with age or, due to folds in the newspapers at the time, indecipherable. In some cases the *Guardian* version has been abridged, and then I have replaced it with a typescript if available, as more representative of Mendes's development of his ideas in arriving at a critical judgement (for example, "Trinidad's First Sculptor", *Trinidad Guardian* 19 October 1947).

As with Mendes's stories, I have arranged his articles and letters in chronological sequence of their appearance, to illustrate the different phases of Mendes's interests, as well as the evolution of his critical style.

Trinidad 1, no. 2 was a much more elaborate production than *Trinidad* 1, no. 1. In his editorial Mendes describes the labour of love that went into its production and the difficulty of financing it, which will probably mean that despite his hopes for a quarterly magazine, this issue will be the last. He refers to the criticism of 1, no. 1, especially of James's short story "Triumph" (which he will address more fully in his "Commentary"), stating: "We do not flee what has been curiously called 'criticism'. There is no closer critic of our work than ourselves." (Despite this brave assertion, Mendes was not always accepting of criticism of his writings from his readers.) He covers the harbour scheme and proposed Early Closing Ordinance, writes approvingly of Soviet Russia and suggests that Christ was the first socialist. He deplores the commercialization of the annual carnival: "All we ask of Mr Wrigley is to stick to his gum and leave Carnival alone in her labour: to the intent that when the tents are struck the long columns may go ringing down the road making a little light of life and singing the last songs." And in welcoming the new Governor Sir Claud Hollis to Trinidad, he takes the opportunity to puncture the pomposity of a certain Mr Charles F. Wood.

Mendes's claim not to object to criticism of his writings is quickly put to the test. Dr W.V. Tothill, who later contributed to the *Beacon*, had complained of obscenity in Mendes's epigrams, and that the blasphemy which he detected in one story, "René de Malmâtre" by E.G. Benson, needed to be humorous to escape censure ("More About 'Trinidad'", *Trinidad Guardian* 9 May 1930). There is no need to read Dr Tothill's article to appreciate Mendes's response. In "A Retort Courteous" he deals with Dr Tothill's objections point by point and demolishes them with tremendous vigour and relish.

Two of the articles anthologized here are descriptions of concerts given in Port of Spain. The first, "They Are Artistes", belongs to Mendes's earlier period, and is a great deal longer than the pieces of the 1940s. He uses the opportunity to ponder the way music as an art form works for him person-ally: "There can be no fixed standards by which an individual's capacity for appreciation of the arts may be measured", a conviction that informs all of his critical writings; and mentions another tenet which he holds dear: great art holds in itself "that touch that makes the whole world kin". He spends so much time pondering the effects of music and discussing the performances of the musicians, a Spanish group named Los Alpinos, that he has very little space to devote to the singer/dancer Mariucha. A decade later, in the pieces which he wrote on Beryl McBurnie and the Little Carib,[11] he will give singing and dancing their proper due.

"Black Dot Quintette Praised" belongs to the period when Mendes was writing regular reviews for the *Guardian*. It is a good example of the occasionally highly idiosyncratic nature of his critical appreciations. The piece is considerably shorter than "They Are Artistes". Mendes wastes no time on one concert, "Calaloo of 1948". It "failed dismally". On the other hand, he remarks of the choral singing group the Black Dot Quintette, "This quintette is good", before he has even heard them. Mendes is having a bit of fun here: he goes on to explain in detail why he likes this group so much. His assertion that one of its members, Ken Oxley, should not sing solos provokes a defensive letter from Oxley's teacher, and the abrupt dismissal of "Calaloo of 1948" a vehement letter of protest from a member of the audience. In his own letter to the editor in response, "Critic Defends His Opinion", Mendes gives short shrift to these objections and reiterates his right to his personal reaction as critic, even though it may differ from that of the audience on the night in question. As, in both cases, it seems to have done.

Mendes wrote a number of articles on Trinidad's art scene. Of the six pieces that deal with art and artists, "The Significance of Mr Vassilieff" and "Art Takes Shape and Form in Trinidad" were written before Mendes left for New York. They are careful, conscientious assessments, but they do suffer from name-dropping, an occasional fault especially in Mendes's early writings, as though he were conducting a conversation with carefully selected *cognoscenti*. Daniel Vassilieff was from the Ukraine. He was very friendly with Mendes, and after he left Trinidad they kept in touch by letter. Mendes says nice things about "Dan", even if he does not afford him the accolade of being "a great painter".

The review of the art exhibition at the Garrett Galleries is important because for Mendes it "unmistakably shows that the amorphous consciousness of the island is beginning to take artistic shape and form". Mendes always claimed that for Trinidad's art to be truly indigenous, it must incorporate a total sense of the island and its peoples. Unerringly, he identifies the paintings of Hugh Stollmeyer as the most significant of the entries. Like "Mr Vassilieff", it contains information about Trinidad's art scene in the 1930s, and the men and women who were painting at the time, which art historians of today may find useful.

The later article on George Herbert, "Trinidad's First Sculptor", is also important historically. It stresses Mendes's firm belief that artistic talent is better left to develop on its own without formal training, and that the artist's heritage must infuse his work. Another important tenet was that great art transcends the boundaries of race and class, and thus is a vitally humanizing influence. These were some of the criteria with which Mendes approached his reviews of artists and exhibitions during his period as an art critic.

Mendes's particular hobby horse, that the true artist needs no academic training, is again referred to in his review of the Art Society Show of 14 November 1948. In support of this, he cites an experiment by the Mexican artist Diego Rivera, who sent his pupils out into the fields equipped with canvases, brushes and paints, with instructions simply to paint. (He refers in greater detail to this experiment in his defence of his position in "Two Cromwells", below.) He writes approvingly of the watercolourist Eric Cameron as an example of the artist abandoning imitations of foreign culture to focus on "the soil and spirit of [his] own folk": "Every work of art is an act of faith." In his review of M.P. Alladin's show on his return from England, "Artist Retains Stirring Qualities", he again states his fear that for gifted artists, studying overseas away from their roots "can often distort the freshness of the talent and sometimes destroy the talent altogether", only to admit, in an ending typical of Mendes in its honesty and generosity, that "Alladin's case fails to prove my theory – and I honour him for it".

Mendes reviewed the Art Society exhibitions faithfully every year, but the exhibition of November 1949 was the last he reviewed before the exhibition of November 1954, for which he wrote the piece "Two Cromwells". The article, written in Mendes's usual idiosyncratic vein, provoked vitriolic reactions from a disappointed artist and a fellow judge who should have known better, and sparked a lively three-week battle of words in the *Trinidad Guardian*.

Mendes had "spotted" Joseph Cromwell in the exhibition of 1949 as a talent comparable to Leo Basso, whom he revered, so it is unsurprising that he should choose to focus on two of Cromwell's paintings, both of which had been selected by a panel of eight judges, including Mendes, the chairman of which was his old friend "Pope" Wharton. The exhibition was formally opened on Saturday, 6 November 1954. The judges selected 162 works of art, two by Joseph Cromwell. All four of the paintings entered by Cromwell were sold within the first hour. On Sunday, 7 November Mendes's review "Vivid Form and a Touch of Cézanne", came out in the *Guardian,* and the following Sunday, 14 November, an article by Brother Fergus Griffin, whose contributions had failed to be selected, launched a stinging attack on Mendes, "Squint . . . and the Masses Vibrate". Brother Griffin wrote: "One might find it possible to ignore the unfortunate choice of two of the beribboned masterpieces as examples of the best paintings of the Exhibition were it not for the general onslaught on the public in an effort to educate the masses and dragoon them into seeing art through the discerning eyes of the judges." Brother Griffin went on to denigrate abstract art, and to claim "irreparable damage to the prestige of the Art Society". He ends the article: "It is good publicity to provoke controversy. But it degrades and belongs to a world far removed from aesthetics."

On Wednesday, 17 November, Mendes responded to the brother's attack with a brisk refutation of the charges, ending with his own attack on Brother Griffin's "good manners": "The tone of his article was in execrable taste", and promising to respond to "its matter . . . such as there is of it".

The next day, a letter from one of the other judges, Colin Laird, appeared: "Freedom of Artist to Express Himself Must Not Be Denied". Laird, according to the *Guardian,* was an architect and artist. He delivered himself of the following: "Of course, we were all amazed by Mr Mendes' fatuous article on the Art Show. It did not even get us hot under the collar, let alone justly [*sic*] an answer." He points out that "Brother Griffin has shot at a sitting target and has stated the obvious only to grind his own personal axe". Laird's quarrel with Brother Griffin stemmed from Brother Griffin's attack on abstract art.

On Friday, 19 November, Brother Griffin said in a letter to the editor, "Nothing Personal":

> I wish to state that my motives were, and still are, as expressed in my original article: the establishment of some permanent set of values which might be applied to the choosing of paintings at the annual exhibitions.
>
> I am concerned solely with the field of aesthetics and therefore refuse to be drawn into any side issues or personal quarrels. Nothing could have been further from my mind than the launching of a personal attack.

On Sunday, 21 November, in *News Review*, journalist Lenn Chong Sing sums up the letters so far, to keep the quarrels fresh in readers' minds. On Thursday, 25 November, Mendes's response appeared, in company with a letter from Don Taylor of Arima, which contributes little to the arguments, but stresses the importance of the abstract in art.

Mendes's response, "My Reply to Brother Griffin", appeared in the *Guardian* as "Critic Says Work of Art Is AN END IN ITSELF, NEVER A MEANS TO AN END". The article is temperate, balanced, restates his conviction that the critic's personal response to a work of art must be seen as valid, and again mentions his fondness for works by untrained or "primitive" artists. He goes into further detail of Diego Rivera's experiment with gifted schoolchildren, and asserts his own familiarity with and fondness for the paintings of Haitian intuitives. His authorities may be somewhat dated: Clive Bell's book was published in 1914, but it is the source of Mendes's criterion of "significant form" when making a final judgement. He magnificently ignores Colin Laird's incredible lapse of taste in criticizing a fellow judge, and heaps coals of fire on Laird's head by making common cause with him in having "no truck with the Brother's standards". And with his response, the debate on the meaning of art and of good manners is brought to an end.

Mendes was away for most of 1950 on his course observing ports in the United States and United Kingdom, and the years leading up to this exhibition would have been fully occupied by his job as deputy general manager of the Port Services Department. As far as I have been able to discover, he wrote no more such reviews.

Three of the pieces, the letter to Dr David Pitt, the head of the West Indian National Party, Mendes's letter of resignation from that party, and the eulogy which he delivered at the farewell function held for C.P. Alexander, were chosen to illustrate different sides to Mendes, and different points in his career. His brush with politics was short-lived. He found the West Indian National Party too conciliatory, and when its executive supported a candidate in the Grenada elections, Mr W.E. Julien, whom Mendes regarded as a "dyed-in-the-wool reactionary", he resigned in disillusionment. However, when Jack Kelshall returned to Trinidad at the end of the Second World War, Mendes helped him to form the left-leaning political party the United Front, and campaigned energetically with him until the general election of 1946.

His party lost, and Mendes seems to have abandoned politics after its defeat.

The address to C.P. Alexander shows Mendes in his capacity of acting Port Services general manager. C.P. Alexander had worked with the Port Services Department, but was now leaving to give more time to his activities as a trades unionist. Although Mendes was "management", he and Alexander liked and trusted each other, and worked well together over the years. Mendes additionally would have had a good deal of sympathy for Alexander's concern over workers' rights and the welfare of the members of his union. The speech is warm and personal, and full of anecdotes. Mendes has come a long way as a public speaker from the neurotic self-consciousness which he describes in his letter to Dr David Pitt as preventing him from speaking out at the meeting. In fact, at this stage in his life, he was renowned for his public speaking.

The two articles which deal with theatre, "Whitehall Group Make History with Their West Indian Plays" and "Henry Hall's English Play Has Definite Creole Flavour" in different ways illustrate Mendes's interest in the indigenizing of Trinidad's theatre. Both Errol Hill and Errol John went on to distinguished careers in the theatre as actors and playwrights, and it is much to Mendes's credit that he perceived their "star" quality in these early curtain-raisers. Henry Hall, an Englishman who wrote an "English" play for his racially mixed students to perform at the concert hall of the Government Training College for Teachers, succeeded in achieving a Trinidadian "flavour" for the performance, thereby earning Mendes's approval. The idea that principal and students could work together like one happy family inspires Mendes to say that certain politicians on the international stage could learn a lot from them. That the arts were a civilizing force was always for him an important credo.

The two editorials for the *Trinidad Singer* were written towards the end of Mendes's writing career, at a time when he was settled and very happy working with Singer. They contrast well with the editorial for *Trinidad*, 1, no. 2, which was the work of a young, brash, edgy writer with his way to make in the world. These two editorials, "Christmas" and "Life, Work and Success", are the philosophical musings of a mature intelligence, reflective and serene, and filled with hope for humanity. "Christmas" in particular reveals that Mendes, although he abjured religious institutions and dogma, and anything that interfered with man's freedoms and development, nevertheless had his own personal devotion and loyalty to Christ and His teachings. "Life, Work and Success" restates his reverence for human life and his value for work. The "restlessness of life and work" which he discerns have characterized his own life and writings, together with his love for, and endless fascination with humanity. Despite his rueful musings on age in "Christmas" (he was to live for another twenty-five years) there is a keen intelligence at work here still, and an unimpaired zest for living.

TWO LETTERS FROM GEORGE PADMORE TO ALFRED H. MENDES

The letters from George Padmore cast an interesting light on yet another of Mendes's many friendships. George Padmore, formerly Malcolm Nurse (1903–1959), was a Trinidadian, a well-known political activist and pan-Africanist. He was living in London in 1950, the year that Mendes was sent by the Port Services Department in Trinidad to study ports in the United States and United Kingdom. They would most probably have known each other in Trinidad earlier in the century, before Padmore left for the United States in 1924, particularly as Padmore was very friendly with C.L.R. James. Oddly, there is no mention of Padmore in Mendes's autobiography, because the letters suggest that there was considerable warmth and affection on both sides.

The first letter was scribbled on hotel notepaper and left for Mendes, together with some photographs and a tie as a farewell present, at the Regent Palace Hotel in London. I have been able to date it to about two weeks before Christmas Day of 1950, thanks to Irene Schirmacher, Mendes's granddaughter, who was "the kid" mentioned by George Padmore. She remembers being brought down by bus from Fife in Scotland by her mother, to meet Mendes in time to take ship with him for Trinidad, and to have landed in Port of Spain on Christmas Day.

The second letter was written on an air-letter form and mailed to Mendes in Port of Spain. Like the first, it is preoccupied with political activity, both in Trinidad and in West Africa, especially in what was then the Gold Coast, now Ghana. There is tremendous energy and vigour in Padmore's writing, suggestive of the ferment among his left-wing intellectual contemporaries, but he spares the time to argue over a critical pronouncement by Mendes with which he does not agree.

Mendes usually erred on the side of generosity when he assessed the work of other writers. For some reason, he cherished an intense dislike for the black American author Richard Wright, whom he had known in New York City when they both worked in the WPA Writers' Project, and Mendes could never be brought to admit that Wright had the "depth and delineative abilities" which Padmore and the South African writer Peter Abrahams saw in him. Padmore and Abrahams both knew Richard Wright, who was then in Europe and active in the pan-African movement. Three years later in Trinidad, Mendes, in a letter to a friend, Bill Collins, thanks him for lending him a copy of Wright's *Native Son,* but dismisses it as "not a good book. The hero of the book appears to me not so much to have been caught up in the tragic conflicts of our world as to have been caught in the confused and amorphous thinking of the author". The occasion for his reading the famous novel was a visit by Wright to Trinidad in the same year and a dinner party in his honour which Mendes, despite his personal animosity towards Wright, attended.

Mendes's family have been unable to supply a reason for this uncharacteristic vendetta. Wright seems to have been of an abrasive character, and perhaps he and Mendes did not work well together on the guide book to New York City which the writers in the Manhattan office of the WPA Writers Project Unit had been asked to prepare. Certainly he is not mentioned along with the writers of the Harlem Renaissance with whom Mendes regularly socialized, Countee Cullen, Claude McKay, Harold Jackman and Dorothy West.

George Padmore's letters are interesting, both in what they have to say about Padmore himself at a crucial historical period, when Europe's colonies in Africa were moving towards independence and he himself had an important role to play in the process, and in Padmore's perception of Alfred Mendes: "Our country needs more Alfred Mendes's [*sic*]." The vigour of Padmore's writing matches that of Mendes. He writes to the latter as to a trusted friend and confidant, and takes a warm interest in the welfare of Mendes's family. Mendes, himself a diehard anti-colonialist, would have been in total sympathy with George Padmore's politics, though as one steeped in the high culture of Europe in boyhood, who fought on her battlefields and in her trenches in the Great War, he may not have been quite so ready to dismiss that continent as "dying".

Despite his sojourns abroad in Europe and America, his enjoyment of foreign travel, and his appreciation of the arts of the Old World as well as of the New, however, Alfred Mendes remained West Indian to the core. Early in his writing career he and his *Beacon* colleagues had set out deliberately to shape and establish a Trinidad-centred literature. The writings would focus primarily on the island's urban and rural working classes, their environments, their problems, and their Creole speech. In the text of the West Indian Symposium, which he attended with other West Indian writers in London on 8 July 1950,[12] he takes issue with Edgar Mittelholzer first for the latter's denial that a West Indian culture exists "in any recognizable form", and in particular with Mittelholzer's statement that [for a writer] "to take thought before you write, to attempt deliberately to produce a work that is biassed in respect to local colour and local folklore is to be defeated before you begin". Mendes's own fear at this time is that younger West Indian writers, many of whom had emigrated to metropolitan centres, may be distracted by international events and influences into "a phase of development beyond the purely regional one". That the writer or artist needs to absorb the texture of his or her immediate surroundings in order to be able to create is a central tenet of his own writing, both in his fiction, where it is put into practice, and in his journalism, where it functions as a criterion for approaching the works of others.

What makes Mendes especially significant in the larger context of Caribbean literature is that his fiction was always strongly autobiographical. He wrote about people he knew or met and situations which he encountered, frequently in his own life, sometimes getting himself into trouble in the process. He was born into the middle class, but with the ability, the sympathy and the intellectual curiosity to move freely across the social spectrum. Many of his short stories are about Trinidad's middle class during the colonial era and the ways in which they interacted both with each other and with the working class. In this he goes beyond the original goals of the *Beacon*'s writers. He was both recorder and interpreter of his own times in the stories he wrote and in the articles about Trinidad's sculptors, artists, playwrights and dancers in which he grappled with his own ideas about what culture should be, at the same time devoting careful consideration to the artist or work under scrutiny. The journalism of the 1940s contains a great deal of valuable information about Trinidad's contemporary cultural scene.

Mendes's enormous energy found outlets in addition to his writing, and in many cases complementary to it, in his challenging job at the Port Services Department, where he, a native Trinidadian, worked alongside English expatriates and succeeded eventually to the top position there; and in public service, sitting on committees for the National Library and for the Trinidad and Tobago Hotel and Restaurant Association. He flirted briefly with politics, was a carnival judge for twenty years, and enjoyed the reputation of a fine public speaker and brilliant raconteur. During the course of a life which spanned nearly a century he watched the islands of the British West Indies moving inevitably towards political independence, and registered the developing maturity of his own people in his articles about their culture. His figure looms large both in the period of the 1920s and 1930s, when the greater part of his fiction was written, and in the decade of the 1940s, when he was transmitting his impressions of the changing scene around him week by week in his journalism. Both in Trinidad and, after retirement from his last position at Singer, in Barbados, where he wrote his autobiography, he was a well-known personality, inspiring both respect and affection in those who remember him.

Alfred H. Mendes was the writer who came back home and stayed.

NOTES

1. Mendes, *Autobiography*, xxiv, 77–78.
2. Ibid., xxv–xxvi, 78–79.
3. de Boissière, *Life on the Edge*, 71.
4. The West Indian National Party, founded by Roy Joseph, Dr David Pitt and Patrick Solomon in 1942, merged with the Indian National Council and the Negro Welfare Association to form the United Front in 1946.
5. Mendes, *Autobiography*, xxx–xxxi, 159–63 (appendix C).
6. These two drafts have been edited and published as the *Autobiography of Alfred H. Mendes, 1897–1991*. Most of the biographical details in the introduction are to be found there.
7. Mendes's grandson Sam Mendes was approached some years ago in a London restaurant by a woman named Jemima Potter, who told him that his grandfather had been a friend of her father's, and that she had one of his stories. She duly sent the story, "Bert and Betty Briggs – English", heavily annotated but minus several pages, to Sam. Unfortunately, Jemima Potter's father was not mentioned by name.

8. There is no connection between these pedlars and Gordon Habib, with whom Mendes became very friendly after his return to Trinidad in 1940.

9. Mendes, *Autobiography*, chapter 10.

10. de Boissière, *Life on the Edge*, 70. Out of their liaison came much of the material for Mendes's barrack-yard stories and his novel *Black Fauns* (see also introduction to *Black Fauns* by Rhonda Cobham, xi).

11. Republished in Mendes, *Selected Writings*, 231–32, 233–35, 238–39, 240–41.

12. The West Indian Symposium, which was chaired by Arthur Calder Marshall, was broadcast on *Caribbean Voices*, 9 July 1950.

THE SHORT STORIES ARE LISTED AS far as possible in chronological sequence, to give the reader a sense of Mendes's development and interests at different stages of his writing career.

"The Cat" was published in the *Trinidad Presbyterian* 24, no. 2 (February 1927) (edited by Reverend Gilbert Earle, Port of Spain). "Lai John" (co-authored with Algernon "Pope" Wharton) was published in the *London Mercury* (January 1929), and in *Best Short Stories of 1929*, edited by Edward J. O'Brien (New York: Houghton Mifflin, 1930). "Jacob Ayoub" was published under the pseudonym "A.H. Seedorf" in the *Quarterly Magazine* (September 1931) (edited by Austin M. Nolte, Port of Spain). "Without Snow" ("Richard") and "Ursula's Morals" or "The Visit" were published in the *Beacon* (edited by Albert Gomes, Port of Spain) in 1, no. 9 (1931) and 2, no. 8 (1933) respectively. "Ramjit Das" was published in the *Trinidad Guardian Weekly* (15 June 1947). "Cold Turkey" was published with slight alterations to the original typescript in the *Trinidad Singer* series 1966–1972, but like "The Larsons at Home", it was written in the latter part of Mendes's New York period 1933–1940. A letter from Mendes to Ellen, dated December 1937, mentions sending "Cold Turkey" to *Esquire* magazine (it was rejected). Since both stories belong to a particular period of Mendes's life, I have preferred to group them together in the sequence.

Of the five remaining unpublished stories, "When My Mother Was Left Alone" and "Caribbean Scare", because of their subject matter, seem to belong to a period slightly earlier than the first appearance of the *Beacon* in March

1931. Mention of the *Beacon* in "Tropic Town" (co-authored with Algernon "Pope" Wharton) dates the typescript as contemporary with or later than March 1931. "Young Da Costa", with its autobiographical image of Mendes as mentor to younger writers, may have been written around the same time. "Yellow Legs", which mentions the Second World War and Oswald Mosley's Blackshirts, was clearly written during the war years between 1940, when Mendes returned to Trinidad from New York, and the end of the war in 1945.

With the exceptions of the editorial notes from *Trinidad* 1, no. 2, a copy of a letter sent privately to Dr David Pitt, a speech given at a farewell function for the union leader C.P. Alexander and printed in *Marine Guide* (October–November–December 1951), and two editorials from the *Trinidad Singer* (Christmas 1965): "Christmas"; and 3, 9 (1966): "Life, Work and Success", all of the articles and letters are taken from the *Trinidad Guardian*. Dates of publication follow each piece.

Short Stories

THE CAT

THE ARRIVAL OF AUNT ELIZA'S KITTEN in the house has always been a memory with me. Such a small incident, and yet there was so much that resulted from it! The arrival was humble enough though highly emotional so far as my greeting of it went. I was only a little girl at the time, not more than nine or ten years old. But then, that is the time of life when each small happening looms largely in the budding imagination. The arrival of a kitten, you will think, should be quite uninteresting because so commonplace. Well, that is so. Still, it all depends, as you will see in the instance of Aunt Eliza's kitten.

It was a lovely thing. Never in my life have I seen such a lovely kitten. There was Persian blood in it. Of that no one could have any doubt. What made it so lovely though was the infusion of common blood in its veins that showed in white patches of fur here and there. For the most part it was dark-grey and fluffy. Oh so fluffy! What a bushy tail! And its eyes – why, they made you dream of things! They were humanly intelligent. That's the only way of putting it. I might have said intelligent in an animal sort of way. But that's not quite what my impression was. As it grew the human look in its eyes grew more and more.

Aunt Eliza seemed to have been suspicious of it from the day of its coming – or was it that she had been intuitively warned of impending disaster by virtue of its presence? I shall never know. The fact remains, however, that she disliked it from the very first moment of seeing it; or I should rather say, feared it. Were it not for my childish enthusiasm over its beauty, the thing would never have remained with us. But Aunt Eliza loved me, in a queer sort of way. Aunt Eliza was always a queer sort of person. My regard for her in those faraway days was itself a strange one, unanalysable. I liked her, but my affection went no further. She was too aloof, too severe, too prim. I always felt that there was something mysterious about her, something unfathomable. My childlike ingenuousness was appalled by her extreme reserve. And her idiosyncrasies – the way she would sometimes stare, her midnight tramps in her bedroom, her fiery temper with the servants – the mere remembrance of them makes me shudder! I didn't think much of them at the time. I was too young to do much thinking. My nervousness of her was an instinctive one. It's a strange thing that I never knew her age. She may have been anywhere between forty and fifty. An old maid. Mysterious. Unfathomable . . .

My kitten developed apace. I call it mine for Aunt Eliza would have nothing to do with it. It was I who prepared its milk in the morning. It was I who saved up morsels of meat for its luncheon. It was I who sat with it on the rug before the fire in winter. Me it followed about the farm in summer. It was more to me, I'm sorry to say, than Aunt Eliza was. A regular companion . . . This was all in the days before it became a full-grown cat.

Then strange things began to happen. Susie – I gave it that name after my one and only sister who had died some years before – would come into the house but seldom. All the loving care which I had bestowed on her as a kitten seemed to have run to seed. Nothing that I could do would induce her to sit with me before the fire, as she was wont to do when she was still a round, fluffy, innocent kitten. I began to feel hurt – as children will feel hurt – and scold her with as much harshness as I could put into my thin little voice. She would gaze at me with a look of infinite commiseration and slink slowly away into the road as though starting off on a pilgrimage. And perhaps she went on pilgrimages, for at intervals I would miss her for days. Aunt Eliza would say:

"Child, please do not encourage that cat in this house any longer. If it wants to stay away, let it stay." Then she would add in a low tremulous voice, "It's a sneaking, treacherous thing!"

"Why don't you like Susie?" I remember one day querying after one of her particularly invidious outbursts.

She looked at me very sternly for a long while with that queer stare of hers, and then ordered:

"Don't ask questions, child. Do as I tell you," and flounced out of the room greatly agitated, as even my tender years could see.

Then Susie had kittens. They were lovely little things, three of them and all like the mother. She had them in a disused barn some distance away from the house, and how they were discovered was a matter of pure ill-luck for Susie. Ill-luck, because her kittens may have lived despite their mother's emaciated condition. Oh, how my eyes must have sparkled with joy when first they looked down on the three fluffy beauties nestling close to their mother's breast! But I grew anxious immediately, for Susie's meagreness was painful to see. I rushed into the house, excited, hot, flushed, to find what milk I could. Aunt Eliza glanced up from the book she was reading. I was wishing that I would not accost her, for I sensed what the revelation of my discovery would mean to her.

"What do you want, child?" She always addressed me as "child". I never heard her call me by name.

I hesitated before replying. The fact is, I was unprepared for this and so at a loss for a suitably untruthful excuse.

"Milk, Auntie," I blurted out, breathless.

Aunt Eliza rose from the chair to her full gaunt height and looked down on me. Really, I felt as a flea must feel at the base of a mountain. She simply looked *down* on me.

"Milk? What for?"

Her voice sounded unpleasantly near.

"For Susie's kittens."

The flush on Aunt Eliza's cheeks went out as quickly as two falling apples. She grew as pale as mist. I thought she was going to faint, but she controlled herself with a great effort and said:

"You will do no such thing. Kittens? Ugh! Where are they?"

I told her. There was a pause.

"How long have they been there?" she then asked in a low voice.

I again replied. She stood as though undecided, thinking, as I could see.

"Go up to your room," she peremptorily ordered. Aunt Eliza's orders were always final, so I went up.

But my curiosity was aroused. I peeped over one of the windows. I saw Alice, the maid, walk across the yard in the direction of the disused barn. Presently she returned, holding in her arms what seemed to me to be Susie's kittens. A horrible suspicion came over me. I banged out of the room, rushed downstairs and arrived just in time to see Aunt Eliza dropping Susie's three beautiful kittens into a large bucket filled with water.

"Oh, you wicked woman!" I cried, beyond myself with anger and despair.

She looked round at me guiltily, and strange to tell, said not a word. I was taken unawares by her silence at the rude truth I had flung at her and stood trembling with excitement, my hair all dishevelled and falling about my face in a golden glory. And then I saw Susie, crouching in between a hedge that grew some yards away, staring at Aunt Eliza with unutterable hate. You could actually observe the intensity of the stare increasing. A human look of hate . . .

That night I wept very bitterly and very long until I fell asleep; and my sleep was troubled by ghastly dreams that only left me when the earliest lark's notes rippled into my room like a silver shower of song.

Time passed by and I saw nothing of Susie. Aunt Eliza's behaviour, to say the least of it, became more strange than ever. At any exclamation of mine she would start and her gaze would wander to the door furtively as if expecting to see some phantom of a bygone sin stepping over the threshold. Her movements were hurried, nervous, like a person in dreadful anticipation of some prophesied happening. With my youthful girlish inexperience I could put no interpretation on her unnatural demeanour.

I had almost forgotten the incident of the drowning of poor Susie's kittens. Little girls don't bear such things in mind indefinitely. I was sitting at the door and the dusk was coming down upon the farm, relentlessly wrapping all the familiar objects in its concealing spacious arms. It was autumn and not very cold. I heard Aunt Eliza's voice from the back of the house calling me, presumably for the purpose of telling me to retire for I had had my supper and was feeling happy, as happy as a child could feel. I rose and was just about to turn my back on the night when two glittering green specks of brightness arrested my further movement. They shone from the hedge at just that point from which Susie had seen her kittens splashed to their watery graves. I was puzzled though not in the least frightened; for a pleasing suspicion had crept into my mind. Still, it was only a suspicion which I could scarcely dare hope would materialize. I hurried across the yard and the two bright specks went out as quickly as two candles being blown upon. That didn't matter. I hurried all the more. How great was my joy in coming upon Susie! Susie whom I had not touched for so many weeks! Susie of the dull coat with white patches on it! Susie of the human eyes that made you dream of things! I held her in my arms. She purred. She rubbed her warm body against my face. She mewed softly, ever so softly. She looked up to me and her eyes glittered like emeralds. She raised her tail into the air and the tip of it brushed my cheek like the soft kiss of a soft wind. I buried my face in her silken down – when my happy excitement was rudely interrupted by Aunt Eliza's voice calling me. What was I to do? I dared not take Susie into the house. I dared not stay with her. Could I conceal her in the folds of my dress? Impossible. Aunt Eliza would notice . . . I could do nothing but leave her in the night, alone. As I placed her down I begged her from the depths of my little soul to come again; to make the hedge our trysting place. I told her I would bring her food every evening at that hour; all the daintiest delicacies I could lay my hand on during the day would be hers in the evening, and I hastened out of the night into the dim light of the house, wretched and happy; wretched because Susie was alone in the dark; happy because I had held her in my arms once again.

I was startled out of my sleep that night by the horrible crying of a human voice. I listened intently. It sounded like a baby crying in pain, a baby out in the night, deserted. A hungry baby crying for its mother's breast. I shuddered. The cries broke the mournful silence every now and again, and I knew they were not a baby's. I listened with all my hair standing on end. It was not a baby crying. It was something else, an animal, a cat. I shuddered. The bed creaked loudly in Aunt Eliza's room. A low murmuring oozed through the wall, the words inaudible. There was a noise in the passageway and my door opened, revealing the gaunt height of my mysterious Aunt like an affrighted ghost. She stole swiftly up to my bed. I made no motion but lay as though asleep. She passed her hands over my prone form, and I felt them shaking violently. Then she eased herself into the bed beside me, shared my cover and put her arms about my neck like a frightened child . . . When I woke in the morning Aunt Eliza was no longer in bed with me. She had gone to her room before the dawn could discover her to me in her cowardice, as she thought.

Things went from bad to worse with Aunt Eliza.

Each night I sat on the doorstep waiting for Susie, but Susie never came. And each night there was that human voice in the sombre darkness. I soon grew accustomed to it. Not so Aunt Eliza. I am pretty far advanced in life now, but I have not yet seen a person change so painfully in so short a time. She seemed haunted by a hovering fear, something that left her for not a moment, something that was sucking the life-blood from her, something that was unmercifully dragging her down to the grave. She thinned perceptibly. She paled visibly. "Ah, my child," she would say, "this thing is killing me." "What thing, Auntie?" I would ask in my childish innocence. She would only look at me and her dry inexpressive eyes would twitch as she moved away lackadaisically to her household duties.

And then it happened. Why it happened I cannot pretend to know. Winter had come. It was some nights since we had heard the dreadful sounds, and I could see that in Aunt Eliza's breast there yet flickered a faint flame of hope. She had grown a little less melancholy and moved around with a quicker step.

The moon was desperately trying to cast its light upon the snow-powdered environment of the farm. The night was bitterly cold. I was wakened by a low scraping sound at my window, and saw by the sickly shine of the moon my own dear Susie clinging desperately for life to the sill, for my window was shut to keep the biting cold out. I flung myself out of bed and, as silently as I could, raised the window. Susie sprang in and dropped with a dull thud of her paws on to the floor. I tried to hold her but could not. She was strangely unstrung, strangely emotional. My movements must have aroused Aunt Eliza from her slumber for I heard her whispering fearfully from her room:

"Child! Child!"

I have never heard a voice so filled with fear. I stood still, not daring to answer. But Susie kept scratching at the door making an awful noise in the dead hush of the house, the hush that houses know when the near-by church-bell solemnly strikes one.

"Child! Child!" Aunt Eliza whispered hoarsely.

Without thinking I turned to my door and opened it. Would to God I had not! But then, how was I to know that Aunt Eliza's door was ajar, she who had been recently in the habit of closing every window and aperture in her room? . . . Susie leapt into the passageway with one bound, wildly; and her mournful midnight incantation rent the deep sombre stillness of the house, its weird echo searching every nook and corner. I stood in fear and wonder. I could make nothing of the strange drama that was being enacted before me. I stood in the passageway, not daring to move. Alice, the maid, had by this time come up and loomed before me like a trembling effigy. Suddenly I heard

Aunt Eliza scream, a sustained scream that trailed off into a low moan. I ran to her door, not knowing what to think, what to do. I saw her standing on the window-sill, her arms raised high above her head like a priestess invoking some exotic god, her night-dress hanging loosely on her bony frame – a pale yellow shade in the pale yellow moon. Susie was immediately beneath her, crouching to spring. Aunt Eliza looked round. It was the last I saw of life on her face, a face twitched with an excruciating fear. As she fell forward and outward, Susie sprang. They both disappeared . . .

How long I remained gazing at the vacant window, I cannot say now. When I looked out with Alice, we saw the pale yellow form of Aunt Eliza lying motionless in the yard. And nearby was Susie, motionless too.

LAI JOHN[1]

THEY CALLED HIM LAI JOHN. It was not wholly his name, but it was good enough; for what could a Venezuelan or a nigger make of a name like Tuen? It was too much of a sneeze. He lay in the bows of the boat cuddling his knees. Cold and wet, he had never suspected that he would ever have left his kitchen to come out on such a tramp as this. His toes, chilled in the ooze at the bottom of the boat, were like ten little icicles, each an agony. Never since he had fled China for the promise of the West,[2] not even in the bitter unsubstantial weeks that had quickly harassed him out of Canada, had his spirits sunk so low. Whatever had possessed him? He put the question to himself in his own oriental fashion; but there was not an answer. He had already considered a variety of ways of keeping warm, but in vain; and each movement was a madness in which the rain beat relentlessly upon him, numbing some new spot hitherto concealed. By now they had long passed beyond sight of land, and there was only the black dripping sky overhead that rocked and rocked until his eyes grew dim and sick, and all about them the noisy hummocking seas that splashed him every now and then, so that he swallowed great mouthfuls of sea-water.

He cursed himself, in a flow of half-audible, choppy words; and then, more emphatically, holding the pit of his stomach the while, he cursed Lucia – the cosmopolitan Lucia, with the black hair and yellow eyes. He cursed her for a full-lipped slut, his black gape of a mouth terrible to see, reviling every part of her, until there remained but a skeleton of the beauty that had trapped him. But it took shape again, and flesh, and she hung above him in the wind, her yellow eyes gleaming, an agonizing laugh on her lips; and his soft flattened little nose itched again at the vision of her firm round breasts, that in a happier moment he had compared to ripe oranges. He screwed up his slits of eyes at the memory of how she had approved of his simile, drooping a shoulder to him and pouting; though the metaphor had come readily enough and, as you might say, involuntarily, he being a cook . . . It is true that he was not master of his kitchen, since a considerable part of his time was taken up peeling potatoes, washing the rice, or skinning shrimps; yet he was a first-class cook, as Lucia could attest. His curry alone betrayed his artistry; it had been indeed one of his early gifts to her – that first night of his scuttling off from work to her alley down-town. He had almost been himself prepared to doubt the age of the hen she had described so delightedly as "chicken". "It is so nice and soft," she had told him tenderly, her mouth running, and his display of tiny, mouse-like, blackened teeth had done scant justice to his ecstasy. He seemed, moreover, to better himself as he went on: he was so well repaid by her amusing attempts at using chopsticks that he contrived the most appetizing dishes with which he thought they might with the most difficulty be used. From curry, and chicken, and shrimps, it had been no difficult step to cakes – and here he was a master. Little corn-coloured puffs they were, with crushed peanuts sprinkled thick and brown, or almonds, just appetizingly burned; then rice cakes, crisp, flaky little squares of puffed rice embedded in honey-coloured sugar that melted in the mouth. And from rice cakes (how she loved them!) it had been no difficult step to Lucia . . .

The women he had known of his own race and station had been altogether too critical and knowing; they left him with no delusions. But Lucia had been different: she had the knack of drawing his confidence by her appealing artlessness and childish delight. She had given him such power; she had made him feel such a man! With what busy swagger he would pass up the dark passage to their trysting place! But such a triumph had been too swift to last, and only this night his eternity had fallen about him in ruins. The bitterness was insupportable when he remembered the ease and eagerness with which she had led him, so unforgivably a path to the night's abomination. He had taken her to the cinema – not because he specially understood the entertainment, but because it was a fine thing to do. Everybody went, it was true; but not everybody, and certainly not any of the Chinamen, had a girl on his arm:

they trooped in as a rule like a flock of geese, gazing about them in blatant surprise. How unique had he been! With Lucia! And the touch of her hand in the darkness had never seemed so firm and strong, and yet so tender. Sitting in the hall, in a sticky ecstasy of some papelon she had brought him, he had been thrilled to feel how alone they seemed in the crowd. And when at last the unintelligible show was over and he had been obliged to inform her that they must part, he having to go on a "job", he recalled how she had clung to him, yielding herself up to a new fear.

"The police . . .?" her soul seemed torn in terror.

But Lai John was game: "No get flighten,"³ he had told her reassuringly, patting her arm, "Opium have plenty cash. Me get lot-a-money, and by-an-by me go countly open shop: you come too."

She had been inconsolable, wringing her hands, and must go with him through the gathering rain out of the town to where his boat would be. And then he remembered with horror the last kiss (her sweet warm breath was still in his nostrils) with which she had yielded him up to the two men under the trees . . .

He sat up in a sudden fury in the boat, about to spit at her; but between them was the black expanse of sea, and between him and the sea was his stomach, and instead, he merely gulped twice, as if the neck-band of his shirt would choke him, and the next moment was very sick indeed.

Till now no one had spoken. The boat lay some five miles to the south of the little islands that lined the northern extremity of the Gulf. Somewhere far in the southern distance was Icacos Point,⁴ impossible to see even in the best light, and between it and the coast the Serpent's Mouth, the narrow channel through which the sloop would come. The west was a black wall, and though there should by rights have been a moon, so thick was the night that even the lights of the town were discernible only as a faint glow towards the east. But every so often the powerful beam from the lighthouse on the cliff stabbed the storm, like a ribbon of liquid light. Drenched with rain and sweat, the other two men had lain on their oars for a space, and then, still without a word but in a cunning silence, Small, the black fisherman, took up his new position at the tiller in the stern, while José steadied the boat with the sculls. There was no light by which to see the men's faces, but Lai John's outrage could not be passed unnoticed, and Small's voice rose ironically above the wind: "You belly belly sick, Lai John – good thing you didn't bring Lucia," and he spat in amused disgust over the gunwale. José showed his appreciation of the joke by a broad grin that wrinkled his face like a baked apple. "Ah, Chinaman," he said sympathetically, "the waters is too strong for you; you ought to take to rum." And he groped to feel for the bottle in the dark. Drawing the cork with his teeth he did not, however, pass the bottle to Lai John, but sucked at the sharp spirit noisily.

"After opium," drawled Small, reaching out to his friend, "rum's dish water, no doubt." And the gesture with which he set the bottle down held every sort of hopelessness.

This play, though Dutch to the Chinaman, was perfectly understood by the two men; among the fine points of the game – ever since a couple of years ago, fishing along the coast, they had decided that in their line two could work wonders where one might fail, and had sworn eternal friendship. There was money in fishing – well, enough to keep you going in the season anyway – but he was a poor fisherman whose only catch was fish; and if without the need for the baser and more laborious work they could, so to speak, take the flower at its bloom, one could not blame them. As it was, they had a double danger: from the real smugglers they could expect very little friendship; and the police – well, one was never sure: even Lucia, versatile, and triumphant on one or two occasions, could never be trusted. But if, again, they seemed to snatch their winnings at the post, effortlessly, it was not without considerable thought and that expert knowledge of every hole wherein stuff like opium could be stowed. They had them all charted in their minds: from Toco to Teleron Bay; and along the east and south coasts from Galera to Soldier Rock they had the eyes out for a gull for "pickings". This labelled them deep-sea folk, and though it was not often they got a hand – that is, not much to speak of – yet they managed! About the workings of the harbour and town "depôts" they knew next to nothing. That was in the hands of the bigger people – the Chinese intermediaries, sloop captains, Mainland traders and the more successful merchants; and it was only when things were dull out to sea, as on this occasion, that they came up, country bumpkins at heart, to see the sights of town.

In the boat José rubbed his high cheek-bones thoughtfully, looking up at the sky in the East. "Soon be over now," he said, "– till it comes again."

The sky had indeed cleared, and the rain came in a drifting drizzle from drifting banks of cloud. Far across the water the lights of the shipping came out slowly, one by one. Astern lay the black masses of the Northern Range, rising sheer out of deep valleys and decaying swamps, with here and there a faint light showing at the water's edge or high up on the hills. Over the bowl-like silhouette of a valley a dark purple pall of smoke marked a spent bush fire. Closer at hand were the islands, rugged and rocky hills, one of them like a gigantic lizard with its long flat tail dwindling away in the wash of the sea. High overhead the clouds hid the moon, and one shapeless mass, fringed with a pale light, glided majestically before the storm, like a magic carpet. A flight of night birds, deftly skimming the water, swept by silently on quickened wings, like lost souls.

Small came to the business in hand: "What about that sloop?" he asked, leaning forward, elbows on knees.

Lai John turned bleary eyes to the west and back again, but said nothing.

"Well, here's the plan," Small went on. "When sloop he come, you go takee stuff from captain; you payee money quick; you sit down damn quiet. If you makee noise you dlink plenty more water." And then in more business-like tones: "Keep your eyes open and your mouth shut, and your stomach silent – see?"

"True," put in José in agreement: "if you going to be sick again get it over now and be done; there won't be no time later on, Yellowbelly!"

Lai John kept his eyes as wide as possible, which wasn't very wide, and his mouth shut tight; but his stomach – well, he begged all the dynasties to witness that over this he had no control. Small stuck his bare, fan-shaped feet along the gunwale of the tossing boat with enviable ease, and looked him up and down in the darkness, as if critically surveying his catch for the first time.

"H'm!" he said, "can you shoot?"

"Levolver?" asked the Chinaman, fearfully, "no, no, never."

"Levolver, yes, yes," came the encouragement, "at least if we've got to – unnerstan?" Then after a pause: "How much stuff's for you?"

"Bou-ten-poun'."

"But you lich man! – How much money?"

"One-hundled-ninety-tollar."

"Good. Well, we'll want a hundred and twenty dollars a pound – sell it where you like, see?" And then he added as if in an afterthought:

"Play square, now, and we, as is usual, will play square too. You can get a damn sight more money than that for it, but all we want is a hundred and twenty dollars – nett cash! So bring the dough over, like a good lil feller, and the stuff's yours – savvy?"

Lai John forced a grin, and Small cast his eyes about before he resumed his instructions: "But if," his voice was casual and almost friendly, "if you ain't square, d'you want to know what'll happen? I'll blow your blasted gold-filled stud clean through your neck; I'll rattle your teeth down your gullet, maybe, like peas in a pod; or stick some lead through your eyes, like a parcel in a pillar-box – all sorts of things could happen, in fact, to make you feel ashamed of yourself."

There was a silence, and now that they understood each other Small saw no need for further speech but patiently went over the night's work in his mind. He took his bearings: the boat had drifted before a running sea; a low peal of thunder ran along the southern floor of heaven like the gentle roll of a faraway drum; the moon peeped for an instant from behind racing clouds, and he could see Lai John glistening beneath its light in the bows, a shiny black and yellow, like a cheap plaster doll. He smiled; and again at José at the engine, whose light merino and flour-bag trousers clung to him like a skin. He himself was fairly clad, in blue serge trousers and a heavy sweater, and this bodily comfort must have gone a long way to ease his mind. He tugged his begrimed felt hat more cosily over his face and let his eyes wander over the sea, sleepily. The visibility was sufficiently bad, but the sharp gusty rain, and salt and sweat, played the devil with his eyes. Yet he had to see for three! For Lai John, stiff with cold and sea-sickness and anxiety, had ceased show-ing any signs of life and lay with his thin little body curled like a bit of gut. José was a mechanic and a great sailor, but not a seaman. He could work all day at an oar or in the rigging, but was as unfitted for the responsibility of the helm, for instance, as Lai John for anything more than a duck-pond. And this consciousness in Small swelled his pride. He had in his early days smuggled with the best of them, rum and cheap jewellery enough to set him up in business had he wished; but never before had there been such promise of gain, nor had things run so smoothly, and his joy for the moment was in the old sense of danger, the splendid trick, the sting of the sodden wind, the smell of the salt sea in his great wide nostrils – and his supreme command. Suddenly he strained forward:

"Better tune her up," he said presently. "Just keep her turning."

And as somewhere in the darkness José stooped to the order, a blinding lightning cracked the sky, and simultaneously, as if through the crack, peal upon pent-up peal of thunder dropped out of heaven. In the flash a form, blunt and black, suddenly swung over their bows; but Small was as quick:

"Let 'er go – hard !" he roared, jamming down the tiller. There was a cry from Lai John that trailed away on the wind, and the swift splash of water, and the next moment they had all but stove their starboard bow. The motor boat rocked as her stern half buried itself in the wash, then steadied herself, running parallel with the sloop. José whistled low through his teeth. Lai John sat up stupidly staring down at the sea; Small's brows knitted a little, but now was not the time for Lai John. He turned to the sloop:

"What the devil're you doing?" he shouted, "Where're your lights?"

"None o' your business. What the hell d'you think I am – a floating hotel, or a Coney Island show,⁵ maybe?"

The voice was unmistakable to Lai John. He sprang up suddenly like a Jack-in-the-Box: "Him sloop, him sloop!" he cried gleefully, desiring to please.

Small's voice sang out again: "Throw a line."

"Not for hell!"

And now Lai John, with strange loyalty, and in a flow of explanatory cosmopolitan chatter, like a river in the rainy season, at last managed to come to terms with the sloop; and the next few moments the two vessels sheared apart.

Even with the wind drumming in their ears a strange, sweet stillness came over the three men. José let the engine hum easily along and reached out his hand to Lai John: "You've earned a drink: rum is good for bad stomach," he said genuinely. The bottle passed, and Small, about to raise it to his lips, kept it poised in the air, his ear cocked like a terrier's. "Hell!" he growled under his breath.

Faintly, just sufficiently to reach their ears, like the echo of their own engine, a low, flowing sound. The engine's roar and the boat's sudden leap testified to José's attention. Down the wind the little boat was flung. In the bows Lai John took a breaker, beautifully, and lay confused and gasping in a new terror. A sharp low command brought him to his senses as an unfamiliar and unwieldy revolver was thrust into his hands. Now Lai John was a cook, and no shot; and the cold touch of the steel burned his numbed fingers; but the strong neat spirit still tingled in his gullet and beat upon his brain. Over the sea a dim form moved – towards them, almost imperceptibly, it gained; and he heard the short sharp blast of a whistle that was the sign of authority for them to stop. Yet he heard his boat's engine roar out a challenge to a chase, and felt the timbers strain and crack against the rushing water. He did not know about these things, but he felt that to dodge the patrol in the darkness was folly; it would be prolonging the night's agony, that should now have been at an end. They should never have tried to escape, but should have given themselves up. They had been caught squarely, and there was no chance, and six months' prison sentence would have been the worst of it; but now there was no telling how it would end, except that the moments were becoming more futile and fateful; and he cursed himself again and again he cursed Lucia. And remembering now only himself and how he might best face it, he clasped convulsive fingers over the revolver: here, perhaps, in his very hands, was his defence. And at that very instant there was a flash and a sharp report as the first admonitory shot was fired by the patrol; and before the others or he himself knew what had happened, he had answered – anyhow, anywhere, so long as his shot would put an end to his terror.

It was the beginning of the end, anyway: and from the pursuing launch came a hail of bullets, and from Small, roaring like a bull in the stern, came a volley of curses. To return the police fire was but a waste of time and ammunition, yet Small himself was shooting rapidly. A quick thought passed through his mind: was there not yet a chance of escape, by silencing the men who had victimized him? What evidence of shooting could there be against him? Lucia . . . Lucia would have her revenge, certainly; but she knew him only as a busy little cook whom she had tricked. Looking at it this way, Lucia might, indeed, be almost his best defence. Besides, the police, he reflected, not without irony, "shoot belly fine!" and some credit for their personal prowess would no doubt be claimed . . . He raised his arm in obedience to a threat from the Venezuelan, and looking along the barrel he suddenly saw Small's vast form square before him. His mind jumped to action, and with the flash from his pistol the black bulk seemed to sag and droop and swing limp, sideways across the stern. There was a cry for his dead friend from José, who was crouching up against the gunwale to leeward of the engine, and Lai John, inexperienced, but now thoroughly amok, steadied his arm for the third shot: and at the instant, José tumbled backwards out of the boat.

Just as a final hail of police bullets shattered the engine, Lai John dropped his revolver over the side and, cold and calculating, watched the little boat take fire. As the flames leapt up, casting crimson shadows in the boat, the only surviving occupant composed himself into a little knot in the bows, and awaited, with an inwardly calm resignation and an expression of unrelieved nausea, the advent of authority.

NOTES

1. "Algernon Wharton and I did one story together. I did the first version; he did the second and finalized it" (Mendes). From Sander, "The Turbulent Thirties in Trinidad".
2. Lai John appears to have come to Trinidad as a free immigrant (Look Lai, *Chinese in the West Indies*, 17). From 1923 to 1947 Chinese nationals were banned from immigrating into Canada.
3. Mendes's working-class Chinese characters have difficulty in pronouncing the letter R.
4. On the south-west tip of the island.
5. There was a famous funfair at Coney Island in New York.

WHEN MY MOTHER WAS LEFT ALONE

WHEN I WAS THREE YEARS OLD my father died and my mother was left alone to struggle along with me. It must have been a hard struggle because my father left nothing and in an island like Trinidad it was difficult for women, and especially for women who have any claims to respectability, to make a living. But somehow or the other my mother managed and sent me to school. Although I am fifteen now I am still going to school and she tells me that she's going to keep me at it until I have what she calls "a decent education".

I am wondering now why my mother never married again. She's forty years old and still very pretty and I am sure of that because I often hear people making remarks about how pretty she is. I can see it for myself too and I can also see from the photographs in the drawing-room that when my father married her she was really beautiful. Her skin has the pale whiteness of the lily, her eyes are very blue, but the blackness of her hair speaks of the Span- ish blood that flows through her veins. I have caught snatches of talk about some exciting romance concerning the way in which my father married her, but I have never been able to get the whole story. Perhaps when I grow up my mother will tell me all about it, although I can't understand why she doesn't give me the story now.

Now and again I go to the pictures and perhaps I know a little more than she thinks I do. Perhaps, on the other hand, there is something to it that I should not hear but that only makes me all the more curious.

My mother is so poor that all she can manage is to send me to school, keep us both in food and things like that. She works in a dry-goods store as a saleslady and I think she's making something like ten dollars a week. She gets up every morning at six o'clock, except Sundays, sees about coffee and tidies up the house before going to work. Once in a blue moon she gets a week's holiday and then she sits at home and makes new curtains and at the end of the week the little house looks spick and span and altogether new.

You will see from what I've said that we're thrown together a great deal. I really don't know what I should do without her. From as far back as I can remember she has made a habit of reading stories to me in the evenings. She's a great reader and I think I have inherited that taste from her because I love books and I have even often thought that I should like one day to become a writer. My mother tells me that my father too was a great reader and all the books she has about the house belonged to him. They were his only legacy to her, but she does not complain. I've never heard her complain about anything; she seems to take it for granted that we were put here to struggle and sometimes I'm very sorry for her.

I have said that my mother once in a blue moon gets a week's holiday from her job, but always she has been so poor that she could never go "down the islands" or to the country for her holiday as other people do. But I do remember how once some friends of hers invited her to spend a week with them in a house on the Mayaro coast.[1] Of course, I went along with her as she had nobody to leave me with. I was only ten at the time but I can remember most of what happened during those few days because it was all very strange and very exciting and very upsetting. At the time, I mean, because I don't think I'd feel the same way about it all now. I might, but I don't think so.

This house of my mother's friends was by the sea and it seemed as if the Halliwells, for that was their name, were very rich indeed because the house was larger than ours by more than four times. And there were lots of beautiful things in it and even a grand piano. I like the piano too and sometimes I even feel that I would like to be a pianist instead of a writer. The big house with all its rich furniture made me feel uncomfortable at first, but as soon as I saw the piano I felt at ease because I knew then that I would after all have something to play with. The Halliwells had no children. As a matter of fact, I soon discovered that Sambo, the old caretaker, had a lot of children but because they were black Mrs Halliwell said that I was not to play with them. My mother said nothing.

The first evening we arrived Mr Deering, a gentleman I had never seen before, said to my mother:

"I think your little girl is very pretty, Tessie-Lou. She's going to be very much like you."

It was the first time I had heard anybody say that I was pretty and I looked up at him. He wasn't a very tall man, just a little taller than my mother, but I noticed that he was dressed well and I liked his face. That night he made much of me before my mother took me up to bed. His name, as I have said before, was Mr Deering and I believe he was a cousin of Mrs Halliwell's. Anyway, he also had come down to spend a week, arriving on the same day as we did, and that first night he told me that we were going to have a great time together, that he would be my friend for the holiday and so on.

When my mother took me up to my room I asked her who he was.

"A friend of your father's," she said.

"I think he's a nice man," I said.

She said: "Now get into bed and sleep well." She kissed me good night and went away.

The very next day Mr Deering told me to call him John and when my mother heard me calling him by his Christian name she was very vexed with me, but when he explained that it was he who had asked me to call him John she said nothing more. But I could see that she didn't like the idea at all.

Mr Deering was awfully nice to me that day and took me to the village that was about a mile away to buy me sweets. While we walked, he holding on to my hand, he talked to me about all sorts of things and I remember he showed me a tree that was covered over with yellow blooms and he said: "That's a *poui*." It was so lovely that I stood up and looked at it and he said: "You like lovely things, don't you, Elizabeth?" It seemed a strange question to ask but I don't remember now what I said back to him. Perhaps I wondered if there was anybody in the world who didn't like lovely things.

And in the afternoon we all bathed in the sea. The wind was blowing very strong and the waves came in with great noises, boom, boom, boom, and Mr Deering found it impossible to teach me to swim in the rough water so he took me by the hand and led me down the beach to a spot where a neck of land went jutting out into the sea and it formed a sort of breakwater inside of which the water was quite calm. There he tried to show me how to swim and we had great fun. He kept saying: "Elizabeth, you'll be a fine swimmer one day," and the more he said that, the more I tried because he said it so often that I actually believed him, but I didn't learn to swim that day, I didn't learn that week at all, not until long afterwards.

When I was out of the water sitting in the sunlight on the sand trying to build sand-castles, Mr and Mrs Halliwell were drying themselves near to me. My mother was in the water with Mr Deering. Mrs Halliwell said:

"Isn't it funny to see John and Tessie-Lou like that again?"

"She's fool enough to turn him down a second time," Mr Halliwell said.

"Oh, I don't think he could ever care again for her in the same way."

Mr Halliwell said nothing, he only smiled.

Sambo's black children stood at a little distance watching us and I was tempted to go up to them, but when I remembered what Mrs Halliwell had said earlier in the day I stayed where I was wishing that Mr Deering would come out of the sea and help me with my sand-castles.

That night my mother allowed me to stay up much later than usual. When she took me up to my room, I said:

"Isn't John a nice man, Mumsie?"

"Everybody is nice, darling," she said. "Now get into bed and sleep well."

The next morning I woke to hear the waves breaking on the beach and the keskidees singing in the trees by my window. The sun was shining outside and the wind blew through my window, flapping the curtains wildly. As soon as I had had breakfast I went into the drawing-room and began to touch the notes of the piano, but Mrs Halliwell came in and told me in a very nice manner that I was not to play with it. When I told my mother about the incident she didn't say anything except to warn me against going anywhere near it in the future. And I was very upset by that because, as I have said before, I love the piano. Now I found that I could play neither with it nor with Sambo's children, but I consoled myself with the thought that I still had Mr Deering.

In the sea that morning it was grander than ever. The sun was shining hot and bright and the coconut trees along the beach shook themselves frantically when the wind came up to them. Some pelicans were high in the air, circling round and round as if they were taking their early morning exercise. Mr Deering supported me beneath the belly with his arms as I tried to swim, and I splashed and splashed, sinking every time he let me go. My mother looked on and laughed and Mr Deering looked across at her and laughed too. The more they laughed at me, the more determined I became to swim before the morning was out. I was surprised to see how happy my mother was. It made me happy to see her so happy. I had never heard her laugh so much and her laugh was clear and natural, like a bird's song is.

I was glad when my mother accepted Mr Deering's invitation to come along with us to the village. Mr Deering said:

"It's nice of you, Tessie-Lou."

"It's a nice day and the walk will do me some good," my mother said.

"Yes, it's a nice day," Mr Deering said.

We walked along the dusty road in silence for a long while and I was beginning to be sorry that my mother had come along when Mr Deering said:

"Fancy, after all these years, Tessie-Lou . . ."

"I'd prefer if you didn't talk about that," my mother said very quickly and in the sort of voice I'd never heard come from her. I was on one side of Mr Deering and my mother was on the other. He held my hand. I looked up at him and saw him give her a long look, but she was looking the other way. Suddenly she began to laugh and when Mr Deering asked her what the joke was she pointed out a litter of pigs all running helter-skelter about a yard. They looked so funny that I had to laugh too. I let go of Mr Deering's hand and started to run after the little pigs, but my mother called me back with a sharp voice.

In the village shop Mr Deering said: "Do you still like chocolates, Tessie-Lou?"

My mother said yes, but she didn't want any. In spite of that Mr Deering bought her some, saying as he handed them to her: "For old time's sake, Tessie-Lou." She took them and smiled up at him.

By the time we started back the sun had risen very high and the heat was terrific. Mr Deering chatted away with me and teased me and laughed, till what with the hot sun and the laughing and the walking, I was out of breath. My mother gave me a look of concern and Mr Deering left me to give his attention to my mother. They spoke in low tones and I did not hear anything they said to each other, but I did notice that he was holding her hand and her cheeks were so red that I said:

"Mumsie, your cheeks are bursting."

"It's so hot," she said, fanning her face with her handkerchief.

"You're very beautiful," Mr Deering said in a low voice.

My mother smiled up at him.

I don't know why, but from that moment I began to feel that I didn't like Mr Deering so much after all. I had heard lots of people tell my mother how beautiful she was and it had always made me happy.

That afternoon in the sea Mr Deering was nicer than ever to me and I tried my best to be nice to him because I didn't want my mother to be vexed with me, but when he suggested going to the calm spot for some swimming lessons, I said:

"No. I don't want to go anywhere with you."

I must have spoken rudely because my mother looked at me and said sharply:

"Elizabeth, I'm surprised at you," at which I ran out of the water, ran up the beach to where the coconut trees started and began to cry. In a moment my mother was beside me wanting to know why I was crying, but I wouldn't say a word. Mr Deering put his arm around me and I heard him say to my mother:

"I suppose I'm the cause of this. I'm dreadfully sorry."

"Elizabeth is being very rude," my mother said.

"You mustn't say that," Mr Deering said. "It'll only make it worse and I want the child to like me." They were both silent for a while and I felt his hand stroking my head. Then he said, very quietly: "It's best to leave her alone, Tessie-Lou. The less notice you take of her, the better."

I peeped at them through my fingers as they walked back hand in hand into the sea. For the rest of the day my mother did not come near me but I caught her glancing at me several times, and I noticed too that she kept away from Mr Deering.

That night as I lay in bed just falling asleep I heard my mother singing in the drawing-room to the accompaniment of the piano. It was a long, long time since I had heard her sing and her voice came up to me in rich tones, full of feeling. I don't know why, but suddenly I felt that I must see her as she sang. All I know is that I felt very sad in an angry sort of way, so I got up from my bed as quietly as I could and tiptoed my way down the stairway. When I got to the drawing-room door, I peeped in and saw my mother standing beside the piano and singing. Mr Deering was at the piano accompanying her and gazing up into her face as she sang. It seemed unfair that he should be allowed to play for my mother and that I should be forbidden to go near the instrument. It was only a glimpse I caught of them, I couldn't look any longer because I had a queer feeling in my heart and I was afraid my mother would see me, so I ran back upstairs, got into bed and cried myself to sleep.

The next day it was some time before I remembered what had happened the day before. Mr Deering was wearing a white suit when he came down and because he did not greet me in his usual friendly manner I remembered what had happened the day before.

"You two would make a beautiful pair," Mrs Halliwell said to my mother and Mr Deering. My mother went red and turned her face away. Mr Deering smiled and so did Mr Halliwell.

The weather had turned and it was raining. At about nine o'clock a lot of people arrived in cars and flocked into the house with a great deal of noise. They had come down to spend the day and soon they were all in their bathing suits and running about in the rain on the beach. I was in the verandah of the house with my mother, looking on at them all playing on the beach. My mother didn't want me to bathe in the rain for fear that I'd catch cold and had decided to stay with me after I had asked her to. We weren't there ten minutes when Mr Deering ran up the walk in his bathing suit and came up to my mother and said:

"I do wish you'd join us, Tessie-Lou."

"I'm staying with Elizabeth," my mother said.

"But surely Elizabeth is big enough to take care of herself. I do wish you'd come, Tess. It'd be so much nicer with you. Do come."

My mother was silent for a moment, then she stooped down to me and said softly: "You stay here, darling, and don't go out into the rain."

In a few minutes she was out on the beach in her bathing suit and I saw her join Mr Deering. I felt very sad and very angry with Mr Deering for having taken my mother away from me. I felt like running out into the rain and catching cold and I hoped I would die and make my mother sad too. Then I knew that I wanted to cry, but I tried my best not to and in the end I succeeded. And I knew too, at that moment, that I hated Mr Deering with all my heart and soul.

In the afternoon the clouds went away and sunshine came back into the world and the strangers and Mr and Mrs Halliwell all went out fishing in a launch.

"Aren't you coming with us, Tessie-Lou?" Mrs Halliwell said.

My mother said: "I have a splitting headache, if you'll excuse me."

Mrs Halliwell murmured something that I did not catch and my mother's cheeks went red.

I don't know what I felt when I noticed that Mr Deering had stayed back too. There was a lovely hammock slung across the verandah and I was swinging in it when Mr Deering came from inside the house and began to talk in low tones to my mother. In a short while they both came up to the hammock and my mother said:

"Run along and play, Elizabeth. It's nice and sunny on the beach."

Without a word I ran out onto the beach and as soon as I got there I saw Sambo's children playing in the sand. I stood still watching them and as I stood like that, the idea came into my head that I should defy my mother and Mrs Halliwell and play with them. I glanced back and saw my mother and Mr Deering sitting in the hammock. They were very close to each other and I am almost sure that they pulled away from each other when I turned to look at them. I ran up to the black children, squatted beside them and took a hand in their game of sand. At first they seemed frightened and stopped in their play to regard me, but after a while they got accustomed to me, became friendly and allowed me to join in their castle-building.

I was very angry because my mother took no notice of my defiance. I wanted to run up to her and say defiantly: "Look, I'm playing with Sambo's children," but I couldn't bring myself to do that.

All the afternoon, I nursed my anger. I suppose I was just as angry with my mother as I was with Mr Deering, but if she had only called me and told me that she too hated Mr Deering, I know that I would have kissed her and hugged her and perhaps cried with joy.

That night I sat up for a long time listening, but I did not hear my mother sing.

Soon after my father's death, something had gone wrong with my knee and every now and again the trouble would return and I'd suffer very much from the pain. The doctor said that I would outgrow it. Sometimes the pain came on if I knocked my knee against something, sometimes it came on just of itself.

The next day was a bright blue sky with the wind whistling in from the sea and the waves breaking on the beach, boom, boom, boom. We were in the sea and my mother was teaching me to swim. I was laughing like anything, and every time I did I swallowed water, and my mother was finding it more and more difficult to keep me afloat.

"You leave her to me, Tessie-Lou," Mr Deering said. "You're tired," and he began to wade his way towards me. But I ran from him shouting: "No, no, I don't want you to touch me." He still kept after me and in a moment we were both on the beach, he in hot pursuit of me. I ran for all I was worth and I was so anxious to escape him that I tripped over and fell. My mother, seeing this, hurried up and found me crying. I was in an awful temper, but as soon as my mother said: "It isn't your knee, is it, darling?" I hugged my knee and moaned as if in physical pain.

"I'm so dreadfully sorry," Mr Deering said, stooping down to lift me in his arms, but my eyes flashed at him and I blurted out:

"Don't touch me, Mr Deering!"

My mother drew back at the words, but immediately, remembering my knee no doubt, she took me in her arms and half-ran across to the house with me, Mr Deering following. She set to bandaging my knee and when she was done she asked Mr Deering to take me upstairs but I wouldn't let him come near me, so she had to take me up herself. We were alone in the room.

"Why are you behaving so rudely to Mr Deering, Elizabeth?" she said.

I wouldn't say a word, I just continued sobbing until I was exhausted, when I lay back on the pillows, my eyes closed. She must have thought me asleep, for after a while she went quietly out of the room.

I must have been alone for about half an hour when I heard footsteps outside my door. I closed my eyes. The door opened and there was a short silence, then I heard Mr Deering saying in almost a whisper:

"I'm sure it isn't her knee, Tess, I'm sure."

"Then what can it be?" my mother said.

"Me."

"You? But why?"

There was another silence and then I heard whispering, but I couldn't catch a word. Soon after, they left me.

That night I again heard my mother singing and although a mad desire seized me to rush down and scream at her, I lay still instead and forced the tears back.

All the next day I limped around the house because the bandage was tight around my knee. My mother was all attention but I gave her no token of affection. Mr Deering did not even try to speak to me and I kept away from him, hating him more and more as the silence went by. I felt that I wanted to scratch him or bite him or do something to hurt him. Once or twice I caught him looking at me and I gazed back full into his face angrily and defiantly.

Our holiday came to an abrupt end that evening. When I think of it, I am ashamed of myself but I really couldn't help myself. Something of the sort had to happen, either that or my mother's telling me that she too hated Mr Deering with all her heart and soul. I can't say why I wanted her to tell me that but I do know that if she had done I might even have liked him again and felt sorry for him.

I have said there was a hammock slung across the verandah. I had noticed my mother lying in it with Mr Deering several times and that afternoon, at just about the time I knew them to be in the habit of occupying it, I went and lay in it myself. Soon enough, they both came into the verandah and I pretended to be busy looking at a picture book. My heart began to beat very fast when I noticed my mother approaching me. She said:

"Get a chair, Elizabeth, and let Mumsie have the hammock."

I knew she meant that the hammock should be given to herself *and* Mr Deering, so I looked at her defiantly.

"Now be a good child and obey me," she said.

"Get a chair yourself," I said

My mother's cheeks flushed.

"Don't be rude, Elizabeth," she said after a pause.

I did not move.

"Leave the child alone," Mr Deering said, advancing.

"I'll do nothing of the sort," my mother said angrily. "She's never before disobeyed me and she's not going to now. Elizabeth, will you do as I tell you, and quickly?"

"I won't, I won't, I won't," I screamed and threw the picture book to the floor.

And then my mother did something she had never done before, she struck me across the face with the palm of her hand, a stinging slap. Mr and Mrs Halliwell were just in time to see her slap me.

It is impossible for me to try and describe what my feelings were. All I can say is that I sprang at her and bit her on the thigh before she could get her hands on me. Then I left her and, screaming, rushed across at Mr Deering and would have bitten him too had he not held me away from him. Instead, I screamed: "I hate you, I hate you!" and raced through the open door, up to my room and threw myself on the bed and shed bitter tears.

That night my mother packed our few things and the next morning, bright and early, Mr Halliwell drove us to the station and we caught the first train back to town.

NOTE

1.   On the south-east coast of Trinidad.

CARIBBEAN SCARE

EARLY THAT THURSDAY MORNING OF 1915 THE RUMOUR started to go its rounds in Port of Spain. The sky was overcast with cloud, and the night before it had rained from dusk till dawn. Oppressed by the melancholy drip of rain and the dark lowering heavens, the people were predisposed to believe a rumour of the kind.

Fernando, being a barber, was one of the first to hear it. As we all know, more often than not it is the barber's shop that sets the ball of news rolling. Fernando's barber-shop, the most select of the city, was in the busiest part of Frederick Street. He had come down particularly early that morning. Indeed, since the war had started he had made it a habit of arriving earlier at his shop than ever before in his thirty years' experience as a barber. The truth is: he felt safer in his shop amongst men like himself. At home, there was only his wife and eight girl-children, and what assurance of safety, in a time of danger, can a man derive from a woman and eight children? And Fernando's nervous condition had been aggravated by the war, especially when the local papers began to report as killed in action young men of the island, young men whose hair he had cut in times of peace. He could scarcely sleep at nights, but lay with his eyes wide open trying to visualize the fields of battle strewn with mutilated bodies; and even when short spells of sleep came to him they were nightmare-filled moments that startled him into perspiring awakedness, and he would call his wife. She, poor woman, exhausted from the suffering she had experienced with her last baby, would then have to put her arms about him and soothe him with comforting words.

On that Thursday morning the shop was agog with gossip of the rumour. Every chair was occupied. Fernando was trimming Mr Hamel-Levitt's hair. His fingers were cold from the excitement bubbling within him, but as it wouldn't do to show that he was excited, he went about his clipping with care and method. Every now and again he paused to survey the progress of his work, a smile spread over his features; and he contrived, as often as he could at such moments, to let Mr Hamel-Levitt see the reflection of his smiling face in the mirror.

"Heard the news, I suppose?" Mr Hamel-Levitt asked at length.

"News, sir?" Fernando said nonchalantly. "Oh, you mean about the German fleet being seen some time yesterday afternoon in the Caribbean, sir?"

"Not fleet," Mr Hamel-Levitt said with a chuckle. "A few ships of war. One version has it six, another . . . oh, damn! You've clipped my ear, Fernando!"

"Sorry, sir, sorry, sir," Fernando said, holding the pair of scissors before him and examining them. "This pair is dull, sir," and he went to the cupboard and extracted another pair.

"Personally I don't believe a word of the rumour," Mr Hamel-Levitt said after a pause.

"Really, sir? That's exactly what I told my wife this morning. Poor woman! She was in such a state, sir. I very nearly had to stay home this morning to reassure her."

"Oh?" Mr Hamel-Levitt said.

"It wasn't in the papers this morning, sir."

"Well, it isn't the sort of thing they would publish for fear of scaring the people. It's all right for people like you and me, but you know: mob-psychology."

"Quite, sir, quite. And who could have started such a rumour, eh, sir? The man should be put into jail if he is caught. Only this morning I was telling my wife that."

"Well, it is my personal belief that it is a rumour. It might be true." Fernando was perilously near Mr Hamel-Levitt's ear at that moment, and controlled himself by shifting his operations to a safer part of the head.

"So that . . . it might be true, sir?"

"It might be, of course. I was talking to the inspector general of police at the club last night and tackled him on the subject. He was very vague. What aroused my suspicion though was that he got a 'phone call and cleared out immediately after. I heard this morning that he has called out the volunteers," whereupon Fernando asked to be excused and went to the back of his shop. He drank a glass of water, then sprinkled some bay rum[1] on to his handkerchief and his head.

"But what can the volunteers do, sir?" he asked on his return.

"I don't know. I know what *I* shall do if German ships sail into the gulf."

"Yes, sir?"

"Pack my family in the car and go up the hillside to my house in Cascade.[2] German shells won't want to bother about that peaceful spot," and Mr Hamel-Levitt chuckled again.

"I hadn't thought of that, sir," Fernando murmured, his heart giving a great bound.

"Yes. Well, don't go spitting it out to everybody who comes into the shop this morning, or else you might have the Cascade road blocked with traffic," and Mr Hamel-Levitt gave a little snort of laughter. Fernando tried to respond to the jest by laughing, and succeeded only in making a hollow sound in his throat.

When Mr Hamel-Levitt left, Fernando went to the back of the shop and sat down, thinking. He was very nervous and dreaded a collapse. Putting his handkerchief to his nose, he inhaled deeply.

Exactly at ten o'clock that morning the rumour was confirmed for Fernando by someone hurriedly stepping into the shop and saying:

"German ships are steaming towards the third Boca. North Post[3] report, I hear. In another hour they'll be in the gulf and then . . ."

But Fernando waited to hear no more.

When he arrived home in a taxi, he was breathless and perspiring.

"But what is it, what is it?" his wife asked, turning pale.

"German ships . . . in the gulf . . . firing just now . . . everybody in the car. Quick, quick."

"But where are we going?" his wife asked, clasping her hands together and calling upon the Lord, as people always do in extremities.

"Cascade, Cascade, up the hillside, the mountainside, away from Port of Spain."

Men were blasting a quarry somewhere.

A hollow boom reverberated over the town.

"Good God, they're here, they're here," Fernando cried.

"Holy Mary, mother of God," his wife murmured, making the sign of the cross. The children, with scared faces, were all about her. They began to cry. The mother and father rushed about the house. Fernando knocked over a chair.

"Ethel, Ethel," he screamed after his wife. "There's time to take nothing. Leave everything. Into the taxi with the children, for God's sake!"

The mother and father hustled the children into the waiting car. In a moment they were off. A few pedestrians glanced at the car as it sped up the street.

Fifteen minutes later they were rushing up the Cascade road, a few miles from town. Suddenly the mother screamed, tried to speak and then fainted. It was the eldest child, Isabella, who spoke instead.

"Papa," she said, her large black eyes filled with fright, "we've forgotten the baby. She was asleep when . . ."

NOTES

1.   An aromatic lotion made from the crushed leaves of the bay berry tree, credited with curing headaches and cooling fever.
2.   A well-to-do area of Port of Spain.
3.   A signal station in Diego Martin.

TROPIC TOWN

I.

At dawn of a Sunday in April the SS *Inania* rode quietly into the First Boca upon a quiet sea. The water parted at her bows in clear-green rolling curves, too lazy, it seemed, to reach even the immediately close shores of Monos[1] or the mainland. But soon a light wash was apparent against the dark rocks. A band of sunlight topped the tall cliffs of Monos in the west. On the mainland shapes took shape: men hauled down their boats for the day's fishing; somebody dived off the end of a pier; a bell rang out from the little church by the shore half-seen through the trees; black women in full white gowns hurried on to pray, under the palms. And as the ship now cleared the Sound the Gulf of Paria lay before her sparkling in the sun.

The ship too sprang to life: stewards rushed busily about; a quartermaster skipped down the companion ladder, sideways; a string of Lascars[2] appeared out of the depths and went off, duck fashion, forward. Two little girls went back and forth between deck and cabin, to enjoy the sight of green hills swinging past the ports. Everybody and his wife came out to see. Everybody, that is, but Mr Smith. He had for some time been standing over the side, blinking reflectively at the sea. He was of middle height, inclined to be bald and inclined to be plump: the inclinations of Mr Smith, indeed, were innumerable. He had a roundish face, a narrow forehead, a roundish mouth and a nose inclined to be long and slightly pinched at the bridge. His small but not unkind eyes looked away from you uncertainly behind powerful horn-rimmed glasses. These were a recent present from his wife, whose felicities were usually of a practical kind; they were the mark of travel: even as Raleigh (and perhaps Columbus!) wore a sword. His new white-duck suit stood out round him like glazed cardboard.

His wife came up wearily, from her last bit of packing. Her face was slightly flushed with her exertions and little beads of perspiration stood out on her lip. She had tinted indifferent hair, was above the average height, slim and pretty. Except her mouth. When she was considering the questions of the horn-rimmed glasses it had been her mouth that decided it.

"Isn't it strange, Bert," she said in a sharp cockney voice. "We left home freezing, and here we are, a fortnight later, in steaming weather!"

"Well, well," said Mr Smith. "And who'd have thought it a couple of months back! Four thousand miles from home! Life's all changes, Betty, all changes!"

"It *was* a drag to leave Ma, Bert; wasn't it?"

"Come, come. Just like you women. Here we are in Tenessa and here we've got to stop, I reckon. But thinking of your Ma won't help. We must make the best of a bad job. The island, you know, Betty, doesn't look half bad."

"But d'you think there are many snakes and scorpions and things?"

"Oh, I suppose there's quite enough of them all right."

"Ugh!"

"Nothing to be afraid of, Betty. Reckon they keep away all right; more up in th' ills I'd say; don't visit the town, so to speak."

"A lot of niggers though, Bert –"

"You mustn't ever call them niggers, Betty. They're Negroes; or better still, just coloured people. And a pretty civilized lot too they seem – judging by what the book said."

"Yes: but don't they come from Africa originally – where the savages are?"

"Well, I expect we must have all been savages once."

"Oh, Bert!"

"But that's true, ain't it? Ha!" he laughed.

"You needn't say it, though."

"And didn't you like the coloured stewards on the ship?"

"Oh, but that's different," said his wife.

"And then there's a lot of East Indians and Chinese, I believe. Pretty cosmopolitan, as the book says. And pretty near every race in Europe, I'm told: us English, and the Froggies[3] and loads of Portuguese."

"Oh, but *they* don't count," said his wife.

"Well; it takes a lot to make a world," he returned in philosophical retreat. "You women *are* funny. People aren't all white, you know."

"But still," said his wife.

"Don't be silly," said Mr Smith, by way of rebuke.

In himself he was inclined to be thankful for small mercies. For the rest, hard work must sooner or later find its due reward. And here on the eve of new things life did not seem so objectionable after all. London, it is true, was far behind, and he would miss a lot: the decent little house with the back garden, and the pictures every Saturday night, and now and then a show in town, or perhaps a dinner at Maison Lyons[4] – in Oxford Street. But still, three hundred and fifty a year wasn't such a lot to run a yacht on. What did hurt a bit, though, was the old firm acknowledging his application for a rise by giving him a month's notice. As he had complained to his wife:

"After all these years."

"I told you that would happen," she had said.

"Why, you never did."

"Well, I hinted it."

"You never did, Betty," Mr Smith reiterated, beginning to lose his temper.

"Well, anyway, I *knew* it would," she insisted.

"Then why the devil didn't you say so!" he flung at her.

But she was not his wife for nothing, and she said:

"You ought to see Mr Hankey at once and tell him straight you're sorry and that you'd made a mistake in putting in your application so soon."

But as Mr Smith had already approached his chief, without success, he said sharply:

"I do that? I demean myself like that? Old Hankey can go to hell!"

And there the matter rested. Until one day, arising out of an advertisement in the press, a new horizon loomed before them.

"Tenessa?" asked his wife, putting down the paper.

"Where's that?"

"Overseas," said Mr Smith laconically.

"Overseas?" she queried again.

"Well – overseas. That is – I can soon find out."

He methodically went in search of an almanac.

"Why, *of course*," he began, adjusting his glasses. "The British West Indies."

"Oh, India," affirmed his wife, in better company than she imagined.

"Don't be silly," Mr Smith corrected her, restored to confidence by Whitaker. "It's one of those islands near South America and all round there."

"Oh, an island. One of those places with *natives*, I suppose."

"Well," said her husband wearily, "we might try it anyway. And the pay's good."

"Yes, the pay's good," his wife agreed thoughtfully. "And I suppose we'll be able to get home pretty soon. I hope it's not a savage place though."

"Who says it's savage? Does well-laid-out streets sound savage? You women *are!*"

A month later Mr and Mrs Albert Haddon Smith sat in the train bound for the West India Docks. Mrs Smith snapped her bag upon a bright new passport book; but not without a compensatory glance at the horn-rimmed glasses in the photograph. Her husband blinked before her from the carriage window.

"Good-bye, Ma," he waved to his mother-in-law. "And don't forget to pass on the *Mail*."[5]

II.

Despite Mr Smith's earlier assurance life was at first a little bewildering. He could better have coped with the straight conflict, as from all accounts in other parts you sometimes got it, between Englishmen like himself and "natives". They kept themselves to themselves. At any rate, you knew where you were. And the progression for instance from the habit of a cup of tea to coffee and cocktails was unequivocal and exclusive: a birthright more or less immediately acknowledged. Not, as here in Tenessa, a mere matter of paying for it: *everybody*, too, was sipping coffee; the most extraordinary people drinking rum-punches. Moreover, coffee upset his digestion; and he had perforce to register a certain regret that he was himself, unfortunately, a total abstainer.

His wife's perceptions were, however, more alive, and with time on her hands she watched, and prayed. At this distance from home her self-reliance and commonsense would soon return redoubled. She accepted with sufficient grace the prospect of the modest boarding-house which her husband's employers had assigned him: "Till you find your feet," the manager assured them. It was unfortunate that her landlady was a Portuguese, but as it happened Miss da Costa was a simple soul, very tidy and obliging, and breast high in the pride of having the "unassuming new English couple" at her house. They in turn liked her, and in the afternoons would often take her for a drive. Miss da Costa, too, was always delighted to show them the sights of the town, or direct the chauffeur to go round the Saddle,[6] or down to Teteron Bay.[7] And often they would return to the Savannah for a last turn round the park.

"This is where all the aristocrats live," she informed them, indicating the fine houses they passed.

"Aren't they grand?" observed Mrs Smith.

"Well, I don't know," put in her husband. "They're not cosy enough for me: too much style."

"There now!" Miss da Costa rejoined. "Humility is a true Christian virtue."

Mrs Smith took her astonished eyes from her husband and turned to their companion. "You are, of course," she hesitated, "a Roman Catholic?"

"Indeed no!" Miss da Costa's voice quickened. "I'm a Presbyterian."

"Well, fancy that now!" said Mr Smith. "So are we!"

"Fancy that!" agreed Miss da Costa. "Do let me take you to *our* Mr Elrae.[8] He'd be so pleased to see you. Our church,[9] you know, has quite a wonderful history. The first refugees driven by the Catholics from Madeira set to and built it with their own hands. They gave their all. Wasn't that grand? Mr Elrae is always telling us never to let that spark die out. It isn't sufficient just to build, he says; we must just as generously maintain." She hesitated. "Unless of course you prefer to go to Trinity Square.[10] They're more swell than we are, you know."

"Don't you worry," Mr Smith assured her affably. "We're not a bit swell."

Mrs Smith stared at her husband.

In this way Miss da Costa's innumerable relatives now heard about the nice English couple staying with her and soon were calling at the boarding-house, "to have a little chat". Mrs Smith was charming to them all. They too were at pains to make it clear how much "at home" she must regard herself. And so in a very short time they were, on all sides, calling one another by their Christian names.

This, however, brought Betty no nearer an understanding of Antonia de Freitas. Antonia's heart was in music. She was an accomplished pianist and used to play to her friend by the hour. And it puzzled Betty to observe the power of this frail and exquisite little creature at the piano. One day Antonia flung up her hands from a chord and said.

"Why *didn't* I learn the ukulele as a child?"

"The ukulele!" repeated Betty in surprise. "But you play the piano so well!"

"Oh, dear, you English!" Antonia rejoined. "That's just what my music master used to say. But you're really quite wrong. The piano merely makes you remember; the ukulele helps you to forget."

And she laughed.

"Were you in England then?" asked Betty.

"Yes." Antonia named a famous girls' school. "And then Paris."

And with the deepest serenity she in turn asked:

"Where were you?"

"Oh, a place in the North. You wouldn't know it."

Betty might more accurately have said "in the north of London". But she conceived that any good school must be situated in the country, and boldly dying for a sheep as for a lamb, presumably, the farther in the country the better. Besides, the difference was a small one and might almost have been a slip. But Antonia passed on to what she had to say.

"Anyway, I'm going to get a ukulele. You see, it's no good playing the piano. Every householder has one. It still remains, despite the efforts of the gramophone companies and the Baby Car manufacturers, the symbol of a more or less successful respectability. And as such, I'm almost beginning to hate it – poor thing!" She let her fingers fall softly on the keys, and laughed a little. "I'm getting up a concert party," she went on, "to play Jazz and Negro Spirituals. You can sing: would you care to join?"

Betty, having reflected that Antonia couldn't possibly mean to include actual Negroes among the performers, smiled her consent. "That would be jolly," she said.

"I'll get Freddie Nunes to come in," said Antonia, counting off her troupe on delicate expressive fingers. "He's a ventriloquist,[11] you know, of no mean parts – dear Freddie."

But when the girl had gone she began to realize that she disliked intensely the fact of her inability to estimate Antonia. This was a blow to her prestige and she was conscious of an actual resentment.

The rehearsals, however, provided an amount of fun, and the Serenaders faced the footlights in unmistakable excitement. The biggest surprise of the evening was Bert's success as a buffoon. He delivered himself of a number of quips altogether unsuspected by the others. And the house was rocked to tears. Congratulations poured in. One paper astonishingly said he was "the greatest exponent of motley that ever graced the local histrionic (if comic!!) stage. It was universally agreed, so far as we could judge, and we interviewed a number of the audience, that Mr Smith's sense of the ridiculous was of the highest order and refreshingly clean – such, indeed, as we should feel no shame in the most innocent of our daughters appreciating."

This was in rebuke of Freddie, one or two of whose jokes could hardly be regarded as fit for the ears (far less the appreciation) of even the more innocent of our daughters. But it ought to be said in fairness to Freddie that on such occasions he, with great skill and precise judgement, had thrown his voice to the farthest corner of the house, where it could be heard only as a very distant whisper. From that quarter, it has also to be observed, he received the greatest applause.

A gossip writer in another daily paper regretted Antonia's obvious (though entertaining) decline; but gallantly emphasized the length of time it was "since the island had seen such a talented English couple on the stage". It was there also suggested that the Dramatic Society should lose no time in securing their services. Whereby Betty was considerably mollified. And Antonia said: "Well, Bert, you have arrived."

At his office next day several people came in to shake Bert by the hand and say a few words. It was fine! Splendid! What a scream! Good old Bert! More, the office itself was pleased. Bert was undoubtedly an asset. And the manager so led him to understand. Nor were things idle at home. Betty was now receiving a long line of callers. She never realized before that there were so many English people in the island – so many, that is, agreeably disposed to herself. She very generously put forward Antonia to share, or at any rate, to mark, her triumph. Antonia herself had derived considerable satisfaction from the event. But for her own slight though highly decorative scene, she had taken the least conspicuous part of organizing and managing the show. And that had been work enough! But it was work on which her spirit fed. It gave her an interest outside of the dull round for which she hungered; and she was already planning a second venture. The curious effect was to send her back to the piano out of sheer delight. Her fingers simply flew over the keys.

Not long after this Bert was very handsomely given an increase of salary. And with this advance it was possible for Betty to move into a house of her own. They found one vacant in the flat and rather congested lands of Woodbrook, by the sea; but the rent was not high and, anyway, it was theirs. Antonia, putting her car at their disposal, helped her furnish it. They shopped for long hours together and attended regularly at all the auction sales. She selected a room for Betty and filled one wall with a design which completely captured Bert. Seeing Antonia for the first time against it, in blue overalls and with her hair flung about in wisps and flushed cheeks, he kissed her ecstatically on the ear. And Betty showed no resentment.

"So I *can* have it, all to myself?" said Betty.

"So long as it's available for rehearsals," said Bert, still somewhat excited and looking at Antonia.

There, of course, Antonia often met Betty's new friends. But the occasions were not altogether happy, and the regularity with which she would, upon passing them in the street, appear entirely to escape their observation was only too noticeable. She went to Betty.

"It isn't as if you were *any*body," said Betty uncomfortably. "But still, I shouldn't mind."

"Oh, I don't mind," Antonia explained. "The thing in itself doesn't worry me a bit. It's simply so hopelessly embarrassing all round."

"Oh, I know!"

"No one is consciously snubbed more than once."

"Oh, I know," said Betty.

But Antonia had cast off her mood and with that unfathomable impetuosity of hers turned lightly on the Englishwoman.

"What a marvellous opportunity you've missed, Betty. You could easily have said that it anyway ought not to be necessary! And now I shall have to add for you again, 'Oh, I know!'"

Betty was slightly bewildered. She never could understand the dexterity with which Antonia, if unprovided with material, would mark down her own puppets for destruction. And the young girl laughed.

But Antonia was not altogether indifferent to her triumph. And when the Portuguese Club gave a special "Ukulele Dance" in her honour, she dressed ravishingly in white. Her wide-fringed Spanish shawl, in apricot and bronze, held her like a lily. She had taken Bert and Betty to a restaurant and arrived at her club between them, adequately late to receive the acclamations of a crowded hall. And now one saw how black and shapely was her head, and the colour of her eyes green-gold.

"Why, there's Freddie!" She exclaimed to Betty. "Dear boy, Freddie; with more qualities than you'd think, but dreadful judgement. He thought an awful lot of your singing."

"Did he?" Betty smiled.

"Yes. I'm really afraid he's falling in love with you."

"Oh, nonsense!" said Betty.

"Ah!" drawled Antonia mockingly, tapping Bert with her fan. "Bert! I'll repose on your virgin bosom for precisely two turns."

Bert thought this an excellent though slightly daring joke – Betty could not have made it – and guffawed with pleasure. One or two of his own friends were there, and he was just a little proud to be the first to dance with so attractive a girl as Antonia. That evening he was completely lionized. Somebody suggested that he must surely have been "on the London stage". And Bert said, well, he had always been keen on amateur theatricals. The rumour snowballed as it went that Bert had been keeping it dark all the time, that he was a real actor, and that he had really been an enormous success "in the old country". Everybody gaped.

At home that night Betty experienced all the sensations of success her husband had been made to feel in the course of the evening. She wished to test him.

"Had a good time, Bert?"

"Not so bad. You seemed to be getting along all right too."

"Oh pretty fair. What a crowd, though!"

"Well, these Portuguese aren't half so bad, you know. Very generous people. And one or two of them – like Antonia, for instance – wasn't she a peach in that frock, Betty?"

"I liked the shawl best," Betty admitted. "Though that colour wouldn't quite suit *every*body, would it?"

"No. Wouldn't suit you, I don't think," said Bert, a little too decidedly seizing the undercurrents of his wife's mind.

"Pity she's not English, isn't it?" Betty put in quickly. "It would make such a difference."

"Yes, of course, it is a pity," Bert agreed. "But still – she's been pretty decent to us, I must say."

"And why shouldn't she, pray?" challenged his wife. "It's not as if we were *local* people."

"Oh, quite," Bert assured her. "I wasn't saying, mind you, that she shouldn't be; only that she was."

"Oh," Betty agreed more kindly. "Only it's not like being with English people, *is* it?"

"Leastways, not those that belong to the Government House set," said Bert.

"Well," observed his wife maliciously, "I don't suppose all of *them* always did."

"Expect not," said her husband. "We've not done so badly, so far; have we, my dear?"

Betty gave him her cheek to kiss.

"By the way," she said. "Hasn't the Dramatic Society asked us to join yet?"

"No."

"They ought to, I think, seeing that the *Beacon*[12] mentioned it."

"They probably will," said Bert. "One or two chaps were talking about it tonight."

"Really! But were they – Portuguese?"

"No. Jimmy Higgins, from Sanderson & Co., was one."

"Why! That would be nice, Bertie, wouldn't it?" And Betty rewarded him with a kiss.

"Switch off the light, darling," she said.

Next day the Reverend Mr Elrae, BA, came round to congratulate him. And Bert increased his monthly subscription to the church fund to ten dollars.

III.

The expected, as usual, unexpectedly happened. That is to say, among his morning mail at the office Bert was surprised one day to find a letter addressed to himself, and marked "Personal". It proved to be from the Dramatic Society. The secretary begged to advise him that it would be a great pleasure to welcome both his wife and himself as members of the society. He took it upon himself further to say that the committee had Bert already in mind for a part of their forthcoming production.

Bert was by nature of the kind that responds slowly, even under the most stimulating circumstances. He read the letter over and over again. All its implications he could not, of course, immediately seize, but a deep sense of pride and satisfaction gradually spread over him. He felt like laughing aloud. He put the letter at a little distance from him on his desk, within sight but out of reach, so that he could get on with his work. But it was no use. So he opened it once more and read it through again; and finally he put it up in the pocket of his jacket that hung on a distant peg. To settle himself a little he ordered a messenger to bring him a glass of iced water.

To his subordinates, however, he spoke that day with a tentative and almost imperceptible ring in his voice, such as had not been noticeable before. And well might he. For to be a member of the Dramatic Society meant that he belonged to the best set in the island. It gave him a *cachet*. The early rising of his sun had not, after all, meant a false dawn. His humble London beginnings might always have been there, to remind him that in the scheme of human affairs he was a nobody. But how different was the fact! In London you had to be altogether too big to be anything at all; and so far as London went distance was beginning at last to lend enchantment to the view. Tenessa wasn't half a bad place. And no mistake, Tenessa for him! Old Hankey-Pankey was a bloody fool. Still, his uppishness had been a blessing in disguise. Sitting at his desk, with a quantity of work unheeded before him, he was grateful to remember what Betty had observed: it was only the English that counted. When he came to think of it, Betty was always right – good old Betty. And he was English – and proud of it: if even in only a Morris Minor key.

It was no wonder, he was beginning to see more clearly now, that all the people they had met had been courteous and respectful to them: at their church, at the boarding-house, at the Portuguese Club. *They* had realized what he had failed to see – though Betty had seen it, he was proud to think – that being English they belonged to the cream of the island's society. And he remembered, too, other incidents by which even Antonia had shown, in little ways only too plain to him now, her fear of one day having to release them to their birthright. And Antonia was undoubtedly clever. Good-looking too, by Jove; beautiful even. But beauty was only skin deep. She was so different from – Betty, for instance. True she had been educated in England – and France, wasn't it? Well, perhaps she would go all right in France. But her English ways and English accent sat so incongruously upon her. And there was Freddie too. Not a bad sort, Freddie; could see a good joke now and then. But that wasn't everything. And what was worse, they both had such queer-looking friends and relatives whose chief employment seemed to be selling salt-fish, onions and potatoes, or keeping rum-shops. He could think of dozens, now he'd put his mind to it, he had met at their club. They seemed to fit in all right *there*. But how would they be at the St Ann's? It is true that at present he knew of that club only from hearsay, and by passing it sometimes on his walks with Betty; but he couldn't imagine how they *could* fit in.

As it was Saturday he left the office early – early for him, that is, at three o'clock. He telephoned for a taxi and while awaiting it showed the letter to his chief, a director of the firm. Mr Croucher slapped him on the back.

"Splendid, Smith! Splendid!" he applauded. "I always knew it. That's where you should have been ages ago. The Serenaders were all right in their way, you know; and that de Freitas girl a pretty little piece. But, my boy, now you're with your own people. And we're proud of you!"

Bert flew home.

He was at first, however, somewhat nettled to find both Antonia and Freddie there – on just this one homecoming when he wanted Betty to himself. But by the time he had changed and was sitting down with them to tea his old mood reasserted itself. After all, these people had been very nice to him.

"Well, well," he said breezily. "Can you imagine it? I've been asked by the Dramatic to help them in their next show."

Antonia suffered a cold spasm down her spine, but she managed to look him in the eyes and smiled. Betty's heart seemed to leap into her throat, but immediately remembering her guests she asked calmly enough:

"The Dramatic Society, Bert?" She hoped all the same that Bert had done nothing stupid without consulting her. "To help them in what way?"

"Why, to play for them."

"Well, I never!" Betty exclaimed. "Why didn't they have the decency to ask you from the start?"

"That could hardly have been possible, Betty," Antonia put in quietly. "He surprised even us!"

"Yes, of course. I forgot that. But I do hope, Bert, you've not gone and made a fool of yourself."

Bert was annoyed. It was hardly what he had expected. "A fool of myself! A fool of myself!" he reiterated, groping for a reply.

"I hope you've written," said his wife slowly, "declining their invitation with thanks." She looked straight at her husband. "Remember you're already a Serenader."

"Oh, no!" said Antonia. "Don't let that disturb you, Bert. You'll be doing much better work."

"Come, come," said Bert taking the crutch his wife offered and thinking what a *sensible* girl Antonia was. "I haven't written yet, but I shall certainly remind them that I already belong to an entertainment party."

He breathed more freely.

"But I insist, Bert," Freddie unexpectedly put in, "that you do exactly as you feel about it. And I'm sure Antonia and the others won't mind."

"Quite," said Antonia.

"Besides," Freddie continued, "it'd make it so awkward for us if you refused."

"You mustn't say that," said Bert.

All the afternoon Betty wondered how much of hope there was in her husband's news, and how much to believe. She watched him closely for the signs she knew well; but not with such success as to dispel the hint of anxiety in her voice, when they were at last alone.

"Well?" she inquired. "You surely haven't refused?"

"No fear," said her husband. "I replied this afternoon. But it was damned awkward with those two here."

"That's fine," said his wife encouragingly.

"But what about Antonia? We've made her believe –"

"Don't you worry about that," put in his wife. "That's the least of it. Our real difficulty will be to get rid of her and her crowd."

This was too downright for Bert, and he winced.

"But d'you think that's quite fair? Hardly playing the game – I wonder."

"You're a fool, Bert. And this is where you're absolutely at sea. We've got our bed to make, and it's just as well we make it as comfy as possible. Don't you realize that if we go on with Antonia and Co. the set we rightly belong to will never take us up?"

Bert fixed his eye on the floor reflectively. Betty was wonderful – the way she put things.

"And here's our chance," pursued his wife, tapping the letter in emphasis. "It's a challenge from our own folk in the island. It's up to us now. But I'm glad you've accepted promptly. It'll show them that we're in earnest."

"No doubt you're right," her husband at last admitted. "But it's all going to be very unpleasant."

And Betty knew she was right.

The following week Bert came in later than usual to announce that Mr Piper, the stage manager, was coming that evening to discuss the show.

"He's bringing his wife."

"Mr Piper?" repeated Betty, knitting her brows. "Is that the tall man with red hair?"

"Yes. He's in the Government, you know. Just back out from leave," he added impressively.

"But Antonia's coming."

"Bit awkward, isn't it?" Bert blinked.

"Oh, *I* know," said his wife.

She flew to the telephone.

"Isn't it wretched, my dear. But the poor man's come home awfully ill. Oh, nothing serious. But a splitting head. I believe it's overwork – this terrible weather, you know. Yes; isn't it *terrible*. What's – Oh, thanks awfully, but we've got some, thanks. And aspirin too – quite; heaps, thanks. Oh, he'll be better in the morning, I expect. Yes, you're right there: wisdom cometh with the morning – good for you! Well, so sorry. Nighty-night!"

It is about the business offices of the town that news takes wing, and Freddie Nunes was among the first to hear of Bert's new role. He thought at once of telephoning Antonia. But such reflection as he could give it told him that he would thereby merely be spending the indignation he felt on her. He was far too upset to realize that that was probably the best thing to do, and probably what Antonia herself would have wished. He saw simply that his friend had been most ill-used, to say the least of it. As soon as possible he took a taxi down to Woodbrook and found both Bert and Betty at home. He refused the chair they offered him.

"Is it true," he began at once, "about Bert and the show?"

"Why, yes," said Betty.

"Bit of luck, isn't it?" said Bert.

"Well, I think it's a bit of damned cheek."

"What's the matter, Freddie?" Bert asked concernedly.

Freddie put his hands in his jacket pockets.

"Why, everything's the matter," he burst out. "What d'you mean by letting Antonia down? After all she's done for you, to treat her like this."

"What do you mean?" demanded Betty in an endeavour to stop him.

"You've let her down; that's what you've done – and you know it. Since you've made a lot of your own friends we're no more use – *she's* no more use to you now."

"Here, calm yourself a bit, my boy," urged Bert warningly.

"Oh, don't you worry: I'm not in a temper. But it's enough to put anybody in a temper – the way you treat people. She's done all your running about for you; fetched and carried for you; and been pleasant to you both, just out of kindness. She needn't have done. *She's* gained nothing by it. She was a fool – we've all been fools. But *you've* gained: you've got the best she had. It's she that's brought out whatever there was in you – and a damned sight more too, you take it from me. If you'd only been straight about it. But you went behind our back, pretending all the time. You're a pair of damned sneaks!" he thundered. "That's what you are!"

They were somehow obliged to listen till he had ceased. The boy was obviously unstrung, with blotches of angry colour in his swarthy face. His usually sleek hair stood about his head in tangles. Betty sank into a chair.

"For God's sake, Bert," she appealed to her husband.

"Look 'ere, young man," cried Bert, his throat working. "Just you take your 'at and go. Get out."

"Oh, I only came to congratulate the two of you! You damned suckers! You damned cads!" Freddie stamped out.

"Get out!" Bert flared after him. "The little cur," he added, turning to his wife.

Betty wondered, indeed, whether that had been the youth to whom she had once softened; with whom Antonia had so often twitted her. He'd been in love with her! And when she raised her head to her husband the distress of the last few moments had already gone from her pretty face. Bert stood before her, loyal, level-headed and secure. Her Bert! She put out her hands with a little sigh.

"The young cur," Bert said again.

"It's the best thing that could have happened, my dear."

"What!"

"Oh, don't be a fool," said his wife.

IV

My dear Freddie – You must by now, I imagine, have purged your contempt, if one may judge by the fact of your writing at all. Thanks ever so much for the long and charming letter. Mine, as you see, is going to be equally long; but I, alas, have lost my charm!

How are the wide spaces? Your days in the saddle must indeed be long, and I shall henceforward always imagine you at the head of your gang swarming into town, like they do at the pictures, with a gun at each hip. But is it necessary in real life to use such weapons for coffee-growing, or cattle-raising? What do you do with them, I wonder, during the time that you and your iron men are at peace? Politely flick a fly off a companion? Or singe the moustaches upon his lip? You tease! Do not be hard on me if I get my "travel" from the films. Do you often go down to Bahia?[13] I hope your life there is in every way edifying. And I sincerely hope your arduous pleasures do not entail holding up the bank, or any of the wilder frivolities which are the tribute you men of destiny pay to civilization.

The past twelve months or so have brought little change to myself, except, as I say, to sober me a little. Things have progressed, however, with some rapidity in other directions. You will be interested to hear of the success of the Dramatic Society with *Charlie's Aunt*.[14] Bert simply brought the house down. And it's really surprising when you consider what he had to overcome. It was a truly great performance in which he surpassed himself. The *Beacon* came out with a wonderful headline: MR HADDON-SMITH'S TRIUMPH. Isn't it marvellous! Of course I've never seen them since, except, perhaps, promenading in the afternoons encased in the refinements of their new saloon. They've now got a house on the Savannah before which my inelegant footsteps falter as I pass. Bert has got a new post as secretary to Caribbean Essences Limited, who deal so delightfully, as you know, in tonka beans, rums, essential oils and spices, and of which he hopes, I am told, soon to become a director. I sometimes see their car outside Trinity Square now, and heard, at first, that he and Mr Elrae had quarrelled. But that proved to be entirely false, their little difference, which I understand related to the old subscription, having been settled in a manner entirely satisfactory to all concerned, and redounding greatly to Bert's credit.

He has also, it appears, lately been made consul for Austria here. This is of the greatest interest to myself, as I contemplate very shortly taking a trip to Vienna. It'll certainly *start* well!

They are of course – I don't know why I say "of course" – both members of the St Ann's Club.[15] This last lustre admirably fits the empty setting in Betty's diadem. As Keskidee[16] in the *Beacon* puts it, "The *plage* at Macqueripe on Sunday was thick with local celebrities and other Saints of the Club. I was particularly pleased to see the Haddon-Smiths with their small son, having a dip in the lovely water. John, who is of course just six months old, was the centre of attraction as he gurgled comically at the capers of his gifted father. Is this a sign, I wonder? The time of their departure, by the way, on long Home leave is fast drawing near, and I hear they're planning a magnificent farewell cocktail party, at which of course I expect to see all the elect."

May not much be done, my dear, in five years?

My news has now run dry; which is more than I can say of myself these sopping days. I have a flame-coloured gown that is a dream. The snag about long frocks is that they're so apt at any moment to revive all the stupid psycho-therapeutic jokes about women's legs which one hoped the short skirts had forever silenced. Thanks ever so much for your recipe for making "real" coffee – you dear boy! But will the ordinary domestic utensils do, unhallowed as they are? I shall certainly try it, and break, with my most excruciating maid, my empty cup towards the South.

Well, my dear, goodbye. Make good. And if you've got the time write oftener. You were never in love with *me*, you know! And I'm so glad of that, because I should have hated it.

Your virtuous
Antonia.

NOTES

1. The largest of the five islands off the coast of the mainland of Trinidad.
2. East Indian sailors.
3. The French, for whom frogs' legs are a delicacy.
4. An inexpensive but landmark London restaurant, one of a chain owned by J. Lyons and Company.
5. The *Daily Mail*, an English newspaper.
6. A narrow pass between two hillsides in the Northern Range.
7. On the north-west tip of Trinidad.
8. An anagram of Earle. The Reverend Gilbert Earle was rector of the "Portuguese Church", St Ann's Church of Scotland on Charlotte Street from 1917 until 1929. Mendes helped him to edit the *Trinidad Presbyterian* 1926–1927.
9. The "Portuguese Church".
10. A probable reference to the older Presbyterian Church, Greyfriars Church of Scotland, which was built to cater especially for English and Scottish settlers in Trinidad. It was located in Woodford Square, as is the Holy Trinity Anglican Cathedral.
11. Like Freddie, Mendes was an accomplished ventriloquist, who had performed to acclaim at his school concert (cf. "Torrid Zone", *Selected Writings*).
12. Mention of the *Beacon* places the story contemporary with or later than its first issue of March 1931. Mendes has in mind the social column of the *Trinidad Guardian*, "The Talk of Trinidad" by "Humming Bird".
13. In Brazil.
14. A farce by an English playwright, Brandon Thomas.
15. A club for expatriates, now the Chinese Association.
16. For "Humming Bird".

JACOB AYOUB[1]

JACOB AYOUB WAS SIX YEARS OLD when he arrived in Trinidad with his father and two elder brothers.[2] Following the Syrian tradition, the two elder brothers went into business with their father in Henry Street. Jacob went to school and grew up to be a dandy. Every year he travelled up to the States to buy "job-lots" for the family business. On all such trips he spent much money and would never let anyone know the sort of business his father owned. He would say vaguely:

"I'm in business with my father," and then order champagne cocktails for the party.

Because Jacob had horse-sense, which is a synonym for business acumen, his purchases were always lucrative, so that his father and brothers spoke of him as being a very clever fellow. When, however, he sent them into bankruptcy because of his aristocratic manner of throwing money about, he promptly looked around for a wealthy girl, found her, impressed her with his glittering style and then married her.

Carmen (Jacob called her Carmeng because he thought it sounded *chic*) was the daughter of Mr de Freitas, a rich Portuguese merchant of Georgetown, Demerara. Jacob met her on shipboard and, in his fashion, fell in love with her. That, of course, was after he had had many a quiet tête-à-tête with her. She was pretty, just returning to Georgetown from an English school, and well-figured.

Old de Freitas didn't want to hear of the marriage.

"Syrian, Syrian?" he said. "That oily man?" and his own shining face wrinkled indignantly.

At last, against heavy odds, he gave in with a flow of abuse for his daughter's sinfulness, and Jacob married Carmen.

Six months later old de Freitas lent Jacob twenty thousand dollars to start him off in business. Jacob started well and continued well. He still travelled up to the States every year and became more of a dandy than ever.

Carmen bore her marital yoke like a patient beast of burden. To everybody she said how happy she was; and if Jacob happened at the moment to be away on one of his "business" trips, she would add how much she was missing him.

Jacob, meanwhile, in a dark corner of the promenade deck, was in the arms of some other woman; and this time Jacob was more in love than usual. Gladys was a very rich Manchester girl, circumnavigating the globe in order to be in the modern fashion of touching life at as many points as possible.

When the boat arrived in Port of Spain, Jacob took Gladys to the Queen's Park Hotel to luncheon. Afterwards, in lending him a thousand pounds Gladys was made to feel just as if Jacob was doing her a great favour by accepting the small sum.

Before parting, Jacob faithfully promised Gladys that he would meet her next June in Manchester. This was September.

Through all the days of her up-to-date pilgrimage, Gladys thought of Jacob. She wrote him often, and some of the post-marks were: Valparaiso, Honolulu, Brisbane, Shanghai, Teheran. She even cabled him now and again:

"Duckey Stop Hell Fire Cannot Melt my Love Stop Glad."

May came and with it an empty pocket for Jacob. In spite of the screams of the last-born from the first room, Jacob's mind, with its business acumen characteristic, waded through the difficulties of a little plan for obtaining money, rejecting and accepting, like a novelist in the throes of creation, until the plan was all cut-and-dried.

The next morning he went to his father-in-law.

"Len' you t'irty t'ousan' dollar? Len' you t'irty t'ousan' dollar?" old de Freitas spluttered.

"That's what I said, sir," Jacob said, full of confidence.

"What about dat twenty t'ousan' you still owesh me?"

"Oh, that," Jacob said nonchalantly. "My business can pay you that now. I didn't know you wanted it."

Old de Freitas looked at his immaculately dressed son-in-law with an expression that struggled to believe and yet dared not.

"Bring me dat twenty t'ousan' dollar first," the old man said at last.

Within fifteen minutes Jacob was seated before the manager of the bank.

"I give you my word of honour, sir," he was saying impressively, and Jacob could be as impressive in his business dealings as in his love dealings; "I give you my word of honour, sir, I shall return you by two o'clock this afternoon – it is now eleven – my cheque for the twenty thousand. Have no fear, no fear. This is a big deal, and I must have that amount for a few hours – until two o'clock." He rubbed his hands together to add: "I stand to make a clear ten thousand, sir."

The bank manager, with the vision of old de Freitas looming up before his mind's eye, gave Jacob his cheque for the amount.

Jacob went straight to his father-in-law and handed him the cheque.

"Dis not good," old de Freitas said, carefully examining back and front of the slip of green paper.

Jacob indicated the telephone with a generous gesture.

"Dat a you, Mr Brisbane?" old de Freitas said, speaking through the instrument at the top of his voice. "Dis cheque dat my son-in-law . . . Oh, you say it good? . . . You sure? . . . No offence, Mr Brisbane, but dese young mensh, you know . . . T'ank you, t'ank you much," and he hung up the receiver. Taking out his pocket-handkerchief, he mopped his brow, the cheque in the trembling fingers of his left hand. Then he let his heavy-lidded gaze fall on Jacob.

Jacob appeared to be utterly unconcerned. He blew smudges of cigarette smoke through gold-filled teeth into the still, salt-fish-smelling air of the office. Then he leaned back and returned the old man's stare.

"I didn' know you was doing so good businessh, Jacob," the old man said ponderously. "I didn' know you was so good businessh man."

"I could have let you have that money long ago, only I didn't know that you wanted it," Jacob said grandly.

"An' now," the old man said, and paused.

"And now," Jacob repeated.

As a matter of fact, the old man meant it when he said:

"Not one damn cent, not one damn cent. You playing smart."

On the following day, the bank closed down the business of Jacob Ayoub and Co. Everybody gave different reasons for the bankruptcy; and one old lady, who had in her earliest days been a spark of old de Freitas, whispered across the tea table that she heard that poor Carmen's father was a bit shaky.

But Jacob rode his troubles like a cork on a bouncing sea. He cabled Gladys, who in return cabled him one hundred pounds. He shook the dust of Georgetown from his feet a fortnight later to join Gladys in Manchester.

He found her in her usual modern warpaint.

She was already planning another tour: to Russia this time for the purpose of studying the USSR's new-fangled marriage laws. On her return she hoped to write a book. A few publishers, learning of her proposed trip and book from the gossip column of a certain paper, made her offers for the book.

Before leaving, she took Jacob to London and showed him the sights of the town. Jacob liked London so well that when the time came for leaving, like a spoilt child he didn't want to leave. The truth is, he had seen so many other Gladyses, each prettier and richer than the others.

NOTES

1. Mendes used the pseudonym "A.H. Seedorf" for this story for reasons that are not apparent. The story's publication in *Quarterly* preceded that of "Sweetman" in *Beacon* by a month (September and October 1931 respectively). He did occasionally ring the changes on his own name: "Hubert Alfred" for "At the Ball", "Profit On Opium", "Sé-Sé" and "Twelve Cents"; "Alfred Hubert" for "The Thief" and "A Thing of Beauty"; and "A.H. Seedorf" for "Escape", all published in the *Quarterly Magazine* (ed. Austin M. Noltc).

2. Settlers from Syria and the Lebanon migrated to Trinidad in the late nineteenth and early twentieth centuries (Besson, *The Book of Trinidad*, 398–404).

WITHOUT SNOW

Albert, after swallowing his whisky and soda with quick gulps, said:

This is a Christmas story without any snow. Indeed, it need not be a Christmas story at all, but as it happened last Christmas Eve night, I suppose I may call it a Christmas story.

It was a very hot night. Perhaps that is not quite what I should say. We had been drinking, and as all the world knows, drink engenders heat in a human body. There is, however, no question of the drink playing any part in the fatal happening of that night a year ago, as you shall see for yourself. Richard was that way: psychic, if you like, with something else added, and what that something else was you will know when I have finished.

I had known Richard for a long time. He was a tall fair-skinned man: white, I think, but you know how difficult it is, in the West Indies, to tell if a man is pure-white or not. He looked Spanish. The hair on his head was as black as the plumage of a black bird and he wore a small moustache of the same jetness. His eyes, almond-shaped and black, were so deeply set that when he fixed them on you he gave you the feeling that he was looking *into* you. I had never liked him, but because he had married my sister, Christmas and such holidays found him, more often than not, at our house. We never visited his house. Quite frankly, I was afraid of the man: in some strange way, every time I saw him I was reminded of Emily Brontë's Heathcliff.[1] He looked malevolent. That my sister, poor girl, was not happy, anybody could see; and the disturbing thing was that nobody could tell why, not even my sister, when asked. Richard was never known to be drunk: he had never in his life gambled: he was not fond of women, and I believe my sister was desperately in love with him – that is, up to the moment before his tragic end; after which, she seemed to have wakened from her trance. Now, I know, she hates his very name to be called in her hearing; and every single thing that could have reminded her of him was, soon after his death, destroyed, sold or given away. I am not so sure, even now, that Richard was ever in love with my sister. Long before he married her, long before he had met her (for she was at school in England for eight years), everybody knew that he was in love with Isabella, my wife. In those days, I was in France with the British army. Richard proposed repeatedly, but Isabella, not caring for him and, like myself, scared whenever he was near, as often rejected his offers. Soon after my return from the war, I fell in love with Isabella and married her.

For a year or so we saw and heard nothing of him. It was said that he had gone off to the Maracaibo oilfields on a most lucrative contract: which must have been true, because when he returned he bought a house, furnished it expensively and did not another stroke of work for the rest of his life. Gossip could not understand this sudden affluence and, as gossip will, whispered all sorts of reasons for it.

Before marrying Inez, my sister, he called at our house once, alone: and I shall never forget the perturbed condition in which I found Isabella on my return to the drawing room which I had vacated for the short space of five minutes in order to ask the maid to mix some cocktails. Isabella was all unstrung, as I, who know her so well, could see; and as soon as Richard left I pressed her to tell me what had so disturbed her. At first, she refused point-blank to say anything; but when I threatened to go to him with my curiosity, she confessed that he had said, malignantly:

"So you married him? Well, we shall see."

As a matter of fact, I was relieved, for I had thought it was ever so much worse – involving my honour and that sort of thing. I tried to reassure Isabella: it was really a very slight matter: perhaps he was jealous: perhaps he was in a bad mood, but Isabella shook her head and said nothing more. From that night I gave the incident no further thought until now.

And then Richard married Inez. No one in Port of Spain had any suspicion that they even knew each other. Inez came to our house the day before she was married. Her face, usually so alive, was pale and listless; and her fingers, twitching, gave another sign of something oppressing her. I asked what was the matter and she said:

"Why?" averting her eyes from mine.

"Because you look out of sorts, not your usual self," I said, putting it as mildly as possible.

She gave a nervous little snort of laughter and turned the conversation, with an obvious effort, to a light topic.

At first, I couldn't believe it when I heard that Inez had married Richard. The fact is: I didn't *want* to believe it; but Isabella, coming into the house that evening with excitement writ large over her face, assured me that it was true.

"Well, people are saying so," she replied to my unspoken question. "But you know what people are: dirty-minded. And we all know the sort of girl Inez is. No, I don't believe *that*; I don't believe that she was forced into marrying him for *that* reason. I believe she was forced into marrying him for *another* reason."

"Oh?" I said, interested.

"Yes, I believe she had to marry him all right"; and then added, quickly: "I'm sure he deals with the devil."

I laughed out at her naïveté.

"You may laugh," she said, bristling up, "but I know what I'm talking about."

"Then why the *devil*" – enjoying my play upon the word – "didn't he force *you* to marry him?"

At that, her face fell; but, recovering herself in a moment, she said, evasively: "Well, you will see, you will see. I don't like it, that's all. Something is going to come out of this. It has happened before . . ."

"With him?" I interrupted.

"It very nearly did with *me*. But I don't mean it *that* way. I mean that it has happened in the world before and it will happen again."

"Perhaps," I added, mockingly. The truth is, I was uneasy.

For a long time that night I was kept awake thinking over Isabella's queer words. What mysterious power had this man, I kept asking myself, that Inez, above all people, should have been led into marriage with him? I was afraid for her; and the very first time I met her after her marriage I sensed that all was not well with her.

And so, let me come down to that last Christmas Eve night.

I do not pretend to be able to give any explanation. But explanation of what? I find myself asking. It is impossible for me to put into words the strange implacable atmosphere that weighed down upon us during the course of that eventful night – and it is that, to me, that needs explaining. How did it come there, and why?" And by whose agency? Richard's – there is no doubt in my mind about that: Richard's, but what reason can I give you for being so sure that Richard was responsible for it? None that I can think of except the vague: intuition. I knew, and Isabella, and Inez too, and all the others that had Richard not been present our spirits would have been, as they ought by all the rules of the game to have been, free and festive. So that I can only state it as a fact: there was something wrong somewhere, impalpable, unseen.

Richard was dressed in a black tweed suit and his tall cadaverous body looked more forbidding than ever, with its stoop and its ridiculous shuffling manner of moving about: a glide, almost. When I saw him entering the front gate with my sister, I involuntarily recoiled, only to get possession of myself after I had pointed out, deliberately pointed out to myself how silly and child-ish it was of me to be behaving like that. At the moment I was playing on the gramophone Ravel's *Daphnis and Chloe*. Richard halted in the gallery, listen-ing; then he glided up to me and said:

"Ravel: I can't listen to Ravel and Debussy and Stravinsky and that modern lot without some drinks. Drink helps one to understand them. They lack emo-tion, and drink supplies it, and what is music without emotion?"

Everybody was looking at him as he spoke, even Inez, but no one said a word. For myself, it was just as if his presence had shut off the flow of music to my brain: I could no longer hear it as music, only as a blur of sound. His eyes were fixed on me: in all conscience a perfectly natural thing for him to do: fix his eyes on me; but still I felt that there was something more in his look than the mere necessity of having to look at me when speaking to me. Isabella rose, glad enough no doubt for an excuse for leaving the drawing-room, and went to the back to help the maid prepare the drinks that were already prepared.

We all sat down, pretending to listen to *Daphnis and Chloe* and I knew, again intuitively, that every single person in the room, because of the pres-ence of Richard's tall, black-clad figure, was in some way or the other put out. Inez's agitation was all the more apparent because of her obvious desire to suppress it. She sat in a corner smiling inanely, her large dark eyes holding a timorousness in them that made me pity her and want to do violence to Richard. I noticed Richard, through the corner of my eye, beating his fingers on his knee to the time of the music – and suddenly the room seemed to empty itself of all life. I felt almost as if I were gasping for breath; and for quite a few seconds I did not realize that the cause of my dark sensation was simply the cessation of the music. In my confusion, I knocked over a glass that stood on the centre table as I hurried to the gramophone. The glass rolled over and, with a crashing sound, fell to the floor. Everybody woke up. There was a patter of human voices running round the room, but all that I caught was:

"Breaking a glass, they say, means bad luck."

Richard said: "That's what they say."

I busied myself gathering the broken pieces, finding relief in my occupation and an opportunity for trying to account for the complete change that had taken place in my mood since the arrival of Richard, not five minutes before. His coming had spoilt the evening for me, for Isabella, for everybody. Gone was the sentimental delight in the remembrance that here, once again, was Christmas!

We strolled into the dining room and all had a drink. The warm alive liquid, flowing down my gullet, warmed me to a sense of my perfectly congruous surroundings. We were human, every one of us; but Richard, because of his deeply set eyes and the dark history of his past, had deluded me and the others into regarding him, for the moment, as something subhuman, or superhuman, or perhaps, not human at all. There he stood, like any one of us, drinking, his long emaciated fingers clasping the glass; and, not knowing how I could have permitted myself the eccentricity, I laughed aloud.

"He who laughs last, laughs best," Richard said, truculently.

"What do you mean?" I asked.

For answer he stared at me. I had to lower my eyes to the sting of his stare.

When, from the nearby Sacred Heart tower, ten struck, I had had a sufficient number of drinks to be merry, but not at all: I was anything but merry. There was a lot of talk and laughter, followed by long intervals of absolute silence; and although I tried my best to enter into the spirit of the evening, dismally I failed. All the time I was conscious of Richard; and once, in catching Inez's eyes, I received, unaccountably, the impression that she was wanting to say something to me which she dared not say. Isabella, poor girl, revealed her discomfiture in some of the fatuous things she said and did. Her mind appeared to be far away, and every opportunity that came her way for leaving the room, she took; and stayed away once so long that I had to go in to fetch her out.

"No, no," she said.

"But you can't leave your guests like that, Bella," I remonstrated.

"I won't go out, I *can't*," she said, helplessly.

"What on earth is wrong?"

"I don't know, but something is."

"Have we all gone mad?" I asked, sensing in Isabella's spiritual collapse (it was nothing else) a substantiation of my own apprehensions.

She said nothing: only looked at me and wrung her hands. We were both trying to avoid calling his name, but inevitably it came, and more as a self-put question.

"Is it Richard?"

She took me up immediately with a disconcerting searching look, then nodded, slowly.

"You mean," I said, hesitatingly, the idea searing my mind, "you mean that you are falling in love with him?"

"Oh, Albert, Albert," she cried, again wringing her hands, "see if you can't get him to leave the house!"

"But why all this fuss?" I said, trying my best to be genuinely annoyed.

"I don't know, any more than you."

"You haven't answered my question as yet, Bella," I said sternly.

"I don't know what is happening, any more than you"; and added, almost to herself: "Such queer penetrating eyes when he looks at me!"

"He's been looking at you?"

She nodded.

"Often?"

"All the time."

"But I haven't noticed that!"

"Do you ever notice anything where I am concerned? For God's sake, Albert, get rid of the man!"

"How on earth can I do that? He's my sister's husband, you seem to forget."

"Poor, poor Inez!"

"Bah, just like you women, sentiment, sentiment all the time! Come, we've been away too long as it is. Brace up yourself and come out."

"Have you noticed that she wants to say something to you?"

"Who?"

"Inez."

"Has she told you so?"

"I said noticed, didn't I?" – and that petulantly.

"You mean . . ."

"Yes. I feel it."

How strange, I thought, but said nothing.

When I re-entered the drawing room, I determined to observe Richard a little more carefully. At that moment he was cracking a nut which must have scratched him, for he stopped, wincing, and sucked the wounded finger – and at that moment, when physical pain had, so to speak, put him off his guard, I divined the perfect humanness of the man. For a fleeting minute, I saw into him and was preparing to enjoy my victory when Isabella, coming into the room almost on tiptoe, roused his slumbering power and shattered my sense of victory. Once more his implacable sinister spell took possession of the room, and with all the greater intensity because of its short eclipse.

"Blood," he said, holding the wounded finger to Isabella's sight. She went pale and I thought she was going to faint, but she controlled herself, smiled wanly and fatuously, and as fatuously stood gazing before her. All held down their heads, bowed as if in prayer, and a sort of darkness crept over my eyes until I could see nothing. I wanted to scream and thought I did, but I heard no sound. How long I sat in my little world of night, I do not know. When I came to myself, Richard was laughing and some others were talking and Inez was playing the piano and Isabella, seated on the sofa, seemed to be quite composed. I rose and went over to Inez and watched her fingers wandering about the intensely white keys. She was playing Chopin's "Raindrop" Prelude.[2]

"Why not something Christmassy?" I asked for want of something better to say.

"This is Christmassy, for me." As she said that, she gave me a quick hunted glance, and I knew then that she wanted to see me alone.

"That's lovely," somebody said when the music stopped.

"I should like to have that played while I am dying," Richard said. "That reiterated note would be like a hand pushing me over the edge of the world into – who knows?"

"A drink, Richard?" I asked; and as he nodded I walked to the back of the house, ostensibly for the purpose of bringing out the drink, but actually to await Inez. In a moment she was by my side.

"Not here," she whispered, looking through the open door into the yard. I went into the yard; but she led me to the back gate, opened it and stepped into the alley. The alley was dark and deserted. I wondered why all this secrecy, but remained silent.

"Even here I'm afraid," she said.

"But surely he . . ." I fumbled and corrected myself: "no one can hear us here."

"He doesn't listen with his ears," she said. "Sometimes he even hears what I *think*."

"Think? I don't believe in all that nonsense."

"Neither did I – until I met him."

"And now?"

She held up her terrified face to me. "I think he's hearing me now."

"You're distraught."

"And why, and who's made me so?"

I did not answer.

"He's a devil incarnate," she resumed, with emphasis on each word.

"What, you too? Then why did you marry him?" I asked, not giving thought to the cruel implications contained in my question.

"Because I loved him, and do still, at certain times."

There was a silence, during which I could hear her breathing.

"And all this time you've kept this to yourself?"

"I dared not tell before. Tonight I had to."

"Why?"

"You really want to know?" – but before I had time to give her my irritable assent, she bared her neck and bade me strike a match. The flickering flame of the match revealed a blue bruised mark running low down around her neck.

"His finger marks when he tried to strangle me this evening in one of his mad fits," she explained.

Suddenly, anger boiled up within me. She laid a hand on my shoulder and said:

"That won't do. You must control yourself."

"Is that what you've called me out to tell me – to control myself?" I asked, marvelling at her self-possession.

"That, and why you must."

"Oh?"

"He means to harm you tonight."

"Me?"

"Or Isabella."

"But how?"

"I don't know. This only I can tell you: besides something else, he's mad," and with that, like a ghost, she was gone.

Standing where I was left, I tried to think over what Inez had told me, but my brain, working as fast as a small wheel in a large machine, jumbled up my thoughts, so I gave it up and went back into the house.

"You've been a long time getting that drink ready," Richard said, as I walked into the drawing-room.

The sarcasm, taking me unawares, left me stammering some unintelligible excuse. The result, however, was that we had our drink. Only once, during those few short minutes, I permitted myself a furtive glance at Richard. His eyes, fixed on me, gave me a shock: they appeared to be sinking deeper and deeper into his forehead. I tried to conceal my uneasiness under what must have been a stupid remark, for he laughed, I remember, and the others laughed with him.

Soon after, midnight struck and all our guests left us with the exception of Richard and Inez. There were now four of us in the house, not counting the maid, who was somewhere at the back dozing, no doubt. That was her favourite relaxation.

It is difficult for me to relate, in proper sequence, what followed.

Our departed guests left behind them a long silence. I could feel the tenseness, like taut invisible strings criss-crossing about the room. An acute immediate alarm, unlike my former forebodings, took complete possession of me.

Why should I have thought of the traveller (in de la Mare's poem[3]) knocking on the moonlit door? Richard, rigid in his chair, was tapping the floor with his feet: a regular monotonous rhythm of dull taps. Isabella sat stiff on the piano stool, her face lined and old with a pain I had never before seen in it. Inez's eyes were large with fear. Gone was the sangfroid she had displayed in the alley. Unable to bear the silence any longer, I was just about to break it when Richard took from his pocket an old gold watch and said:

"Time is moving and you've not as yet played for me, Isabella. Inez has played for Albert, remember."

"She didn't play only for me; she played for everybody," I put in, my nerves fearful of a return to silence.

"I really don't play: not well, that is," Isabella said. "And how would I sound after Inez?"

"But you will play for me," Richard said rising from his chair and going over to Isabella, who, without another moment's hesitation, swung herself round on the stool and began to play. Richard stood over her, his tall body bent, his feet tapping the floor to the time of a Bach prelude.

My eyes caught Inez's and she shaped her lips into the fashion of a sentence which I failed to read. Just then, Isabella ceased playing and Richard said:

"Play me that stereotyped thing: the Rachmaninoff prelude."

"I don't know it, Richard."

"Play it," he said looking down into her upturned face.

"How can I when I don't know it?" she pleaded.

"Play it," he repeated; whereat Isabella tentatively touched the keys and struck the opening chords. For a moment or so she was uncertain, then went on. I listened, trying to remember if I had ever heard her play this prelude. I was certain I had not. I looked at Richard: his back was turned to me and he was tapping the floor with one of his feet – evidently a habit of his, I decided.

Inez's warning kept passing through my head in a light persistent way: light in the sense that I could not dwell upon it. Indeed, I found it impossible to concentrate: I could only glance from Inez to Isabella, from Isabella to Richard and give myself up to the strange premonition of some impending disaster. Isabella's odd behaviour, Inez's strangulation marks, my own alarming nervousness, and now this: Isabella playing something she had never before played – all these things conspired to put me into a frame of mind fit for the anticipation of some evil happening.

I turned my attention to the music in the hope that I would find relief. Immediately the room filled with ominous sounds. Before this, I had many a time listened to Rachmaninoff himself, on the gramophone, playing his famous prelude, but never did the music affect me in quite so uncanny a manner. I felt as if I were sinking into deeper and deeper gloom, until there came a moment when, in some untranslatable way, I became a part of the circumambient night, lost and utterly frightened. What pulled me to the surface of conscious life again, I do not know. All I can remember is seeing Richard's right hand resting on Isabella's head and his body bent over so that his eyes were gazing into hers.

My first impulse was to rush at him and seize him by the throat. As I attempted to rise, something, to my horror, held me fast to the chair. I made another effort: in vain. A third: again in vain – and I looked to Inez for help. Her eyes were wide open, staring, and in an instant I knew that she was fast asleep. I tried to scream: no sound rose to my throat. And then I realized, inwardly struggling against the approaching sensation, that I was once more sinking down, down, down . . .

Suddenly I was awake and a scream tore the silence into shreds. Perhaps it was the scream that wakened me. I rubbed my eyes violently and glanced about me. Inez was there, sitting where I had last seen her, immobile, her eyes fluttering into consciousness. I remembered the piano, but where was Richard? Where was Isabella? They were nowhere to be seen. And what was that weird scream I had heard a moment before? Was it human or could it have come from some prowling cat? Leaning forward, my hands gripping the rest of the chair, I strained my ears to catch the slightest sound. A minute crawled by as slowly as a year, my heart pounding against my breast, fright in every fibre of my being.

Another scream, and this time there was no mistaking it: Isabella was somewhere in distress, but where? I could not even tell from which direction the scream had come.

I rose, tense, and started to the sound of a rustling dress and feet pattering across the floor. It was the maid, her eyes two white blotches on the background of her black face.

"You hear dat, sir?" she said in an awed whisper.

"Who is it, where?"

"Is madam." She was shaking like a blade of grass in the wind.

"But where?" Frantic now, I shouted at the woman.

"In dere, sir, in dere," said she pointing to the adjoining room.

With incalculable quickness I sprang to the door. It was locked. I banged on it with my fists and my banging was answered by another scream.

"De oder door," I heard the maid saying. "Perhaps it open."

I ran across the drawing-room, through the dining-room and so into the back bedroom. Sure enough, there stood the door ajar. With long strides I was before it and jerked it open.

The scene that met my affrighted gaze I shall never, to my dying day, forget.

Isabella, stark naked, lay on the bed, the floor littered with odd pieces of her garments; and bending over her was Richard, his jacket off, his long emaciated fingers wrapped around her neck. Isabella's tongue was already sticking out of her mouth.

Richard threw his head back and saw me. For a second I was completely off my guard, for the man before me was stark staring mad. His eyes bulged, his hair was dishevelled, his mouth foamed.

Releasing Isabella, he stiffened himself up to his full gaunt height and laughed out hideously. Realizing, in a flash, that this was my chance, I caught hold of a chair beside me, raised it above my head, leapt at him and brought it down on him with all my strength. The chair crashed through him and he fell.

There is only this to add: he died two days later, as he should, don't you think? Anyway, a jury of twelve good men and true thought so.

NOTES

1.   In *Wuthering Heights*.

2.   Frédéric Chopin, "Raindrop" Prelude in D-flat Major.

3.   Walter de la Mare, "The Listeners" (1912).

YOUNG DA COSTA

I WAS SITTING ONE EVENING IN the little room I am pleased to call my "study", a room of which I am very proud, for in it there are shelves containing about a thousand books, and in it I entertain my literary friends, and in it, too, I attempt to write poems and short stories, when my wife announced that young da Costa had called. I asked her to show him in. He entered soon, and sat on the chair which I offered him; but I saw at once that he was nervous about something or excited over something for he crossed his legs and uncrossed them, shifting his position in the chair with a restless frequency; and although he spoke about books with his usual fluency and soundness I knew that he was preoccupied and only awaiting an opportunity to tell me all about his preoccupation.

Young da Costa had always interested me. He was a queer amalgam of literary talent and business acumen. Of the former there was no doubt for of the dozen or so short stories which he had so far written there were at least two that gave promise of fine things to come. I knew of his business acumen from my uncle who employed him and spoke to me about him with undiluted admiration. He was a clever boy, my uncle said, assiduous in his work, conscientious and all that sort of thing. At the time of which I write he could not have been more than nineteen years old, and although so young he was the sole support of his family: a blind father, an anaemic mother, and a sister still going to school. He was very proud of his premature responsibility and his ugly face would become quite attractive because of the glow that suffused it when the matter was discussed with him. He was extremely short, perhaps five foot three, and squat, of a dark olive complexion that told you unmistakably that he belonged to the Portuguese race, of which there are so many families in the island.

We talked of this and that relating to books but all the time I could see that there was something at the back of his mind. He was buoyant, vivacious, staccato-like in utterance, quite unlike his usual placid manner of talking.

"My dear boy," I said at last, "you seem to be rather excited. Anything up?" I regarded him closely as I spoke. He showed not the slightest sense of discomposure. Rather, his small beady eyes danced more, if that were possible, and an elated expression leapt into his face. I realized immediately that I had given him the opportunity for which he was longing.

"Well, if being in love is something up," he said slowly, toying with a volume of Force Stead's poems[1] the while, "there is."

"Oo!" I said, "that's it, is it?"

He glanced quickly at me. Perhaps he thought my intonation of voice was not quite to be trusted; and perhaps that was so, for the declaration, coming from him, sounded rather ludicrous, to say the least of it. I could not conceive of his sallow, pimply face reflecting the passion of love. It was simply incongruous, something like the sun shining when the rain is falling.

"Oh yes," he said, "I am in love. And what is more" – he paused for a moment and sought my eyes before continuing: "I'm thinking seriously of getting married."

"Don't be a damn fool, Joe," I blurted out. The words came to my tongue involuntarily. I knew immediately that I had pained him and hastened with: "You know, my dear fellow, you are young, fearfully young, and I can see no reason why you should be wanting to harness yourself so early in life. Of course, Joe, it is a stage through which we all pass," I continued in a moralizing tone. "Ten years ago there were three or four girls with whom I fell head over heels in love and each one I vowed to myself I would marry." As an afterthought I added: "And then, your position."

"Ah, but you don't know the girl," he said, disregarding my last warning. "I have thought myself in love before this, but this . . . Ah!" He shook his head violently as though trying to get rid of something from it and leaned towards me, his hands clasped together tightly in his lap.

"Come, come," I said, speaking lightly and smiling incredulously, "isn't this another of your passing fancies?"

"Passing fancy?" he threw at me venomously as though that was the most horrible thing that could happen to him. "Chut!"

I saw his seriousness. His small eyes were half-closed, ecstatic, his hair all awry. He was apparently under the influence of a profound feeling, and I realized I had to be extremely careful, for I had no wish to hurt him by anything I might say.

"Do I know the young lady?" I asked.

He did not reply immediately. He appeared to be thinking, to be undecided as to what answer he should make.

"Yes," he said at last.

"That makes it more interesting," I rejoined.

"It does," he said with an unaccountable emphasis.

His expression became bitter and I began to wonder what it all meant. He rose abruptly and threw himself on the sofa in a dejected attitude. I took my pipe from the desk that stood nearby, filled it and lit it.

"Now tell me more about your trouble," I said, making myself comfortable and puffing wisps of smoke into the warm room.

Again there was a pause, and I was deciding to let the matter drop, when he said:

"You know her casually: Irene Thompson."

For the moment the name seemed vaguely familiar but I really could not remember the girl to whom it belonged. I told him so.

"She lives in Belmont," he explained.

"Ah yes, of course," I said. "I remember her now. But surely she is much older than you are and . . ." I paused in time to notice a keen look of expectancy in his eyes that told me how anxious he was to hear what I was next going to say.

"Yes, Alfred, that's what makes it interesting: she is coloured, slightly coloured, and that's where all the trouble lies, and my mother and sister are giving me hell over it."

"Your mother and sister? So they know about it?"

"And why shouldn't they?" he asked pettishly. "They had to know sooner or later, for I am going to marry Irene." He rose and began pacing the room like an old philosopher. He stopped for a moment to tell me in an impassioned voice: "She's the most wonderful girl in the world!"

"Come, come, Joe, calm yourself. I know that you are disturbed, but you must have control over your feelings."

He looked at me contemptuously and sat down. "Control over my feelings?" he said, leaning back tiredly. "What's the use of a friend if I cannot let him see how I react to certain experiences?"

His ponderous way of putting it amused me, but I would not let him see that I was amused.

"Oh no, no," I expostulated. "By all means let me share with you your worries, but please, let me do so in a sensible manner."

He shot a suspicious glance at me and asked me what I meant.

"Simply that I should be allowed to know the facts and give you my opinion of them."

The changes of his mood were startling to observe. His despondency dropped from him like a cloak, and his ugly face brightened in the anticipation of telling me something about the affair.

He leaned forward so much that he was almost kneeling.

"I met her six weeks ago, and from the day I met her I knew that I would grow to care for her. I tried my best to ward it off, to keep it from ever coming near to me. I stopped visiting her. It was no use. The longer I stayed away, the more I ached to see her. And then my sister got to hear of it and told my mother. There was a hell of a row at home, because Irene's father happened to be a slightly coloured man. It's a damn shame that a girl should suffer for her father's drop of negro blood; just as if it is syphilitic blood." He had flared up in a moment and as quickly cooled down. "And Irene got to hear of it. I believe my sister must have told her something. If only I were certain of that!" He clenched his right fist and brought it down on the palm of his left hand with a sharp exploding sound. His voice was calm when he resumed.

"However, Irene got to hear of it and refused to have anything more to do with me. She told me that if she were not good enough for my mother and sister she wasn't good enough for me. And this to happen when I was bringing her round to my way of thinking! As you probably know, she is Catholic."

"I wasn't aware of that," I interrupted. "Really, I know Miss Thompson only by sight."

He said nothing for a while.

"Yes, she is Catholic," he continued, "but I was making her realize how absurd is her God, her immortality, her Bible. I was making her see how cruel, how dangerous her confessional box is. She's intelligent, you know, intelligent." He repeated the word as though it was a beautiful word and he loved it. "She's amenable to reason. She listened to me attentively when I spoke to her and tried to show her the futility of all organized forms of religion. She knows it now, deep down in her heart she knows it now, but her training, her tradition will not allow her to break away quickly."

"You were saying: your sister . . ."

He glared at me and then collected himself. "Ah, yes. Irene was hard against my people, myself. She said she would never see me any more. I begged her. I implored her. I got on my knees and implored her. I threatened to kill myself, and I believe I would have done it. I was frantic, like one crazy, for I realized I was losing her. And then at last she relented, and I told my sister and mother they could do what they liked. What could they do but eventually reconcile themselves to me marrying a coloured girl? They are dependent on me." He chuckled as though it were an exhaust for his seething cross-currents of feeling. "Now!" He gazed at me defiantly, challengingly. I pondered for a minute or two. Then I said:

"But Miss Thompson: isn't she older than you are?"

"Yes: what of that?" He was still glaring at me. I saw it was useless; he would have his own way in the end, and so I said, as nonchalantly as I could under the circumstances:

"Oh nothing, Joe – if you think so."

"You have nothing more to tell me?"

I glanced at him quickly. "Except that I wish you luck," I said.

He bade me goodnight soon after that and left me in a turmoil of conflicting ideas; but above them all was the thought of youth and love together overcoming all obstacles.

I had almost forgotten Joe and his impassioned confession, when one night, about a month later, I was strolling round the Pitch Walk with my wife. It was a fine night. The moon was at its full, and across the Savannah floated on the tranquil northern breeze the strains of the Constabulary Band, which plays once a month at night for the delectation of the people of Port of Spain. The moonlight made every object clear: the range of mountains to the north and east; the trees scattered about the Savannah; almost the blueness of the sky; the grass bordering the walk on either side. My wife and I were silent, overcome by the tropic beauty and peace of the night. Now and again we passed a solitary walker, or a couple, and sometimes a group, with the children full of laughter and happy noise. As we approached the Queen's Royal College I saw young da Costa coming towards us. His squat figure I could recognize anywhere. There was a lady on his arm. At first I thought it was his sweetheart, Miss Thompson; but on nearer approach I saw it wasn't. This girl was much shorter; indeed, no taller than da Costa himself. We said "Goodnight" to each other. I turned to my wife and remarked:

"That's young da Costa with his sister."

She said: "His sister leaning on his arm? Hm!"

Da Costa called in to see me a few days later. Naturally I opened the conversation with him by asking him how his love affair was progressing.

"Splendidly," he said, in good spirits. "I am thinking of marrying some time next month."

"Good," I said. "And I see you are reconciled with your sister."

He looked at me with a puzzled expression on his face. "How do you know that?" he asked. For a fraction of a minute I hesitated before asking:

"Wasn't that your sister I saw with you on the Pitch Walk last band-concert night?"

"My sister!" he said contemptuously. "Of course not! That's the girl I'm going to marry!"

I was thunderstruck.

"But Miss Thompson?" I said feebly.

"Oh, she," he said, snapping his fingers, "I've done with her. This is the most wonderful . . ."

NOTE

1.   William Force Stead (1884–1967), an American poet.

URSULA'S MORALS

AT LAST!

Ursula Aranguez sighed as she shut the door after her mother's retreating figure. At last! – for she was beginning to think that her mother wasn't going out again, it had taken her such a long time to tidy herself before the mirror. And what a narrow shave she herself had had! She could hear her mother's voice now:

"Ursula, come wit' me. I goin' see you aunt Carmen."

But wasn't Antonio coming in tonight? She simulated a headache; and the mother, gazing at her only daughter with concern ,had suggested aspirin. And perhaps Ursula would not like to be left alone?

"No, no, Mama, you go. I'll be all right. I'll try and sleep," and her mother had said:

"Well, child, if you insists I'll go. An' besides, a girl twenty years old can take care of herself, I says." She paused and added: "Tony comin' tonight?"

"I don't know, Mama."

Poor Mama! Ursula had thought, watching her through the corner of her eye. Mama was placing all her hopes on her marrying Tony one day. What a triumph that would be for Mama! – for Tony Gravo,[1] the son of one of the richest Portuguese merchants in Trinidad, to marry her daughter Ursula, a poor coloured girl! She could hear Mama gloating over friends whose daughters were all married to ordinary coloured fellows with hand-to-mouth jobs. Marriage with Tony? Ursula toyed with the phrase in her mind. She had never thought of it seriously. How could she have done so when Tony was white, high up in society, superior in every way to her? If Mama was simple, she was not. And marriage for itself she had no use for. What, tie yourself up to one man for all your days? She couldn't imagine herself doing that sort of thing. And besides, Tony was at least two years younger than she was. She liked him; certainly, she liked him and gloried in thinking over how she had seduced him. At such moments her heart swelled with pride. And so easy it had proved that night six or seven months ago! Ever since then Tony had visited her occasionally, and they had always taken full advantage of those nights when they found themselves alone together. Ursula was quite satisfied with things as they were. What more can any girl want? she asked herself time and again. It was a pity, though, Mama would never hear of her going out alone with Tony. That would have solved the present difficulties of their intimacy. But Mama was so strict with her, so prim and proper!

"What will people say seein' you two alone together in the t'eatre or at dances, eh child?" Mama would say. And Ursula would think: "Poor silly Mama for supposing that Tony would take a coloured girl like me to dances and the theatre! As if I don't know what Tony's friends would think of *him* then!"

Reclining on the sofa now, she smiled. Tony was coming and her mother was out, would be out for at least two hours. She glanced at her cheap wristlet watch: ten minutes to eight. Tony would be here at any minute, so she would have to make everything ready. Rising, she crossed the room and closed the window that gave to the street, clapping the jalousies to at the same time. The room was warm, nice, but the tips of her fingers and the tips of her toes were cold from excitement. Then she went over to the pitchoil lamp that stood on an old wickerwork table in a corner and lowered the wick. Everything became dim and looked cosy. Her own face, as she passed the mirror hanging against one of the walls, seemed like a ghost flitting across it.

As she lay back on the sofa she closed her eyes and tried to imagine how Tony would behave when he arrived and found her alone. He was so timid, so difficult to arouse! She hoped he would be bold and rough for once.

There was a gentle knock at the door; tap, tap. She rose quickly and opened it. Tony stood outside, blinking shyly at her.

"Come in, darling," she said softly to him. He entered and she could see that he was admiring her beautiful figure set against the dim squalid background of the room her mother called the drawing-room. Shutting the door after him, she put an arm around his waist, drew one of his around her waist and led him gently yet firmly to the sofa. There she held his face to hers and kissed him passionately.

"Your mother out, Ursula?"

"Yes, darling, she left a few minutes ago and she'll be away for two whole hours. Tell me you're glad."

"Sure," he said. "It's such a long time since we've had a chance of being alone together. And you know, as I came along just now, I felt that we'd get an opportunity tonight."

He glanced timidly around the room.

"Ursula," he almost whispered, "why have you put the lamp so low? Aren't you afraid?"

She laughed softly at his vacillating mood.

"Afraid, darling? O, you silly, silly sweetie boy! What is there to be afraid of? Come, come to me and let me show you how much we're going to enjoy ourselves tonight."

But Tony drew himself away, murmuring:

"I'm afraid, Ursula, afraid. Not now. Just now. You never know. And put up the lamp in case your mother should return."

"Not now, darling?" she asked naïvely, disregarding his injunction about the lamp. "Why sweetie, why?"

Tenderly and timidly he put both hands to her cheeks and pressed his lips against hers.

"Not now, Ursula, darling, not now," he whispered. "Suppose your mother should return now, sooner than you expect?"

"But Mama isn't coming back now, I tell you," she answered pettishly. "She's gone to see Aunt Carmen."

"Aunt Carmen? Where does she live?"

"Quite in Belmont,"[2] she said, pouting.

He was silent for a moment, gazing at the door through which he had entered.

"Are you sure?" he asked at last.

For answer she put her arms around his neck and kissed him on the lips, the eyes, the ears, murmuring all the time:

"Oh, sweetie, oh, sweetie, oh, sweetie!"

She saw that he was succumbing to her blandishments when suddenly he pushed her from him and stood, listening intently.

"What was that noise?" he whispered hoarsely.

"Noise? I heard nothing."

"Yes, in there," he said, pointing to the open door that led to the bedroom.

"You're a little idiot, Tony," she said, piqued. "I'm sure it was the cat you heard."

"Go in and see, Ursula," he insisted.

When she returned, she noticed that he had raised the wick of the lamp, for the room was brighter than it was before. She was annoyed.

"It was only the cat you heard, you little fool."

"Don't be angry with me," he said, and sat beside her on the sofa.

Although she was quite accustomed to this kind of behaviour on his part, for this was exactly what happened every time he met her alone, she could not help once more thinking what a slow effeminate boy he was. But she knew him well and leaned towards him and kissed him desperately on the lips, breathing into his nostrils the while and drawing him against her breast with both arms. One of his arms groped about her body and the other drew her legs over his until she was sitting on his lap. Hoarsely he kept whispering: "Be careful if your mama comes in, be careful if your mama comes in." But all the time he was kissing her and passing his fingers tenderly through her hair. Then he lifted her and just as he was about to pass with her in his arms through the door leading to the bedroom, there was the sound of an approaching step at the front. He dropped her and hurried back into the drawing-room. Ursula disappeared through the door, pulled it ajar after her and stood behind breathing heavily and peeping through a hole in it.

When Mrs Aranguez entered she found Tony leaning back on the sofa with a strange expression on his face. To Ursula she seemed to be undecided what to say, for she looked at Tony suspiciously and then around the room. It was the first time, Ursula realized, she had ever allowed her mother to find Tony alone with her in the house.

"Why, Tony, you here," she said after a little while.

"Goodnight, Mrs Aranguez. Didn't Ursula tell you I was coming?"

The fool! Ursula thought, standing behind the door.

"Tell me? No."

"Oh, of course not, Mrs Aranguez," Tony said with a snort of laughter. "How could she when I didn't tell her I was coming?"

"But where, where be Ursula?" she asked, still looking around the room.

"Somewhere in the house, I suppose."

Ursula, very still, was thinking of the narrow escape she had had. She would have to be more careful in future: find out definitely where her mother was going to. The slightest cause for suspicion and their liaison would be brought to an abrupt end. Oh yes, she knew her mother all right!

"But has you been here long?"

"Well, yes."

"But who opened the door for you?"

"Ursula, of course. I saw the room lighted and I thought you were here too. Soon after I came in she left me and went inside."

Mrs Aranguez called out: "Ursula, Ursula!"

And Ursula, turning her head away from the door, answered:

"Coming, Mama."

As she entered, her mother asked: "Is this how you treats your guests, Ursula?"

"But Mama, you were not here," and Ursula hung her head demurely.

"I see," Mrs Aranguez said, in her voice the ring of a mother's pride for her daughter's sense of discretion.

They talked of this and that, Mama fawning over Tony: Tony nervous, as Ursula could see: and she, Ursula, casting surreptitious glances at him every now and again. Once, when her mother was not looking, she half-closed her eyes to him, dreamily.

At last Tony rose to bid goodnight, but Mrs Aranguez, turning to her daughter, said:

"Go inside for a moment, child. I wants to speak private to Tony."

Ursula's heart gave a great bound and the tips of her fingers and the tips of her toes went cold suddenly, this time from a different kind of excitement. What could Mama be wanting to tell him alone? Surely not . . . She left the room and could almost feel that Tony too was frightened. But she didn't go into the bedroom. She stood at the door instead, her eyes to the aperture as before, listening. Her heart pounded in her ears.

"I wants to speak to you, Tony, about Ursula."

Tony moved about the sofa uneasily. "Yes, Mrs Aranguez?"

"Yes, Tony, Ursula." She paused. "You understands, I'm worried about something and her."

"Yes, Mrs Aranguez?" Tony said again, moving his lips up and down.

"You understands, Tony, this is something that happen about two years ago, a long time ago, Ursula was only eighteen then, when her cousin come from Grenada to Trinidad to spend some time here, with us. That's my sister's son, you understands?"

Tony nodded. Ursula was amazed: she didn't know she had a cousin, not before this moment.

"You understands, Leslie, that's her cousin's name, my sister's child, Leslie, fall in love with Ursula then, but Ursula didn't like him." Mrs Aranguez paused and glanced at the door behind which Ursula stood. "Yesterday," she continued, "I receive a letter from his family in Grenada asking to let Ursula go there to spend some time there with him. Now, Tony, what you thinks I must do?"

"I . . . I don't know, Mrs Aranguez. That's between you and . . . and . . ."

Mrs Aranguez, regarding him fixedly, interrupted:

"Ursula don't know nothing of this invitation as yet, you understands? I thought to speak to you first and hear what you have to say. And between you and me and the doorpost, Tony, I don't want to let her go. A mother should always be near to her child, I always says. Look tonight. I couldn't leave Ursula alone with her headache. I had to come back. God put us here to look after our children, I always says, and especially our daughters. And you knows Ursula, Tony. You knows what a good, quiet girl she be. For her to go to Grenada now? I'm scared stiff, yes, stiff. You can never tell with people you don't know good, except Leslie. And even him, well, I don't trust him further than I can see him with *my* daughter. Her morals, you understands . . ."

NOTES

1. In an earlier typescript Tony is given the surname Vierra. The name was connected with Mendes's family. His aunt Louisa had married Ray Vierra. Their son Ray married Lea Franco. After Ray's death Lea Vierra later married Alfred Mendes senior, her uncle-in-law. She was his fourth wife. It seems likely that Mendes wrote the story sometime before the "Sweetman" libel case in October 1932, and changed Tony's surname to Gravo for its publication in February 1933.
2. A working-class area of Port of Spain.

THE LARSONS AT HOME

MRS LARSON, MY LANDLADY, WAS SITTING on the couch smoking a cigarette and resting in the midst of her housework. It was five o'clock in the evening but Mrs Larson's housework was never done.

"Lord," she said. "Work, work, work!"

"You make it for yourself," said her husband from the dining room.

"*I* do!" She flicked her ash into the tray beside her. "You'd think I love work to hear you speak."

Roger, the younger son, was sitting before the radio listening to some chamber music.

"Please, please, Roger," said Mrs Larson, "That thing is driving me crazy. Can't you turn it off now!"

"Oh, Mum," said Roger, "you listened to your *Voice of Experience* today, didn't you? Why can't I hear what I want to hear!"

"Turn that radio off, I tell you!" shouted Mrs Larson.

Roger sat still, his ears glued to the instrument. I was trying to read a village paper, but what with Mrs Larson and the radio it was impossible to understand the printed page before me.

"Any news?" Mrs Larson said to me.

"There might be," I said.

"Not even the paper I get a chance to read. It's work, work, work."

"No rest for the wicked," said Mr Larson, *sotto voce*.

"What's that you say, Boswell?" demanded Mrs Larson.

"Oh, Mother, please be quiet," Roger put in. "This is a lovely Mozart string quartet."

"Mozart! Huh, what about your mother?"

"Please, Mother, *will* you be quiet?"

"Have you ever seen anything like this in your life?" said Mrs Larson, appealing to me. "I have no say in my own house."

"A little too much, you mean," said Mr Larson, good-naturedly.

"See, there's a conspiracy against me in my own house," said Mrs Larson to me.

I kept silent. I had been living with the family long enough to know when to speak and when not to.

"I don't see how I can get this report done with everybody talking at the same time," grumbled Mr Larson.

"Listen, to him, will you. You know where to go, don't you, if you want quiet and peace. Go to your room upstairs."

"Sure, and freeze," said Mr Larson.

"Well, and whose fault is that?" snapped Mrs Larson. "To hear you talk you'd think you were making a fortune with that WPA job, you'd think you were giving me gold instead of copper."

"Oh, Mum, please. How can I hear this thing with you . . ."

"Roger, no impertinence from you. I won't stand for it."

"Who is being impertinent? I'm only asking you to let me listen to this Mozart quartet."

"Well, listen," snapped Mrs Larson – and rose with a determined look in her eyes and continued her housework. She was a woman of about forty, still attractive but greying rapidly. I had known the family for some time, and when my brother and his wife went to live in the city I got a job with the WPA Writers' Project and I asked Mrs Larson if she would board and lodge me and she said yes. The arrangement was a happy one for me because I liked them and I knew that they liked me.

Mr Larson had seen better days. For years he had brought in three and four hundred dollars a week as a theatre manager and play producer, but when the Depression came along the bottom was knocked out of the show business and Mr Larson with it. In no time they had lost their house to the mortgagee, their furniture had all been hocked and they had lived on relief until Mr Larson got a job with the WPA Adult Education Program. Obviously, it was impossible to manage on ninety-four dollars a month with three children so it wasn't surprising when I learned that they owed almost every tradesman in Baldwin.[1]

"Not a stitch of clothes to my back," said Mrs Larson, sweeping like one of the three Furies and raising the dust with a vengeance. I coughed, discreetly, but Mrs Larson was far too annoyed with her circumstances to take any notice of me. "Not a pair of shoes, my toes out . . ."

"It's a pity you didn't save some of the money you threw away when Dad had it in barrels, Mum," said Roger.

"What's coming over this boy at all, can you tell me?" Mrs Larson asked of no one in particular. Then turning to her husband, she shot at him. "D'you know that we have nothing, no money for dinner tonight?" Mr Larson was silent. "I'm speaking to you," Mrs Larson said. "Are you deaf?"

"No, worse luck," said Mr Larson, "but I have no money."

"Have you ever heard anything like that in your life? Boswell, when will you come to your senses and send that job of yours to hell?"

"Such language, Mother!"

"Language? Huh, it's a wonder I'm not crazy, it's a wonder your mother isn't in the bughouse."

"A pity, you mean," murmured Mr Larson.

"Yes, go ahead. Make fun of me. Laugh at me . . ."

"Can't you take it, Mother? Dad was only making fun."

"Fun? Huh, if that's his sense of humour then your father has something of the sadist in him." Before marriage Mrs Larson had been a trained nurse and she had picked up a number of the words employed by the psychoanalysts and she was never tired ringing their changes. Sometimes it was amusing.

"Please, Mum, won't you let me listen to this Mozart?"

"Ask your father that favour, not me. Boswell, what are you going to do about dinner? Bless me, I'm not asking you for a bottle of perfume . . . you were glad enough to give me bottles and bottles of perfume at one time . . . I'm asking you about dinner, something to eat, not to smell."

"We'll have to smell for a change."

"Smelling never filled anybody's belly, I'd have you know, Mr Larson. You've got children with appetites to feed, I'd have you know, Mr Larson. If you don't get out of that damn charity job before they throw you out and look for something . . ."

"You don't have to swear about it."

"You and your Christian Science, huh! Has it ever brought you anything?" Mrs Larson was now holding her broom beside her like a rifle and firing her words across into the next room without being able to see her husband. "Don't swear, don't do this, don't do that . . . that's all your religion is fit for. If it would tell you to *do* things it might be better for yours if not for you, bless me. Boswell, will you please tell me how your children are to eat tonight?"

"All right, Mother," said Roger, breaking away from the radio in disgust and pulling out a little purse from his pocket. "How much do you want to borrow *now*?" Roger was sixteen, tall and with the pink cheeks of a girl.

"Borrow? Huh, you'd think I was begging you, the way you speak."

"Mother, please, I want to listen to this Mozart. Will you . . ."

"Where did you get that money from, Roger?" said Mrs Larson, fixing her blue eyes on her younger son.

"Do I have to tell you again that Mrs P. paid me what she owed me?"

"Mrs P.! Now, Roger, *must* I keep reminding you that it isn't nice to call Mrs Partridge P.?"

"Hear who's talking about what's not nice!" murmured Mr Larson.

"Keep your thoughts to yourself, Boswell Larson, if you must mumble them so that I can't hear them. So Mrs Partridge paid you what she owed you! Huh, time she did – and I don't want you to go and mind that woman's baby again while she goes gallivanting at nights – if she can't pay you without keeping you waiting weeks for it."

"Only two days, Mum," said Roger. "And who minds Mrs P.'s baby, you or I?"

"No impertinence, young man."

"And if I didn't mind the baby, where would we get dinner tonight?"

"Shut up, Roger – and turn that radio off before it drives me crazy."

"This is the *Voice of Experience* speaking, my friends," mocked Roger.

"Well, he has a *nice* voice."

"A nice voice that talks nonsense."

"When you get to my age . . ."

"Please, Mum, will you tell me how much you want to borrow?"

"Give me a dollar."

"That's all I can give you because that's all I've got." He handed his mother a dollar bill. "That makes three dollars and fifty-one cents you owe me."

"Tell your father that, not me. Boswell, you owe Roger three dollars and fifty-*one* cents, d'you hear? When's your next cheque coming? It's six days overdue already."

"If you want to know, ring Albany," said Mr Larson. "They *might* be able to tell you. That's what we get with a Democratic administration. Red tape, red tape – and red of another kind. A socialist for our president![2] It's a disgrace to these United States."

"*I* shall vote a straight Communist ticket next month," Mrs Larson announced with venom.

"You would," said Mr Larson.

"Oh shucks, Mother, Dad, will you please shut up and let me hear this Mozart quartet?"

"Yes, I would. You've said it, Mr Larson. You and your Republicans, like you and your Christian Science. You and your Landon.[3] What's Landon got that Mr Roosevelt hasn't got? Huh!"

"I can tell you the other way around. I can tell you that Mr Landon hasn't got Mr Roosevelt's *colour.*"

"Damn nonsense! Have you ever heard anything like that in your life, Fred?" said Mrs Larson to me.

I laughed. I knew my landlady well enough to know that she would never move a step to cast her vote. She was thoroughly indifferent to the political differences in the country and knew little or nothing about them.

"I guess," said Mr Larson quietly from the next room, "I guess you'd like to see Russia in this country."

"Russia?" cried Mrs Larson. "Who's talking about Russia? This is America."

"Thank God," said Mr Larson.

"Your eldest son doesn't seem to thank God for it," said Mrs Larson sarcastically.

"Aw, shucks, Mum, Dad . . ."

"Malcolm is a chip off your block, not mine," said Mr Larson sadly. "All the way back in my family we've been Republicans and I'm proud of it. It is the only form of administration that has ever given this country prosperity. Look at what the Raw Deal[4] has done for America. But Americans are waking up. Americans can recognize an enemy when they see one. Next month Landon . . . we'll see, we'll see."

I had an idea that Mr Larson intended his little speech for me but I sat tight and pretended to be engrossed in the paper before me.

"But if Landon gets in, Dad, won't you lose your job?" Roger asked unexpectedly.

"Why so? Why should anyone think . . ."

"And is the WPA a part of the New Deal, Dad?"

"It will be different under President Landon. It will become a Republican New Deal."

"Aw, shucks," said Roger, "what's the dif?"

"Bless me," said Mrs Larson, "by the sound of it you'd think this was Congress. And in the meantime no food bought as yet and Malcolm running in from his skating this minute or the next, and as hungry as a lion." She went and stood over the register, broom in hand, and exclaimed: "Roger, I thought I told you an hour ago to see to the furnace! There's not a drop of heat coming up, not a drop."

Roger sat at the radio just as if he had not heard his mother. Mr Larson limped across the room on his wooden leg and his wife looked at him solicitously. Years before he had lost a leg in a train accident and had not been able to afford a better artificial one since the Depression. The present one had been giving him trouble some time now; and often, in the evenings after dinner, I had seen him trying to patch it up.

"What shall I get?" said Mr Larson, putting on his jacket and his overcoat.

"Two pounds of chop meat," said Mrs Larson, "and . . ."

"Aw, nuts on chop meat, Mum. Only last night . . ."

"What do you think a dollar can buy, Roger?" Mrs Larson wanted to know. Then she put the usual question to me. "Is there anything you'd specially like, Fred?"

"Anything will do for me," I said, and I meant it. My two years in the trenches in France during the war had taught me a lot.

In came running little Margaret, Mrs Larson's six-year-old daughter, banging the door behind her. She was a pretty little thing, as pretty as a picture, her cheeks bursting with health. "That's what scientific feeding does for a child," Mrs Larson had said to me time and again.

"My Popeye programme," she cried, skipping up to the radio.

"Nuts on Popeye," said Roger. "I'm listening – so shut up."

Margaret tried to turn the switch but Roger pushed her aside.

"Roger, don't you dare," Mrs Larson warned. "You've been at that thing long enough and now it's your sister's turn."

"Two pounds of chop meat," said Mr Larson patiently, looking at me with a smile. "That's as far as we've got."

"Aw, shucks, Mum, I can never hear anything through to the end. If it isn't Margaret, it's you with your *Goodwill Court;* if it isn't you, it's Malcolm with his jazz, jazz, jazz; if it isn't Malcolm, it's . . ."

"Not me, son," Mr Larson put in. "I can listen to my own choice only when I'm *alone* in this house. Two pounds of chop meat and . . ."

"Leave your little sister alone, Roger, and go and attend to the furnace right away! I told you about it half an hour ago. Will you do as you're told? Bless me, what are children coming to these days? When I was a girl . . ."

"I'm waiting," said Mr Larson, winking at me. "Two pounds of chop meat and . . ."

"Did I say chop meat? Bless me, it's nearly six o' clock and there's no time to do chop meat now. Get some frankfurters and two cans of pork and beans."

"How much frankfurters?"

Mrs Larson gave her husband a sharp look to say: "Boswell, must I tell you *every* time how much of *every*thing you must buy? . . . Don't mind us, Fred. We're neurotic, just a neurotic family . . . Boswell, have you never bought frankfurters before?"

Popeye the sailorman was now bassoing over the radio and little Margaret stood rapt before the instrument, her huge blue eyes popping out of her head.

"Yes, I guess I've bought frankfurters before," said Mr Larson with resignation. "Frankfurters, pork and beans, what next?"

"Bread, butter, milk . . . Roger, if you don't attend to the furnace this minute, this very minute, I'll bash your head in with this broom. Hurry up. You've got to go with your father."

"Aw, Mum . . ."

"Don't you start complaining, child! Don't you know that your father's leg has been giving him trouble? Do you think he can walk all over the town for the likes of you? He'll stay in Goliath while you buy the things."

In the family the old 1926 Nash, with its gaping hood and sputtering motor, was called Goliath. Mr Larson had paid twenty-five dollars for it in four instalments.

Roger ran down into the cellar to attend to the furnace. "I'll be ready in a minute, Dad," he called out.

"Frankfurters, pork and beans, milk, bread, butter," said Mr Larson. "Is that *all* you want to get for a whole dollar?"

"Can't you put the balance on the cuff?" Mrs Larson demanded.

"Sure, I can on *my* cuff – but will the clerk put it on *his*?"

Mr Larson and I laughed and in another moment Mrs Larson joined us. She was that way, she could always laugh at her own expense; and when she did laugh, she laughed, make no mistake about that.

Goliath was already sputtering to a false start when the mother rushed to the door, flung it open to let a cold blast in, and screamed: "And don't forget a can of coffee, Boswell." The next moment Goliath was coughing his way down the road.

"Lord, have you ever seen anything like this in your life, Fred?" Mrs Larson said, banging the door shut. Mr Larson was the only member of the family who could shut the door softly. "Frankfurters, pork and beans . . . who'd ever have thought of *that* five years ago! Bless me, I remember the time when I bought nothing but the best, the very best, and ordered it over the 'phone at that. If I'd only known this was coming!"

"It's easy to be wise after the event," I suggested.

"You've never said a truer thing in your life, Fred. And it's strawberries and cream now compared to what it was before we got on relief, not to speak of now with Boswell's WPA job. You know what Boswell is. Have you ever met a man more full of pride? Bless me, even when we were starving, with nothing to eat but porridge and a little milk for the baby and us all hugging ourselves over a stove for warmth, d'you know that even then he wouldn't go to the relief office? Have you ever heard such a thing in your life? I said to him: 'Boswell, if you don't go, I will.' D'you know what he said? You'll never believe it, Fred. He said: 'Don't you dare!' Christian Science! Huh, much good it did him then! Much good it's doing him now with that leg of his. Refuses to see a doctor. Can you imagine? Dying with pain, but go to a doctor? Not Boswell Larson, not on your life. Instead, some old fool of a Christian Science woman comes to see him and what they say to each other only the four walls know. What else can you expect? Christian Science! Huh, have you ever seen anything like it in your life?"

Mrs Larson sighed. I had long since put aside the paper. It was impossible to read, it was impossible to write, it was impossible to do anything that required mental effort in the house. You were either hearing the blare of the radio or willy-nilly listening to the family talk – and more often than not you heard both at the same time. But I enjoyed it, it was exciting. And to me, who had an insatiable curiosity about people, it was intensely interesting.

"What worries me more than anything else," Mrs Larson continued, fussing around in a mechanical dusting of this and that, "is Malcolm. What's to become of that boy, I ask you? I guess you know how crazy he is to go to college. But how? 'No money, no college,' I tell him, 'and the sooner you get that into your brain,' I tell him, 'the better for all concerned.' Malcolm's going on twenty, he's willing to work. Last summer he got a job with some building contractors, and what do you think they put him to do? Dig ditches for foundations, tote cement, an ordinary labourer's job! And he a high-school graduate with ambitions to become a doctor! Have you ever seen anything like it in your life? It nearly killed the spirit and heart of the boy – as it nearly killed mine. Which boy's heart, what mother's spirit wouldn't it kill, I ask you? What's this country come to that its sons with ambitions to become doctors, lawyers, engineers, must dig ditches and tote cement for a living? Is there any wonder that Malcolm has the ideas he has? That's what I say to his father, but Boswell can't understand. Show him a socialist and you make him mad on the spot. And he a Christian Scientist! And I? – nothing. No church for me, thanks. But I'm tolerant. And Boswell? Christian Science! Huh, what's happening in this country today is what is putting all those wicked ideas into young men's minds."

"Wicked, Mrs Larson?"

"I know you think like Malcolm, Fred. I know that and I guess I can't blame you. Why, it makes *me* see red too – sometimes. I know how *much* the rich have and how *little* the poor. D'you know what Malcolm did about a year ago? Bless me, he wrote to Morgan, to Rockefeller, to Strauss,[5] begging them to give him his course in medicine and he would repay them as soon as he could. And I know that Malcolm would. Though I say it myself, he's an honest boy. *Can* you believe it? They refused! Dirty rich dogs! And Boswell, when he got to hear of what Malcolm had done, was mad. That's his pride. There's pride for you. Damn nonsense I call it. Fancy him daring me to go to the relief office! His pride can starve him, if he wants it that way, but it won't starve me and mine. Not on your life."

There was a heavy thud of feet on the porch outside and the next moment Malcolm, with skates slung over his arm, burst into the room, banging the door behind him.

"I'm famished, Mum."

"You famished! So are we all. Go upstairs this minute and change your clothes. No sickness in this house for me. I've got enough to do without having to bother my head with you in bed. And wash your face. By the looks of you, you'd think you were skating on dirt, not ice."

"Oh, Mum, will you shush and get dinner ready?"

"With what, I ask you? I can't make dinner out of fresh air, boy."

"What, didn't Dad's cheque come today?"

"Dad's cheque! Huh, what do you think of that!" Mrs Larson laughed. "The day his cheque arrives on time I shall die of shock. But we'll all be dead before that happens."

Malcolm threw his skates into a corner and moved across to the radio.

"Leave my Popeye alone!" Margaret cried.

"Malcolm, don't you dare touch that child!"

"All right, butch," said Malcolm to Margaret.

"Butch yourself," said Margaret, pouting.

"Now, now," warned the mother, "aren't you too big to be teasing your little sister, Malcolm?"

"She's getting too fresh," said Malcolm.

"Fresh yourself," said Margaret, her blue eyes defiant.

"Margaret, don't you speak to your oldest brother like that. I'll spank you."

"Tell him to leave my Popeye alone. He's always doing me that."

"Mercy, there's never any peace in this house," Mrs Larson cried. "Don't mind us, Fred. We're a neurotic family and you must take us as you find us."

"Speak for yourself, Mum."

"Yes, your father is a paragon of all that's right and peaceful," Mrs Larson replied sarcastically.

"Pop's too peaceful," said Malcolm. "That's what's wrong with him. People like Pop never get anywhere in the world."

"That's a mouthful of truth, Malcolm," said the mother. "I should have been your father and he your mother."

Malcolm and I laughed.

"Be quiet, you," said little Margaret. "I can't hear."

Mrs Larson went into the dining-room to get the table ready for dinner. More fun started then. Everything Mrs Larson did she did with a vengeance, and setting the table was no exception. Only the week before Mr Larson had gone into the five-and-ten and bought a dozen cheap cups but already she had broken three. Grabbing the small table, she dragged it from the wall and across the floor into the centre of the room, kicking up a tremendous noise. By this time Popeye had gone off the air, little Margaret was squatting on the floor cutting up bits of paper into dolls and Malcolm had turned on the radio full blast to some jazz music. The music jumped and pranced and bounded through the house.

"For Christ's sake, Malcolm, turn down that thing!"

Mrs Larson might just as well have spoken to a mule for all the obedience she got. Instead, Malcolm began to hop-dance[6] about the room, shaking the whole house. Mrs Larson in the dining-room was banging plates together. Crash!

"Malcolm," she cried out, "will you please come and pick up these pieces at once!"

"Mum's on the warpath," Malcolm said.

Roger and Mr Larson returned. Mr Larson closed the door quietly behind him.

"Another cup gone?" said Mr Larson, glancing in at the dining room. "Oh, it's a plate this time. I think it would be cheaper to buy paper ones next time."

"Not for this house," snapped Mrs Larson. "This is a civilized house, not a picnic bungalow."

"It might be a picnic bungalow and worse than that for all the noise and confusion it produces from morning till night."

"If you think you can do the job better, take it and I'll take yours. There's one thing sure, I can do yours better than you can."

"I couldn't get the coffee," Mr Larson announced – to change the subject, I was sure. "Fifteen cents short . . ."

"And with only fifteen cents short you couldn't get the coffee!"

"Fifteen cents short of thirty is fifty per cent," Mr Larson announced.

"Very clever reckoning but very dumb behaviour," Mrs Larson shot back at him.

"Aw, shucks, Dad, if you'd left it to me I'd have gotten the coffee all right," said Roger.

"That's it, boy. Teach your father how to live."

"A nice thing to tell the children," Mr Larson murmured.

"A nice thing – what?"

Mr Larson was silent.

"We've got to live," Mrs Larson said after a pause, "and if we can't by fair means, then . . ."

"Rose!" said Mr Larson, unable to conceal his horror.

"Fiddlesticks!" said Mrs Larson. "Too much righteousness is worse than all the religions – and they are bad enough as it is."

By this time Mrs Larson was busy preparing the dinner and she could get things done more quickly than almost anybody I had ever met. The cooking was done to the accompaniment of banging of pots and pans together, but it was done and done well, turkey or frankfurters. In a short time we were all seated at table, the radio still pounding out its syncopations.

Little Margaret sat next her father and he attended to her as if she were a baby. He was an affectionate man and because his other two children were grown up, he showered all of his affection upon Margaret. For the months I had been living with them I had never once seen Mrs Larson kiss Margaret or show her any tenderness, and yet you couldn't have desired a better mother. She did all the washing of the house. It was a pleasure to watch those strong arms of hers attacking the laundry like any washerwoman's straight out of Zola's *L'Assommoir*.[7] At times she would order an electrical washing machine from a shop in an outside village, where she was not known, and keep it "on trial" for as long as she was allowed to. And she made the best of them for as long as they lasted. She sewed, she darned, she ironed, she even made little Margaret's dresses. That her house was clean is putting it mildly. Some mornings she would get up and, with a terrific burst of energy, wash and scrub the floor of every single room.

For a while we were too busy eating to talk much. I swallowed the food to the jagged rhythm of the music.

"Shucks," said Roger, "can't we have a little quiet music to eat by? Bang, bang, bang – that's all that noise says."

"Stop up your ears if you don't want to hear it," Malcolm retorted.

"Now that's unreasonable and unkind," said the father.

"Have you ever known him to be anything else?" said Roger, reddening. The two boys were always at each other. "He's the only one in this house that likes jazz and he's always pushing it down our ears."

"You play what you want, don't you?" Malcolm said.

"Now, you two," Mrs Larson put in, "let me eat my dinner in peace. It's the only meal I can *sit* down to."

"I play what I want, but how often?" Roger persisted, bridling up. "I'm at school all day, you're at home all day, you can listen to what you like all day. You don't even help Mother with the housework. You're too damn lazy . . ."

"Roger!" the father rapped out. "I'll have no swearing at this table," and he glanced across at his wife as if to say: "That's your example."

"Is 'damn' a nice word, Roger?" said little Margaret accusingly.

"It is *not* a nice word, honey, and no good child ever uses it," said the father.

"So you're not a good child," said Margaret to Roger with sound logic for one of her age.

"Too lazy even to work," Roger mumbled, determined to have his say out.

"Repeat that and I'll slap you," Malcolm said, quietly but determinedly.

"I'd like to see you try," Roger shot back.

"Boswell, can't you keep your sons in order!" Mrs Larson shouted across the table. "Roger, another word from you and . . . why can't you two brothers act like brothers towards each other?"

"Let him and I will. Because he's bigger than me he thinks . . ."

"Silence, I said, Roger!"

Roger was itching to say something more but one look at his mother was enough. He sat silent for some time, sulking.

"I'm announcing it now so that all might know and take note," Mr Larson said in the lull that followed.

His wife gave him a quick look. "Announcing what?" she snapped.

"I want the use of the radio at nine o'clock. May I have it, please?" he said in mock humility.

"You announce and beg in the same breath," said Mrs Larson. "That's you all over, Boswell. People who beg seldom get."

"Dad wants the use of the radio!" Malcolm exclaimed. Even Roger looked up in surprise at his father.

"I want to listen to Landon's broadcast," said the father, trying his best to put some authority into the request.

"That reminds me," said Malcolm, laughing, "In tonight's *World-Telegram* Heywood Broun[8] calls Landon average Alf."

"Heywood Broun is a fool," Mr Larson ejaculated in an unguarded moment.

"Is 'fool' a nice word, Dad?" Margaret asked.

"It isn't a nice word, honey, but it suits Mr Broun."

"Oh," said Margaret, obviously unable to make four of one plus two. Then she asked: "Does Mr Broun live on our block, Dad?"

"No, honey," said Mr Larson patiently. "Mr Broun lives in the city."

"Who is Mr Broun, Dad?"

"I don't know, Dad," Malcolm put in. "I think the expression both clever and true."

"Heywood Broun is a menace to our American ideals," Mr Larson said severely. "I'm sure he's a Jew."

"Nothing of the sort," said Malcolm. "Broun is a full-blooded, one hundred per cent American."

"Then he writes like a Jew," said Mr Larson, "and that's as bad as being one."

"Oh, come, Dad . . ."

"I like Jewish doctors," Mrs Larson put in just in time to avoid high words between father and son.

"Jewish doctors?" I said, puzzled.

"Not because they are Jews and not because they are doctors," Mrs Larson explained, leaving me more in the dark. "I just like Jewish doctors," – and she burst out laughing.

"I guess Fred finds that very amusing," the husband said drily.

"I . . . I don't quite get it," I said.

"Who does?" said Mr Larson. "That's Rose's sense of humour."

"For one thing, Jews make good husbands," Mrs Larson said. "For another thing, Jews are usually successful. For a third thing, a good husband who happens to be a successful doctor any woman would jump at. That's why I like Jewish doctors."

I laughed and Mrs Larson roared.

"Very sound," I said.

"Very sound – for Rose," said Mr Larson.

"Just fancy how close I came to having a Jewish doctor as my father," said Roger, unable to sulk any longer.

"That might have been better for you," said Mrs Larson.

"And for me," Mr Larson put in quietly.

"I don't see why the Jews are so despised in this country," Malcolm said. "As a race they have contributed more to our culture than any other . . ."

"Yes, Communism," said Mr Larson.

"So what?" said Malcolm.

"So everything," said Mr Larson with spirit. "Karl Marx, the anti-Christ, the anti-God, the . . ."

"You're forgetting Christ Himself," said Malcolm. "If you despise the race for Marx, at least admire it for Christ."

"I love Christ for what He is, not because he's a member of any particular race."

"And you hate the race for Marx because of what he stands for."

"Every Jew in this country is a red. There's no place in this country for Communism and . . ."

"That's exactly what is wrong with this country," said Malcolm, warming up to his argument. "You know, Dad, I can't see how you, who have suffered so much from the American system as you have, can sit there and talk as you do. And the tragedy is that nine hundred and ninety-nine out of every thousand think as you do."

"Thank God for that tragedy," said Mr Larson fervently.

"Thanking God for it still leaves it a tragedy."

"Tragedy? Nonsense," said Mr Larson with heat.

"Millions of unemployed, slums, child-labour, strikes – pour them all into a pot, stir and if you don't get a tragedy then I'm nuts. And this is the richest country in the world."

"Shut up, you two," Mrs Larson shouted across the table. "You're old enough to know better than to argue with your son, Boswell."

Mrs Larson's interruption came just in time for I could see that Mr Larson was losing his temper. This sort of close approach to a row between father and son had happened time and again with Mrs Larson always butting in just in the nick of time. But I felt that the flare-up was bound to come and as I didn't want to be held even partially responsible for it I made it a point of keeping my mouth shut whenever politics was being discussed. The more I saw of Mr Larson the more amazed I became that he could lose his temper – and over politics at that! He resented intensely the ousting of the GOP by Roosevelt in 1932. His resentment was so intense that he was willing to see in the New Deal a danger to the whole country, a danger of the introduction of insidious forces that had come straight out of Moscow. He read the Hearst papers,[9] of course, and accepted them without question. "Look at this," he said to me one evening, "look at this reception Roosevelt got in Cleveland yesterday. What do you think?" I thought a lot but said nothing. "I'll tell you. I know this for a fact and it's here in the paper. Every single WPA worker was ordered, yes, ordered on pain of losing his job to attend the procession that greeted Roosevelt. Talk about Hitler!" That was the sort of thing he believed and was willing to defend with hot fervour. And yet Mr Larson was a quiet-going man, a lover of peace in the house and peace in the world, a good man at heart. It seemed to me that he hated Communism more than he loved conservatism, and in him I understood as I had never before understood the dread of the middle classes for liberalism and leftist policies. It threatened their whole background, all the weight of the tradition in which they had been bred and on which they had been nurtured. It didn't matter how much they suffered because of the system they espoused, they were willing to suffer still more for it. Change, change of any sort was what they looked upon with terror. America was safe for the mildly middle way so long as the Mr Larsons remained in their legions.

I have said that the flare-up between father and son was bound to come – and it came that very night. After dinner there was the usual fight over who should help the mother with the dish-washing. I solved the problem by myself offering to help and Roger, sensitive to my offer, gave a hand. Malcolm disappeared in Goliath to the house of one of his ice-skating friends. "There he goes again," said Roger. "Too lazy even to wash the plate he ate out of. I don't know why you don't *make* him help, Mother."

"I can manage my own family without any suggestions from you," Mrs Larson snapped.

"It's as much my family as yours," said Roger.

"Listen to that!" cried Mrs Larson. "Have you ever heard anything like it in your life?"

"And I have to help wash, to help with the housework, to see to the furnace," Roger complained, "while that lazy bum never budges to do a thing."

"No bumming in this house, young man," said Mrs Larson. And to me: "Isn't that awful?"

"What do you expect Fred to do, agree with you?" said Roger. "Aren't I right, Fred? Have you ever seen Malcolm do anything in this house?"

I didn't like being put on the spot, so I smiled. That was my favourite way of escape.

Just at that moment Mr Larson looked into the kitchen to ask: "Where can I find a needle, Rose?" A pair of trousers was slung over his arm.

"Why ask *me*?"

"I guess I shall have to find the haystack before knowing where the needle is – in this house," Mr Larson remarked good-naturedly, "and *then* the search for the needle begins."

"What a house!" Roger ejaculated.

"Yes, we *all* live in it," Mrs Larson said.

"But we all don't take care of it," Mr Larson rejoined, smiling.

"You'd think I was the maid here to hear you speak."

"How did your lecture come off today, Dad?" Roger asked.

"Pretty good, son."

"I'd give anything to hide behind a screen and listen to one of those lectures of your father's," said Mrs Larson.

"Why not sit with the rest of the audience?" Mr Larson suggested.

"What, and look at you! I'd have you know, Boswell, that I've been looking at you for twenty years now and I'm sick to death of looking at your face."

"Which leaves me nothing to say about you," was the husband's retort – and he went off, presumably to look for the haystack. He must have found it, *and* the needle, for a few minutes later I saw him in the dining room sewing buttons on to his pants. A heap of dry washing stood in a corner of the room and soon Mrs Larson, with those strong arms of hers, was ironing away as if her life depended on it. Little Margaret was listening to an adventure story on the radio and the hero was rescuing his friends from a band of brigands to the accompaniment of shouts and pistol shots. The house rang with them. I again settled myself on the couch to try and read the paper, but the hero's triumphant cries of victory over his enemies held my attention and the next moment I was listening with the excitement of a child to the thrilling yarn of rescue. Roger, itching to get at the radio, hovered around with a look of annoyance and disgust on his face. Malcolm returned, banging the door shut after him. Roger gave him a contemptuous glance.

"That furnace," cried Mrs Larson. "The house is an icebox. Roger, Roger," – you'd think Roger was up the street by the way she shouted out the name – "attend to the furnace this minute!"

"Aw, shucks, Mum, it's Malcolm's turn now," Roger replied, shouting to let himself be heard above the din of radio battle.

"Turn for what?" said Malcolm, truculently. "I put out the garbage last night."

"Garbage! Last night! This is the furnace. Now." Roger's cheeks reddened.

"Mum spoke to you, not to me."

"I heard her, I heard her."

"Well?" screamed Mrs Larson.

Pistol shots rang out from the radio. Little Margaret's blue eyes were popping out of her head.

"I think it's really Malcolm who should attend to the furnace this time," said Mr Larson quietly. His remark went by unheard.

"Boswell, will you please speak to your son?" Mrs Larson demanded.

"Which one?" Mr Larson asked.

"Which one! Isn't that awful? Boswell, are you deaf?"

"I believe I've answered that question already, dozens of times," said Mr Larson, rising and limping across the room. He went down into the cellar and the next moment we heard him attending to the furnace.

"Lazy pig!" said Roger, looking daggers drawn at his brother.

"Say that again and . . ."

"Lazy pig!"

Bang, bang, bang – from the radio.

In a jiffy Mrs Larson was in the room and between her two sons. "No Cain and Abel stuff here," she cried. "Another word from either of you and I'll bash your heads in with the broom. I didn't raise you both to be enemies, God knows. This is a Christian house and I'll have you get that into your thick skulls." She turned to me. "Isn't this awful?"

"Boys will be boys," I said.

"Yes, bad boys will be bad boys," she added – and returned to her ironing.

Mr Larson came up without a word, sat down and continued his sewing job. Malcolm and Roger took seats as far away from each other as the room allowed. Little Margaret's programme came to a roaring to-be-continued-tomorrow. Malcolm sprang to the instrument and switched on some jazz music. Roger groaned, rose and stamped his way upstairs to do his homework. Malcolm took a book and started to read and how he could read with such syncopated noises in his ear was always a source of wonder to me.

"No shoes to my feet, my toes sticking out, not a stitch to my back," Mrs Larson soliloquized loudly enough for her husband, who sat near her, to hear, and ironing away in a sort of fury. "A maid, that's what I am, nothing but a maid in this damn house. Work, work, work from morning till night. Jewish doctor? Huh!" Through the corner of her eye she glanced at her husband. Mr Larson was putting the final stitches to his button. "Bless me, I might just as well talk to myself," said Mrs Larson, banging the iron down on the table.

Mr Larson looked up to say: "Certainly – if you can think of nothing better to talk about."

"But I have no clothes, Boswell, nothing on my back!"

"And what about the single decent suit I share with Malcolm? And look at these shoes." He raised his good leg to expose the broken sole of the shoe. "The slightest drizzle and my foot is wet through. What's the use of complaining? It's a long long time since the day manna fell out of heaven – and it's not going to now. When I had it I gave it to you."

"I'm not complaining," said Mrs Larson, trying her best not to show contrition and ironing furiously.

"No, you're not complaining," said Mr Larson with quiet irony.

"Malcolm, will you please lower that radio?" Mrs Larson cried out.

"How can I do my homework with that noise down there?" Roger shouted from the top of the stairs.

Malcolm buried his head deeper into his book. Mrs Larson pounced into the living room and turned off the switch. The sudden silence was startling. Then she returned to her ironing. No one spoke. There was a profound peace in the house, unbelievable because of its rarity. It reminded me of those moments in the trenches after the abrupt cessation of a heavy artillery barrage.

The silence didn't last long, for without any warning Mrs Larson remembered that it was past the time for putting little Margaret to bed and she came into the living room and said, grabbing the child by the hand: "Come on, come on. It's past your bedtime."

Little Margaret set up a howling and protested that she didn't want to go to bed so the mother lifted her from the floor and, with a clatter, ran up the stairs with the struggling child screaming in her arms.

Malcolm turned on the radio and the house once more became its noisy self. Mr Larson, now done with his button, took out his papers, placed them before him and began to write. In a few minutes little Margaret was quiet and Mrs Larson came downstairs and threw herself onto the couch. Picking up my discarded paper, she began to read it.

"This house is like Spain, fighting against itself,"[10] she said after a while. "Germany, France, Russia re-arming. And look at this – Russia is conscripting women and children. Isn't that awful? Europe should blow up into bits," she snapped, angry with the news.

"It will," I said, "and soon."

"If Hitler thinks he's going to cakewalk into the Soviet Union," said Malcolm, never able to resist biting at political bait, "he's got another thought coming. They're letting him get away with too much as it is."

"I don't love Hitler," Mr Larson put in, "but I'd like to see him destroy Russia."

"You can't destroy a hundred and sixty million people, Dad. That's what the Versailles Treaty[11] tried to do with the German people. You know what's happened, I guess."

"Versailles Treaty or no Versailles Treaty, I repeat, I'd like to see Hitler crush those vandals," Mr Larson said with some heat. "People who try to destroy God destroy themselves in the end."

"Perhaps," Malcolm said. "But the Soviet Union has never tried to destroy God, Dad. They've . . ."

"What do you call the destruction of religion and the churches?" Mr Larson demanded.

"Neither religion nor the churches are God . . ."

"Isn't that awful?" said Mrs Larson to me.

"I suppose you call Communism God!" Mr Larson said, the manuscripts before him now forgotten.

"I don't know what you mean by God, Dad, so I can't say. But if God is anything like the teachings of Christ then I can see some sort of resemblance between Communism and God."

"That's blasphemy!" Mr Larson said. I could see he was trying his best to control his temper.

"You shouldn't talk so flippantly of God, Malcolm," Mrs Larson put in, "and you should have more respect for your father and I."

"But surely because I express difference from Dad in his views I'm not disrespecting him! And as for you, Mum, I can't differ from you because you have no views at all."

"Just listen to that!" said Mrs Larson to no one in particular. "Have you ever heard anything like that in your life?"

The radio was blaring away.

"Communism is the enemy, yes, the enemy of God and religion!" Mr Larson announced rhetorically.

"But why, Dad, why? D'you know what Communism is? For that matter, d'you know what God is?"

"Malcolm!" cried Mrs Larson.

"You keep out of this!" Mr Larson said angrily to his wife.

"I'll do nothing of the kind! This is a Christian house and I'll have no barking and biting between brother and brother and father and son!"

"I'm neither barking nor biting," Malcolm said. "I'm talking sense and I'm old enough to hold my own views and express them – even if they annoy my father."

"I'll not have such views expressed in my house!" Mr Larson said, rising in anger.

"Then I'll leave," Malcolm said, the colour drawn from his cheeks.

"Sit down, you!" Mrs Larson cried to her son. "What the devil do you mean . . ."

"Let him go! Let him leave before I lift my hand against him!"

Mrs Larson pushed her son back into his seat, then she turned to her husband. "Boswell Larson, I'm surprised at you, I'm ashamed of you! Is that what your Christian Science teaches you . . ."

"You leave Christian Science alone!" It was the first time I had ever heard Mr Larson shout. "You, *you* are the one responsible for all the barking and biting in this house with your swearing and your godlessness and . . ."

Mrs Larson didn't wait for more: she sprang at her husband and gave him a resounding slap on the face. It was just at that moment that the jazz music ceased and a voice announced Mr Landon at the microphone. Mr Landon began to speak and while his voice drawled on in its pedestrian manner, I sat thinking of the thousands of families like the Larsons in this country, the elder members of which still cling tenaciously to the old way of life, fearful of change, while their children snatch at the new ideas and look ahead with new hope in their hearts, their minds a-flutter with the excitement of change.

NOTES

1.   In Long Island, New York.
2.   Franklin D. Roosevelt (1882–1945).
3.   Alf Landon (1887–1987), the Republican candidate defeated by Roosevelt in the election of 1936.
4.   For New Deal. President Roosevelt's New Deal 1933–1943 was a series of social programmes intended for the relief of Americans during the Great Depression.
5.   American millionaires: John Pierpont Morgan (1867–1943), John D. Rockefeller (1839–1937) and (presumably) Levi Strauss (1829–1902). Since Strauss died in 1902, Malcolm could hardly have written to him.
6.   The Lindy hop or jitterbug, a lively dance that evolved in Harlem in the 1920s and 1930s, and remained popular throughout the 1930s and 1940s.
7.   Emile Zola's *L'Assommoir* (1877) is a grim tale of drunkenness, sadistic cruelty, and grinding poverty.
8.   Heywood Campbell Broun (1888–1939) was a journalist in New York City. He wrote on social issues and championed the underdog.

9. William Randolph Hearst (1863–1951) established a newspaper empire. His publications were characterized by "yellow" journalism.

10. The Spanish Civil War lasted from 17 July 1936 to 1 April 1939.

11. The Treaty of Versailles on 28 June 1919 ended the war between Germany and the Allied Powers. The Allies, worried about the spread of Communism from Russia, hoped that Germany could provide a buffer zone. However, the terms for peace were harsh for Germany, and when the Nazi party came to power after 1933, it abandoned most of the conditions of the treaty.

COLD TURKEY

FOR TWO YEARS I HAD BEEN editing one of the series of guide books being sponsored by the WPA. That folded up and I was out of a job. Every day I bought three papers to see what the ad columns had to offer. For three days they offered nothing, but on the fourth I noticed an advertisement which aroused my curiosity with the sentence: "Only those accustomed to large earnings need apply." I applied – although I had not been accustomed to large earnings. It would be grand, said I to myself, to own two cars, frequent the best nightclubs, go south for the winter, get married for the sake of getting divorced, and so on. You know how a man will dream big dreams when a match lights the spark of his imagination. You know the things a man will say when asked: "What would you do if you came into a fortune suddenly?" True enough, the sentence that fired me wasn't quite the same thing as the question every man has delighted in answering at some time or another. Instead, it trumpeted a challenge for it seemed to imply: *you* have never earned largely but you *can.*

I applied.

At once I saw that the promise offered by the challenging sentence was no empty boast – if appearances had anything to do with it. The office I entered, as offices go in small American towns, smelt to high heaven, not to speak of my earth-bound nostrils, of prosperity. Three smartly dressed young women were smartly tapping away on three bright typewriters. The room was large and sunlight came slanting in through many windows. The furniture shone. A thick rug covered the floor. Before entering, I had noticed the name of a large vacuum-cleaning establishment imprinted on the door, but it conveyed no meaning to me. As I sat there waiting to be interviewed, I felt like a Don Quixote[1] standing on the edge of a new adventure. That's how I felt, and you may call me a fool for feeling so – as I have since called myself. But let that pass.

"Have you ever done any selling?" the manager shot at me.

We were seated in another room before a desk which glittered in the sunlight. A large print of the president of the USA hung on a wall. The manager, whom we shall call Mr Anderson, was immaculately dressed. Tie, socks and shirt matched. His hair was cut just so. His manner was brisk, his voice crisp.

"No," I said as he eyed me up and down.

"What have you been doing?"

I told him.

"What were your average earnings during the past year?"

I told him.

He screwed his face up to ask: "Do you want to make money, real money?"

"Sure," said I without batting an eye.

"Fine, fine. Do you think you can sell?"

"Why, yes, I have been dealing with human beings in my fiction and there's no reason why I shouldn't be able to deal . . ."

"Fine, fine," said he, rubbing his hands together – and he proceeded to give me a recital of the glorious past, present *and* future of his firm. With the enthusiasm and gusto of a man declaiming over his favourite book, he talked on and on.

I left him in a daze. I tried to piece together what he had told me. I tried to decide what sort of job I was being called upon to do. The impressions he had left me with were a jumble, but above them all rose the picture of a world filled with houses all waiting open-doored for vacuum cleaners of his firm's make to pour into them. Lock, stock and barrel, he had sold me his firm.

The next day at the appointed time I was back in Mr Anderson's room. He greeted me with a mechanical smile and shook my hand violently.

"Have you thought it over?" he asked before I had time to sit.

I didn't know quite what I had had to think over, but I said: "Yes."

"Fine, fine," said he. "No man with an eye to making money, more money than he has ever made in his life, passes up an opportunity like this. Money is what makes the world go round. Money is power. But you'll have to *want* to make it. Our product is the finest dirt-digger in the world, but you've got to *sell* it. It's a matter of mind over body. The mind is the power-house, the machine is a dead thing without *you* to put it over. Get me? And you can do it. We've got men here who've been consistently making a hundred and fifty, two hundred a week. They've got nothing that you haven't got. Guts, that's what you need, the guts to succeed. Look at our president there, look at Ford,[2] look at Rockefeller, Morgan, Napoleon[3]: guts, that's what they had. Can you do it?"

Of course I could do it! Two hundred a week? Who wouldn't have guts to make two hundred a week? I thought of the stories I had sold for twenty-five and fifty apiece, stories that had taken me two and three months to write. I thought of the novels that had taken me six and eight times as long to write and the proportionately less money they had fetched me. Think of it: on the one hand fifty dollars in two months, on the other two hundred in one week! The prospect was positively thrilling.

That morning I was passed on to the selling instructor. Now I must tell you something of Mr Van Druten, the name I have chosen to give him.[4] He was a Dutchman. He had lived in this country for years but his accent still marked him loudly for what he was. Perhaps he was forty-five, perhaps fifty-five, a large dark man with the face of a martinet. His gait was slow, deliberate, his posture erect. He looked like a Junker.[5] His eyes were like two ovals of grey-blue steel.

The other newcomer and me he led into an adjoining room. The walls were plastered with large sheets of paper bearing the inscriptions of slogans and mottoes: "Middletown is famous for its friendship", "This is your golden opportunity", "Make more money than you have ever made in your life", "Money paves the path to power", and so on. "Touchdown!" one picture, with the figure of a triumphant halfback, screamed at you. The room was cold, uncomfortably so. It was intended to be cold for what human being, salesman or otherwise, would not lose his pep in a comfortably warm room?

"Gentl'm'n," Mr Van Druten started quietly enough, "I teach you today how to sell. You got to sell an' sell some. Yessir. Dis unit is a hon, a real honest-to-Gott hon. If you was to say: 'I cain't sell,' you cain't sell. You got to say: 'I can sell.' You got to say dat once, two times, t'ree times, all de time. Stand in front of a mirror an' look at yourself an' say: 'I can sell.' Say it loud, like I saying it dis minute: "I can sell!' De mind, gentl'm'n. De mind is your power-house. Let me tell you. Eight year ago I vas in my garten. I lofe de flowers, I lofe to shoot de birds an' de ducks an' de wild fowl. I vas in my garten eight year ago when a salesman come to me wit' one of dese dirt-diggers to gif me a demo. Gentl'm'n, dis is de finest dirt-digger in de whole world. Yessir. Dis salesman, he come. Dat time I vas vurking in a office, gentl'm'n, fifty dollar a veek. Yessir, fifty dollar a veek. I look at dis salesman, gentl'm'n, an' I tell him: 'I don't want to see vat you got. I busy. I got no money.' All alibis, gentl'm'n. But dat salesman, he vas a salesman. Yessir. He give me a demo. I buy an' den I say: 'You can get me a job selling too?' Yessir, dat's vat I say. Ven you say a t'ing an' you mean it, you bound to get it. De power-house, gentl'm'n. An' dis machine, it's a hon, gentl'm'n, anoder power-house. An' you got de finest company in de world behind it. Yessir. Dey want to see you make money, big dough. You like money, ein? Sure. If cows an' dogs could think, dey'd like dough too. Look at dat picture dere. Dat's de president of our company, one of de richest men in de world. Yessir. Look at de power behind de face. He's a great man. He should be president of de country too," at which he threw his head back and laughed, a gush of sonorous laughter.

He continued talking, getting more and more excited until he was almost shouting. And the more his voice rose, the more difficult it became to understand him. He waved his arms. He laughed. He stamped the carpeted floor. He paced back and forth, banging the table every time he got within reach of it. He looked like an evangelist preaching to an unregenerate crowd. Towards the end of his tempestuous monologue, I found it impossible to understand a single word.

Then he showed us how to demonstrate the machine. Taking his coat off, he went to work with tremendous energy. In no time he was sweating. He pulled up pile after pile of dirt from the carpet and deposited each pile back onto the section from which it had come.

"When you in a house, gentl'm'n, put de dirt back from where you get it. Dem piles of dirt vill make her buy. If she don't want to close, dig more dirt. Dig dirt , gentl'm'n, an' more dirt. Every pile is gold dust – for you. Money to spend. Yessir. Qualify de prospect. Say, 'Mrs Jones, you don't want dis condition in your house, ein?' Make her answer your question. If she don't, answer it for her. Have your order book before her eyes all de time. Let her see it, let her get accustom to it. Yessir. And don't leave until she give you her OK, not even if it take four, five, six hours. When she ask you: 'Vat is de price of dis machine?' take your order book, valk up to her slow, kneel down beside her an' say: 'How you vant to pay for it, Mrs Jones? Most ladies give me twenty, twenty-five down.' Don't say dollars, say as I say: 'Twenty, twenty-five down. Dat vill leave a balance of fifty-one. Six dollars a month an' de machine, Mrs Jones, is yours.' All de time you speaking, you filling out de order. Yessir. Ven you finish speaking give her der book an' pencil, show her where to sign, but don't say: 'Sign'; say: 'Your OK here, Mrs Jones.' If she don't want to sign, dig more dirt. Go to a chair wit' upholstery. Put de dirt back in der chair. Tell her to sit down in it. Ven she refuse, laugh an' say: 'But dat's vat you been sitting in all dis time, Mrs Jones!' If she have a child, boy oh boy, make a fuss over it. Ask her how old it is. Tell her vat a pretty child it is. Tell her: 'You value de health of your child, ein Mrs Jones? Vell, dis machine is dust-proof, Mrs Jones.' Yessir. If she haven't got a child, look at a picture. Admire it. Ask her if she buy it. If she say yes, tell her she have goot taste. Dat vill flatter her, dat vill put her in a goot mood. Look at de picture a long time den dig more dirt. If she say: 'I haven't no money,' laugh, laugh out loud and say: 'Neider have I, Mrs Jones. But suppose de doctor order a extra bottle of milk for your child every day, you'd buy it, ein Mrs Jones? Vell, dis is all dis machine vill cost you, a bottle of milk a day an' it vill keep de doctor avay.' Make jokes. Laugh. Dominate de situation. Don' show too much politeness. Den close her.'

He paused to pant for breath. I felt out of breath myself. The room seemed to be going round and round with the violent echoes of his voice. Dragging out a machine of another make, he proceeded to make a comparative demonstration in which the rival was ignominiously outclassed. Where the day before Mr Anderson had done everything in his power to sell me his firm, Mr Van Druten was now moving heaven and earth to sell his product to us – and succeeding with a vengeance. He treated us as if we were prospects and began to qualify us: could anything be better? Wasn't it the best in the world? Did we ever see such power? Wasn't it a "hon" to sell? Didn't we think we could make bigger and better money than we had ever made in our lives? Yes, yes. Sure, sure.

All fine and good, said I to myself in a moment of respite from his hard attack on us, but how get *into* the houses? It was obvious at this stage that my job would be one of selling, and cold-turkey selling at that, selling from house to house, the toughest game in all Christendom for those whose spirits are sensitive to rude knocks. Seated there and panting with that dynamic Dutchman, the realization came to me with a little shock. Could I do it? Two hundred or two thousand a week, could I do it? Could I go out and knock on doors, push bells, face strange women and force them into buying what they hadn't dreamt of buying up to the moment before I had come in from the street?

"An' now, gentl'm'n," Mr Van Druten's pugnacious voice chased away my rising doubt, "it is very important to know how to get into der houses." I sat up. "Before you can sell a lady, you must get into der house. An' dis is der approach I recommend. I hold in my hand a tube of Brite Shampoo. I vill show you how to use it just now. You take der case wit' der machine from der car. Rest der case on der side der door opens an' ring der bell. If dere is no bell, knock an' knock hard, like dis. Stand avay from der door so dat ven der lady open der door dere vill be room for you to make your forward motion, like dis. As soon as she come, smile, smile like dis, gentl'm'n. Yessir. Dat smile vill vin you money. If der sky is black an' der rain is falling, smile. 'Goot morning,' you vill say to her like if you have known her all your life. Yessir. Say it natural an' loud. 'Have you receive your free tube of Brite Shampoo yet?' Free – dat vord vill get her. 'Here it is,' you vill say, giving it to her. She vill say: 'But vat is dis for?' 'Ach, Mrs Jones,' you vill say, 'perhaps you don't know how to use it, ein?' Den take your vatch out an' look at it in a hurry. 'Mrs Jones,' you vill say, 'I have a few minutes to spare. I'll just step in an' show you how to use it.' Den grab your case an' walk in, like dis. De forward motion. Smile an' say: 'My name is Van Druten. An' vat is yours?' Gentl'm'n, get her seated. Yessir. You have to command der situation from der start. An' de best vay to do dat is to get der lady in a chair an' you standing up. You command den. Look round der room. Choose a small bright rug wit' a lot of colours. Tell her: 'You got a vacuum cleaner, Mrs Jones? A Hoover, ein? I must get dis rug clean before I can shampoo it, Mrs Jones.' Den get to vork wit' her machine an' while you are vorking ask her if she bought it herself an' if on time or for cash. Dat, gentl'm'n, is useful information for closing. Yessir. Ask her to tell you ven she t'ink der rug is clean; an' ven she say it is clean, tell her you must make a test. Den bring *your* machine out and make der test an' dig more dirt an' more dirt. Take your coat off. Put pep into der demo. Show her how her machine is not doing der vork. First, you paint der black picture wit' *her* machine, den you paint der bright picture wit' *your* machine. Seeing is believing, gentl'm'n. She vill see for herself. An' don't forget, gentl'm'n, command der situation an' put pep into your demo. Den close her. A knockover, gentl'm'n. Yessir."

We listened, fascinated by his laugh, the wry faces he made, his gusto, his energy. Then he began to put us through our paces by playing the part of the prospect and having us rehearse the approach. I was terribly self-conscious. "Don't be afraid," he commanded me. "Vas Napoleon afraid to vin his battles?" I tried again and did a little better. He kept us there all morning and afternoon, talking, shouting, instructing, laughing and striding the floor. The last thing he did was to tell us what our commission would be: about twenty-five dollars per sale. The figure took my breath away. At that moment, inspired by Mr Van Druten's enthusiasm, it seemed a simple matter to go out and sell a machine per day, two per day, perhaps three per day. Figures kept mounting and mounting in my mind.

On the strength of my potential earnings, I went out that night and spent the few dollars I had left. I felt rich. I felt fine. I felt like a man with power. I thought with contempt of all my previous efforts at making a living. And yet, at every unguarded moment, there jumped into my mind the picture of myself knocking on strangers' doors and entering their houses unwelcomed. I tried my best to obliterate the picture, but still it kept coming.

That night my sleep was fitful. I dreamed of doors and in my dreams they took on tentacles that reached out to crush me implacably.

As instructed, the next morning I was in the office at eight o'clock sharp. The salesmen had already begun to gather for the morning's pep meeting. I tried to take stock of each and was puzzled by the diversity of types. Some were tall, others short and stocky. Some were in their twenties, others grey enough to have already passed fifty. Racially, they perhaps represented every European group. As I learned later, they had come from widely different fields of activity. But in one respect they nearly all seemed to be alike: they had had very little education. They spoke with a great deal of vivacity and colour and there were some who could turn a neat phrase – but they most of them spoke ungrammatically. The lower middle class I judged to be their background.

In little groups they foregathered to relate their experiences of the day before.

"I knocked hard on the door," said one tall good-looking fellow. "But nobody come, so I knocked again, harder this time. Soon I heard a heavy step coming down the stairs and a woman come to the door. I could see she was as sore as hell. She pulled the goddamn door open, looked at me like hell let loose and said, hard-like: 'You've woke my baby, son-of-a-bitch! Go away!' and banged the door in my face. Boy oh boy, that nearly knocked me over. But I laughed and after a while went to the back and knocked on the back door. I wasn't having any goddamn woman put one over on me. She musta thought it was the milkman or somep'n because pretty soon she opened the door. But before she could say anything, I said: 'Madam, I have come to beg you to pardon me. You didn't give me time in the front to tell you how sorry I was to wake your kid.' She looked at me kinda funny and I smiled and she said: 'Come in,' and I went in and, believe it or not, I left with a sale."

Said another: "The day before yesterday I jumped a red light. In a second a cop come up and started to bawl me out. 'Officer, I know I was wrong,' I said. 'I won't do it again.' He looked at me and said: 'You're one guy who is honest with me and didn't try to argue. I'll let you off this time.' Jesus Christ, that was a knock-out, boys, and I had to think fast, fast as hell. I said: 'Thanks Officer. You just done me a favour and I'm going to do you one in return. You played ball with me, I'm going to play ball with you. What's your name and address?' He musta thought I was going to bring him a present because he give me his name and address quick. Then I asked him when he would be home and I went to see him yesterday. Fellahs, I sold him a machine. Jesus Christ! Can you beat that?"

"Last week I made a peach of a sale," an ex-violinist chimed in at this point. "I found the husband home with the wife and started to go to town on them. He was a small cocky guy with a loud voice, as tough as hell. 'You bastard,' I said to myself, 'I'm going to get you yet.' I demonstrated. I dug dirt, more dirt than you'd find in a garden. 'No money,' he said. I dug more dirt. 'No money,' he said. After every pile of dirt he said: 'No money, no money, no money.' He was driving me nuts with his no money. At last I got him to ask me the price of the machine and I knew I had him then. 'Ten dollars,' I said, sorta off-hand. 'Ten dollars?' he said. 'Ten dollars,' I said, still sorta off-hand.

As I dug more dirt, he asked me the price again and again and each time I said: 'Ten dollars, ten dollars, ten dollars.' Then he went upstairs and come back with ten dollars which he offered me. You bet your life I took it. Then I made out the contract and gave it to him and said: 'That leaves a balance of . . .' 'Balance!' he shouted in his cocky way. 'Balance, hell! You told me the price was ten dollars!' I kept my trap shut. 'Was you lying?' he shouted. 'Sure,' I said, looking him in the eye. 'But you lied to me first when you told me you had no money. One lie deserves another.' All the bastard could do was laugh and sign the order."

"Jesus Christ!" said the man of the cop story.

And now for the pep meeting. First, however, I must tell you that the sales force of my unit is divided into two teams bearing popular sobriquets like the *Royal Oaks*, etc. These teams are in turn sub-divided into three groups each, all with leaders chosen for their past performances in the field. The national force is broken down into "divisions". One glance at this dispensation will show how cleverly it lends itself to rivalries and competitive struggles. Add to this the fact that "group leaders" all the way up to "division governors" receive commissions on every sale made within their respective divisions and sub-divisions, and you will immediately understand why prizes in money and kind are the rule rather than the exception. And more, the salesmen are the sole advertisers for the firm of which I write – which is only another way of saying that the money which would have gone into expensive newspaper, magazine, radio and screen advertisements is channelled instead into commissions and prizes.

And now for the pep meeting. It would be something new to me and I was all agog with excitement as I walked into the room set aside for the purpose. The room, with chairs placed in orderly rows on each side, was bright with sunshine falling through a skylight. One team sat on one side, the other on the other side. The men smoked. Team and group leaders tossed taunts at each other. Success mottoes stared us in the face.

Then a door opened and in walked Mr Anderson, followed by Mr Van Druten. Did I say walk? They *strode* in, pounding the floor with their heels, wearing broad mechanical smiles. Like one man, the forty-odd of us rose and let loose pandemonium. Mr Anderson dropped his bundle of papers with a bang onto the table before which he stood, raised his hands, broadened his smile and began to clap for all he was worth. Mr Van Druten bawled, holding his head high in the air. The room quaked with the noise. Then Mr Anderson called for order and we all sat.

The next moment he was in full blast. His speech was a gem of sound and forcefulness, sprinkled with a little salt of humour. Each word was an explosion, each sentence a barrage. He shouted at us, he swung his arms in violent arcs. I tried to take the show good-naturedly by objectifying it. It was amusing at such moments; off-guard, the ritual struck me as being crude and vulgar. I couldn't see the necessity for the waste of such valuable energy in the cause of vacuum cleaners: what a tragic commentary on our social order! But Mr Anderson was obviously not thinking the thoughts that came willy-nilly, skipping into my head. There he stood shouting to us of the great opportunity we had of making money today, of the mind that can be our master or our slave, of the honour and glory of work, of the necessity for it – "twelve, fourteen hours a day, and push those bells and knock on those doors, doggone it, and how do you feel today, gentlemen?" "Fine!" in one thunderous chorus. "Right! God darn it, this is the day to bring the money to the wife and kiddies. Canvass tonight, canvass every night. You get the husbands home then. No husband alibi? Haw-haw, it's a cinch then, a pushover! And don't be scared to push those bells until you wear your glove out. I knew a guy who used to take a block, look it over and say: 'I have four sales here. Every refusal I get will make me happier for every refusal will take me nearer my four sales.' Get the point? That's guts, that's the thing that makes great men, that's the thing that makes a success of life." On and on he went, a spate of words with the speed and fury of a flood.

Then, to whip up the spirit of rivalry between the two groups, he gave the sales standings of the day before. One team was leading the other by a small margin (terrific applause from one side of the room); two groups, one from each team, were running a neck-and-neck race high up in the national report (every man to his feet and a deafening medley of shrieks and stamping and whistles). He then proceeded to the drawing of a raffle to the accompaniment of boisterous banter: the man whose name was drawn was richer by five dollars if he had made a sale the day before.

The opening business done, he called upon some of the more successful men to speak. One small Scandinavian youth with the face of a boy of eighteen (he had gone to sea as a lad and vagabonded about the world) belied his placid-looking blondness by galvanizing us into tiptoe of excitement with a short and fighting talk. More handclapping and applause. He was followed by another youth with a voice of thunder and an earnestness that was impressive. Phrases like "work and more work", "the mind is a power-house", "the finest dirt-digger in the world", "the greatest company at back of us" ran in refrains through every speaker's exhortation.

The final speaker rose. It was Mr Van Druten. He sprang to the table, threw his great chest out and his Junker head back and began his stormy oration. His pitch rose and rose and rose until I feared for the ceiling above our heads. He flung his arms upwards in the gesture of a new creator of a new earth; then he brought them down with all his force on the table before him. The table rattled and one leg flew out. That didn't disturb Mr Van Druten. He bellowed. He ranted, he raved, the blood rose to his face to bursting point. I couldn't understand a word he said. At last, with one final magnificent bellow, he collapsed into his chair, shaking in every limb, gasping for breath. Every man rose and let loose another pandemonium of noise.

Mr Anderson raised his arms for order. We sat. Dead silence. Then this from Mr Anderson, like a musket-volley:

"What are you going to do?"

"SELL!"

There was a wild scramble for overcoats. In double-quick time we were out in the streets making for our cars.

Another day of cold-turkey selling had begun.

NOTES

1. The eponymous hero of Miguel de Cervantes's novel (1605, 1615).
2. Henry Ford (1863–1947), the founder of Ford Motor Company.
3. Napoleon Bonaparte (1769–1821), the Corsican general who became France's first emperor.
4. Mendes earlier chose to give the name Van Druten to the unpleasant Dutchman in "Torrid Zone".
5. A German nobleman.

YELLOW LEGS

SOME YEARS AGO AN AMERICAN JOURNALIST, vagabonding his way north-wards from Trinidad up the almost unbroken chain of West Indian islands, landed for a few hours in St George's, the capital of Grenada. Stepping ashore, he admired for a while the lovely blue, pink and white façades of the quaint buildings, reminders of the early French occupation of the island, giving onto a curving road embracing a bay as blue as blue can be. Then he approached a coloured chauffeur leaning indolently against his taxicab. "I want to see the Carib settlement," said he. The chauffeur screwed his eyes in the blazing sunlight, stared in puzzlement at the stranger for a moment, scratched his kinky head, and said: "What you say, mister?" The visitor repeated his request. "Hunh-hunh," was the non-committal reply. "Jump in. T'ree dollars to take you there an' back." And off they went at dusty speed, along a narrow gravel road flanked on one side by a sea that shone blue and green in turn, and on the other by soaring cliffs that looked like the battlements of the gods.

"Dis is it, Mount Morris," said the chauffeur twenty minutes later, mispro-nouncing the name. The American alighted, mounted the gap, and started to walk through the settlement. Strolling along, he watched the men, women and children as they crowded to the doors of their huts. At first he was puz-zled, then amazed. At length he turned to his guide. "But these are *white* people," he blurted out, "and I asked you to take me to the Carib settlement!" The black face of the taxicab driver wrinkled into a crooked smile. "Is like dis, borss," he explained. "De Carib settlement is in St Vincent, anodder islan' up dat way," and he pointed to the north. "Times is bad now an' we got to make a livin', borss. You did ask me for a settlement, an' dis is de onlyiest one we got here. Mount Morris, borss."

When I landed in St George's recently, I made no mistake. I wanted to look into the Mount Moritz colony of whites I had heard so much about, so I began by asking this, that and the other question before visiting the place. It didn't take me long to discover that the "yellow legs", as they are called by the Negroes in the island, are despised by Grenada's sixty-six thousand people, all of whom, but for a few families of European descent, are negroid. Their contempt is expressed, among a number of other ways, in a couplet that runs:

> Cricket-gill an' dry bonavista (cheap fish)[1]
> Good enough fo' po' buckra (poor whites).

Sung to any member of the settlement by an outsider, it has the effect on him a red flag is said to have on a bull. To veil the allusion, the two final words are at times changed to: "Say fo' who, nuh!" But the tune to which the couplet is sung is so well known throughout the island that the words are not necessary for recognizing it.

Some months ago a string band of three blacks was hired to play the music for a Mount Moritz celebration. In the small Society Hall the sweating whites gyrated in pairs, dancing to the sensuous strains of the calypso tunes so popular in those islands where the annual carnival fete is still observed. All had been drinking "mountain dew", the musicians so much that they grew bolder than proved safe for them. Toward midnight, when the revelry was at its swirling liveliest, the band, by way of a tease, stopped in the middle of an encore and swung into the familiar air. Immediately the celebrants stood as if petrified, twigged the insult being stringed at them, and then with one accord fell on the members of the band and beat them up with a will.

The settlement is spread out on the ridge and sides of a hill called Mount Moritz and lies about four miles to the north-west of St George's. The gap climbing up to it is long and steep. A painted bay glimmers a thousand feet below, blue where the water is deep, green where shallow, golden-brown where the coral reefs sleep. The white arc-line of surf uplifts no sound to you. With the quiet around and the green arch of overhanging branches, the sensation is that of ascending into a faraway world.

The colony consists of about eight hundred whites in all. The first thing you notice about them is their poor physical condition and the dirty garments they wear. Nearly all are barefooted, and almost everyone has a leg bandaged with a soiled rag; later you learn that this is the result of cuts received in the underbrush. Some of the babies are beautiful, their chubby bodies exposed half-naked to the sun, their fair hair unkempt and matted with dirt, their blue eyes bright with the wonder of all children. Speaking to the adults, you are at once struck by their dull voices and the vacuous expressions on their faces. They look moronic, some of them, and even the brightest individuals reveal traces of mental retardation, obviously induced by inbreeding, malnutrition and the climate. It must be remembered, too, that the original stock – yokels from Devon and Cornwall – was itself not too intelligent.

They are the descendants of those cargoes of rebels shipped out from England to "the Barbadoes" by "Bloody Jeffreys"[2] chief circuit judge of Britain during the Assizes of the 1680s. The English Revolution, a bitter and prolonged struggle between authoritarianism and democracy, was in full violent swing. The head of Charles I had already rolled off the executioner's block; Cromwell had died in 1658 and with him his military dictatorship. The restoration of the Stuarts had been established with Charles II, that wittiest of all monarchs who never said a stupid thing and never did a wise one,[3] ascending the throne. He was succeeded by James II, a stiff-necked Roman Catholic who soon roused the opposition of the parliamentary people and the Protestants. A group of the disaffected plotted to overthrow him and place in his stead the Duke of Monmouth, Protestant Pretender and natural son of Charles II. The rebellion, supported by a tatterdemalion army of farm labourers armed with scythes, spades and forks, raised its standard in the West Country and marched to ignominious defeat at Sedgemoor.

Packing the prisoners into the holds of ships, Judge Jeffreys ordered them exiled to the West Indies island of Barbados, outlying bulwark of Royalism, whence he had just had news of a shortage of labour on "His Majesty's sugar plantations". After a voyage of ghastly sufferings, they were disembarked on the island. "Unfitted for work in the fields under a tropical sun," records one chronicler, "the banished men and women became dependents, loafers, doers of odd jobs and in the end were squatters of the most dejected type. Pitied by the planter, held in contempt by the negro . . . they yet kept alive . . . the memory that they were white men. They married only among themselves, held aloof from the blackamoor and went their own way, such as it was." One of their number, however, rose to lasting fame. Making his escape, he became a buccaneer, threw open the Spanish seas to trade, sacked Panama, was knighted by Charles II, and lived to be elevated to the governorship of Jamaica. His name was Sir Henry Morgan.[4]

It wasn't until the early 1870s that the Barbados colony broke from its debilitating isolation of more than 180 years, a largish group migrating to the neighbouring island of St Vincent. There they settled in Mount Dorchester and, just four years after their arrival, a hurricane destroyed their homes and fields, so some of them packed up their bundles and sailed for Grenada.

"I was one of those," said Fitzy Greaves, the oldest citizen in Mount Moritz. "We landed at Molinere Bay, down yonder, and when we came here the land was nearly wild and there was only a few families, including my uncle. They had come from Barbados about ten years before, and they was the first folk here." He stood in the midst of a litter of pigs as he spoke, his wrinkled face ruddy-brown, his emaciated body bent, his blue eyes vacant. The clothes he wore may have been taken from the body of a tramp. "We brought a new kind of eddoe, tannia and prickly yam plants in our pockets from St Vincent. We planted them. All them you see hereabouts come from the plants we brought . . . Sick? I was sick about ten years ago, feelin' as if I'd nivver git up from my bed. I wrote an astrologer in America somebody told me about. He wrote back that I was lazy, to git off my bed an' go to work. I did. I been feelin' better ever sence."

The Mount Moritz houses, scattered about without any plan, except that they stand at intervals facing the narrow winding road, are ramshackle affairs roofed either with thatch or the heat-attracting galvanize sheets so unaccountably popular in the West Indies. Incredibly small for the most part, they nevertheless give shelter to families of six or more. The kitchens, mere boarded-up sheds hard by the huts, are horrible to see. In one I watched a mother, with three filthy but beautiful children clinging to her tattered gown, cooking a mess of vegetables in a cracked blackened pot over a coal fire that smothered the enclosure with evil-smelling smoke. Some provisions lay in a heap on the bare ground.

"Yes, sir, the children eats what we eat," she told me. "When the goat is giving milk, they get some, but we can't give them the cow milk because we can sell it. We gets four cents a bottle in town, but we have to pay one shilling (24¢) a month to deliver every bottle. Sometimes we eat meat; no, not beef, that's too expensive, but manicou" – a sort of glorified rat with a really tasty flesh – "and tattoo" – its back is shelled and its flavour is good. "My husband catches the manicou when the moonlight is strong." She stood there talking timidly in a monotone, her face the epitome of despair, her belly big with child, her skin browned by the sun, her children seeking to conceal themselves behind her gown.

"Yes, sir, we have midwifes here, but I had a good time with these three an' I didn't need one. Just as well, for my husband didn't have the money to pay for one. Them from here charge eight shillings ($1.92); from town they charge one pound ($4.80) . . . My husband is out on Mr Greaves estate, droguin' (carrying) cane. That's down the other side of the hill yonder. When the cane is out, he traffics between here an' Trinidad with goats, and sheep and pigs. Sometimes he makes a few shillings that way, but sometimes it's difficult to get the stock. Last week he walk for miles around," and she waved an arm to the mountainous east, "and all he could pick up was one goat. Miles an' miles of walkin' for one goat. Life is hard for us, sir." She couldn't have been more than twenty-five, but she slouched as if she carried the world on her shoulders. "My husband name is Dowden, but we're all connected here . . . That? That's the Society Hall, sir. The dues is one shilling a month, but when we're sick we have to be in bed before we can git help. That's where we hold our dances, at Christmas an' harvest time . . . Some of the men does a little fishin' in the bay down yonder. No, they don't sell the fish; they eat it with their families."

Most of the land is under cultivation. From points of vantage you can see the patches of ground provisions, cocoa, coconuts, cane, corn, nutmegs, peas. The bulk of the vegetables is taken to St George's, but the big proprietors, who are now planting similar crops, and for whom the Mount Moritz farmers are no match, are implacably destroying the small man's market. It's the old story of "shark eating little fish", as the poor whites phrase it.

In another kitchen the mother was grinding corn into meal in a rusty machine attached to a post. Her eldest girl stood at the coal pot attending to the cooking; eight other children, all filthy, clustered around the kitchen door to gape at the stranger. "Yes, sir," Mrs Winsborough said, "the children go to school sometimes. You'll pass the school house higher up yonder, near the old water cistern where we use to collect every afternoon for our supply of water. When the hookworm got real bad they didn't give us no more water from there. They put up pipes with running water, four public ones along the road. Some of the houses have private pipes, but they're the rich Mount Morris folk. Things is so bad now with us that the children have to work when they can. What they do? They help put manure in the fields. They lift the baskets with the cow dung, put them on their heads an' drogue them to the fields. It's all right when the weather is good; but when it rains, the water comes through the baskets and covers the children from head to foot with the stink manure water. It's a job to clean them when they come home. They git twelve cents a day for that. My husband is out of work. Look at him coming there."

A man entered the shed. He wore a bristly red moustache and his parted lips revealed a toothless mouth. He came in with a slouch, mumbled something that I took to be the greetings of the day, and sat down to gaze at the miserable scene, himself the most miserable-looking object in it. "We livin' on charity now, sir," Mrs Winsborough continued. "No, we don't get help here. Mount Morris people are turrible to each other. Mrs Frederick Greaves up the road yonder is the richest lady here, but she'd quicker help a stranger than us . . . Yes, sir, we hear about the war. Why we shouldn't want England to win? We're English people after all." The afternoon I visited the school house, the exhortation: "God bless our King and Save the Empire" was inscribed in large letters on the blackboard.

I met Mrs Frederick Greaves another day. Her painted cottage of four rooms, curtains fluttering at the windows and an air of cleanliness about it, was something different from what I had so far seen. I knew her the moment I saw her. She was standing in the yard, bony hands resting on hips, wiry body erect. Two greying plaits hung on her shoulders and framed a thin red face with thin lips, knife-sharp nose, and beady blue eyes. She was so obviously the prosperous virago that her rasping authoritative voice caused me no surprise.

"No, I have no children I can call my own," she announced, observing my questioning glance in the direction of the two coloured girls looking out a window of her house. "Them's my adopted. Yes, white folk here started to marry an' to live with the Negroes about twenty years ago. As you move round

Mount Morris you'll see a lot of that; but mostly they're just livin' togither, not married. Outside children? Flocks of them, all over the place.

"Goin' to church . . . yes, we're nearly all Anglicans. A few are Seven Day Adventises. No, we haven't a church buildin' yet; we worship in the school house yonder. It's about twenty years ago we started to put the pillars for a church, but when we was finished with the pillars – you can still see them opposite the school yonder – we had no more money. We started to put aside the money we made with the harvest festival every year to finish the church, an' we saved about eighty pounds ($384), but the school house needed rebuilding, so we did that with the money instead. As I was tellin' you, going to church don't do the girls no good. Almost every family have outside children an' a lot of them is *mustis*. That's the word we have for coloured. But we don't make no difference between the white an' the coloured. All is one in the sight of God." Later I discovered that the issue of the mixed unions are much brighter and less afraid of taking their chances with the outside world.

The story of a brother and sister illustrates this. Their father was white, their mother a mulattress from St George's, and the two children had straight hair, olive skins and good features. An American woman of wealth some years ago visited the island, took a fancy to the girl, and made the necessary arrangements for taking her to the States. At her new school she displayed a talent for painting and was sent off to an art academy in Italy where she carried off all the academy's awards. A young officer in Mussolini's fascist army fell in love with her and married her. The boy, not to be outdone by his sister, went off to Jamaica where he landed a job. Saving his money, he sailed for England just before war was declared and there married a blonde girl. Then, strangely enough, he joined the Mosley Blackshirts.[5] "Nobody has heard from him since the war," Mrs Greaves told me. "We suppose he must be in jail." "So you've heard of Mosley?" I asked. "I can read *and* write!" she shot back at me with dignity.

Mrs Greaves continued: "That's my sister, Mrs Gay, livin' yonder," and she pointed across the road to a hovel from which smoke was rising in thick blue spirals. A tall slim woman emerged, her gown soiled and tattered, three children in her wake. One was a lanky boy of about fifteen, and in his hand he held a bleeding manicou. For at least five minutes, he stood staring at me blankly, a sheepish grin on his face, the blood dripping from the dead animal.

"Don't you go to school?" I asked him. The grin vanished from his face. "*He* go to school!" his mother said. "All he want to do is stand around all day long. No, sir, the schoolmaster isn't one of us; he's black."

Then she sidled up to me, glancing through the corner of her eye at her sister now busy sweeping out the yard across the road. "Don't believe everything Mistress Greaves tell you, sir," she said, *sotto voce.* "She's my sister, same mother, same father, but she's the stingiest woman in Mount Morris. She has so much money an' land and she never even offer me a bread," at which she snapped her fingers. "It's only the poor who helps the poor in Mount Morris, sir. Yes, her husband alive, but she rules him with a iron fist, although it's him who make all the money for her. I hear her tellin' you about those two *mustis.* They're her grandchildren; and if *musti* an' nigger is the same in the sight of God, why she don't admit they're her grandchildren? No, we don't harbour no bad feelings here against the niggers and I must say I see the *mustis* here more ambitious than all of us put togither. Her daughter took up with a black man working there an' she had those two children with him. They're smart children an' she ought to be proud to say they're her grands. The daughter? She now livin' in St George's. She's a wild girl . . . No. Very few of the young men here have jobs in town. I know only two. Both of them are Bedfords an' they working in dry-goods stores as clerks. Every morning they walk to work and back in the evening from work. Their salary is about three dollars a week. I trying to get my son, Henry there, to look for a job in town too, but he has no ambition. All he want to do is to play cricket on the ball pitch."

Henry, abetted by a tip, took me to show me the cricket ground. The young men of the settlement had built it on a slope, the only space available, so I wasn't surprised when he told me: "We win every game we play here. Yes, we play sometimes in other town, St George's an' sometimes Grenville and Sauteurs, but they always beat us then. *Their* ball pitch is level an' we accustom to this leaning ground."

The people are so poor that they're unable to support a single shop in the settlement. The only attempt ever made at establishing one was done with a black woman's small savings. It happened this way. A Mount Moritz married man fell in with a negress, deserted his wife and five children, and went to live with his paramour in the settlement. With her money, about fifty dollars, he opened a little shop stocked with matches, lard, candles, tinned milk and butter, and so on. No sooner had the venture failed than he returned to his wife who consented to a resumption of the intimate relationship only when she saw he was willing to continue tending the vegetable garden in their yard. The day I met her she was pregnant, but every morning she placed a basket of the garden's provisions on her head and trudged, barefooted, all the way into St George's to sell them in the market, the eldest girl taking care of the younger children during her absences. "What will you do when your wife has her baby?" I asked the husband. He shrugged his shoulders and smiled inanely.

At one time the "yellow legs" made their own rum in a still hidden away in a cocoa patch that grew in the valley. To protect themselves against surprise, they arranged that whoever happened to be the first to know of the arrival of a raiding posse of police was to blow his conch shell as a warning. One dark night, as the men were busy with their illegal game, the distant sound they always dreaded to hear and never heard reached their ears. At once they doused their flambeaux and slid into the opaque blackness of the cocoa field. All night they lay there, shivering with fright, every sound a menace, every movement of the manicous in search of food a threat. When they emerged the following morning and learned that one of their own young men had sounded the warning by way of a lark, they gave him the thrashing of his life.

Adjoining Mount Moritz is the Mount Willis settlement of Negroes who also fermented their own "fire water", as the blacks call rum. The two colonies had come to an agreement of mutual assistance in case of an emergency, and the conch shell was to be used as the call for help. The night the SOS floated faintly to Mount Moritz, the whole settlement, men, women and children, grabbing whatever sticks and stones lay at hand, rushed off in one body to honour their pact. They got there too late, for the police had already rounded up the offenders and marched them off to prison.

As most of the cultivation is in cane, more families are supported by mus-covado, a sort of wet brown sugar, than by anything else. The set-up is not new. The few owners of the land rent it out at $4.80 an acre per annum; and when the sugar is made in the mill of the land owner, he retains half, the other half going to the grower. Cash is so scarce that, more often than not, the yearly rental is paid in muscovado. All of it is consumed in the island. A fertile acre will yield about twenty kerosene tins, the measure used in the settlement. When I was there, the market price hovered around $2.40 per tin; some years ago it had dropped to $0.72. A simple calculation shows that at the $2.40 figure, the grower earns $24.00 per acre, minus the rental of $4.80. It's no fun ploughing an acre, planting it and cutting the crop; indeed, it's extremely laborious work in fair weather and foul. When rain falls, the donkey paths serving the fields from the mills become dangerously slippery; when the sun is shining, the heat is terrific. The cutting season extends from December to May.

The settlement boasts two or three motor-driven mills, but I saw the more primitive method in operation. The cane is fed into the "squeeze" and the contraption is turned by a horse. The juice is then taken and boiled in coppers for about three hours, after which it is poured into the tins to cool. The cane flavour is unmistakable to the tongue and quite delicious. There's no better sweetening for coffee.

The men were working under a boiling sun when I came upon them, midway down the hillside, after a hazardous descent. 'Way down in the valley I could see other figures moving to and fro, and once in a while an upward surge of wind brought me their chattering voices. The group I talked with were renters and their hired hands. Only one of them looked strong, but when he turned his face to me the same vapid expression met my inquiring eyes. They were all dripping with sweat.

Two donkeys transported the faggots of cane up the precipitous incline to the spot at which we talked; from there to the mill, transportation was the land owner's responsibility. It was pitiful to watch the donkeys labouring up the hill, the men behind encouraging them with shouts and pushes. Smaller faggots were drogued by some women and their children. Work commences at eight and ends at dusk, the women receiving twenty cents, the men twenty-four cents per day, plus a meal at midday. The land owners find it cheaper to add four cents to the wages and supply no meal. "They won't even give us cold water," said one man. "They don't want to see us come up in the world. You ask them to give you something for nothing, an' they press their heel 'pon you. They like to keep you down. It's the big people who are making us see hell, sir."

"What do you call big people?" I asked. "Mr Frederick Greaves, for instance; I understand he's the richest man here. How much would you say he's worth?" They put their heads together and began, with my aid, to compute his wealth. "With land and everything," one announced at last, "he has about seven thousand dollars. Then there's his brother, Mister David; he has about five thousand dollars. Mister Edward Searles is a rich man here too, nearly as rich as Mister David. Them are the three richest men in Mount Morris. But, sir, they won't help us if they saw us starving with our children."

"Don't you fellows ever work outside Mount Moritz?" I then inquired. "Some of us," was the reply. "Loading bananas in St George's." I had heard about this from a merchant and had been told that, although the Negroes are stronger, they aren't half as willing as the poor whites. "We gets that job about once a fortnight, sir. The work is turrible hard. We have to lift an' turn round every one of them banana stems for the clerk to grade them. Then we put them in the lighters, go out with the lighters to the steamer outside the bay, an' unload them into the ship. Sometimes we handle five thousand stems an' we get about two dollars for the job. It takes us about two days, working practically all the time without even sleeping. It's turrible hard work, sir . . . No, we don't know how they figure our payment. We take it an' have to be satisfied. We can't make a noise, else they won't put us to work."

The evening I left the settlement for the last time, the bay below, reflecting the flaming sunset, lay like a sheet of burnished gold. A few of the "yellow legs" stood on the crest of the hill to wave me goodbye. I pointed to the west and asked them if they often saw so beautiful a sea and sky. They glanced at the conflagration then turned to me without a word. They may have been a little sorry to see me go, for we had spent many a pleasant moment together; but a miracle of colour, there for them to gaze at with rapture until it melted into coming night, seemed to burn beyond the compass of their comprehension.

NOTES

1. The glosses are by Mendes.
2. Also known as "Hanging Judge Jeffreys".
3. A memory of "The King's Epitaph", presented to Charles II of England by John Wilmot, Earl of Rochester (1647–1680):

    > Here lies our sovereign lord, the King,
    > Whose promise none relies on
    > He never said a foolish thing
    > Nor ever did a wise one.

4. Sir Henry Morgan was born in Wales *c.*1635 and died in Jamaica in 1688. Not much seems to be known about his early life in Britain. He may actually have been shanghaied and sold into indentured status in Barbados. Alternatively, he may have gone out to Jamaica in Penn and Venables's expedition of 1655. He was certainly active in the Caribbean long before the Duke of Monmouth's rebellion in 1685. The sack of Panama occurred in 1671.
5. The English peer Sir Oswald Mosley (1896–1980) organized the British Union of Fascists. His followers were known as Blackshirts, in imitation of Adolf Hitler's Brownshirts.

RAMJIT DAS

AS A BOY OF SIX, BHAGWANT DAS came to Trinidad with his parents who were indentured to a cocoa estate in the Manzanilla district. It wasn't long before he himself was earning thirty cents a day as a labourer on the estate. Every morning he rose with the sun, drank his coffee and ate his roti, and went into the green shade of the cocoa to pick or gather or weed according to the need of the season. And Bhagwant Das very early in life decided that he would better his position, so he began by saving half of his earnings.

At seventeen, his father married him off to Moonia who, because of her beauty and the attentions of the young men on the estate, was a harum-scarum sort of girl, and all the old women round about wagged their heads and murmured that no good would come to Bhagwant Das when he took her for wife. But Moonia settled down and was a faithful wife, and for once the old women were disappointed.

When Bhagwant Das was forty years old he took his savings buried away in his mattress and bought a cocoa estate. He worked harder than ever, mixing his sweat with the soil of his holding, and from time to time bought up the surrounding acres. And the day came when Bhagwant Das was looked upon as a rich man.

His worry in life was his only son, Ramjit. One night, when Ramjit was sixteen years, he said to Moonia: "Our son runs wild with the women and doesn't want to work, so we must find a wife for him."

Moonia said yes, and ventured to suggest that Shamiran, the ten-year-old daughter of Ramnarine, would be just the girl for Ramjit. She had to admit that Shamiran was not pretty, but hadn't old Ramnarine recently sold his oil lands for a lot of money? The dowry would be handsome. And anyhow there was much to be said for a little ugliness in a wife.[1]

Old Bhagwant Das rubbed his bony hands together, and the very next day went to the neighbouring village where Ramnarine lived to discuss the subject of joining their families by marriage. The two old men squatted on their hams for a long time talking in low tones.

That evening Bhagwant Das was able to say to Moonia: "It is arranged. The wedding is fixed for two weeks from today. I must send for the priest and make a big fee. Ramnarine has promised a dowry of ten thousand dollars, to be paid when Shamiran enters our son's house. In another year she ought to be ready for that. You must speak to Ramjit."

Ramjit came home late that night and found his mother sewing by candle-light. She glanced up at her son and knew instinctively that he was happy and she wondered why.

Now Moonia loved her son. She loved him with a greater feeling than she had ever been able to give anyone, including Bhagwant Das, and she recognized in him something of that joy of life which she herself had had before her marriage. But she was afraid for him and wanted to see him mated safe from danger.

"You are late," she said to him. Ramjit was silent, his tall body stooped in the low-ceilinged room. She looked up at her son and found him good, for in his face she saw the reflection of her own.

"Your father and I have chosen a wife for you, Ramjit," she said at last in quiet tones, but firmly and decisively.

Ramjit gave his mother a quick, furtive look, then held his eyes away and answered nothing.

So Moonia talked on. She told him that Shamiran was the one selected: and as Ramjit had never cast eyes on Shamiran, had never even heard of her, Moonia chanced the remark that Shamiran was a lovely girl, meaning, of course, her character. Still Ramjit answered nothing, so Moonia gave him the news of the dowry.

"But I've never seen this Shamiran," Ramjit said at last, his voice bitter.

"Remember that your father had never seen me before he took me for wife," Moonia replied.

"Mai," (which is the Indian word for mother) said Ramjit, "I do not want to marry like that. I must choose my own wife."

"That is not our way, son," Moonia said sadly. "Your father has been good to you, he has given you everything you wanted, even a bicycle, and now you must follow the custom of our people or else bring down the wrath of your father upon your head."

So Ramjit bowed and listened to his mother until she was silent, and said goodnight and went into his room. And after that night he showed neither joy nor sorrow, and from his lips there came no word, and Moonia was gladdened by the thought that he had decided to submit himself to the wisdom of his parents in so important a concern as the choosing of a wife.

The sun was pouring down streams of bright heat on the little village as Moonia and all the other women were busy getting ready for the day's wedding: and in the neighbouring village Shamiran, open-eyed with wonder, watched her parents and all the members of her father's household making preparations for the ceremony. Fatted calves were killed: each household slaughtered two goats and the cooks were busy in their respective kitchens. From all the neighbouring villages and hamlets the people began to arrive early, for the news of the big wedding had spread far and wide. Some went to Shamiran's village and others to Ramjit's. And the old women who had heard gossip of the bridegroom knocked their heads together and whispered that Shamiran would come to no good marrying him.

By two o'clock the guests had assembled and the rites begun. Old Bhagwant Das, a new turban on his head, observed that the white overseers of the large estates in the vicinity had brought their wives along, and he felt proud.

Ramjit, with only a loincloth on, was bathed in the middle of a circle of chanting women who cast copper and silver coins into the bucket from which the water was being scooped to wash him. And then they dressed him; a long and mysterious ritual it was, Pundit Hari Narain intoning a prayer in a sepulchral voice with the adjustment of each piece of garment.

At last Ramjit, in all the colours of the rainbow and with countless beads and jewels bedecking him from head to foot, was ready to meet his bride; so after a great feast, they lifted him into a car piled high with presents for Shamiran, and drove off.

Ramnarine and Bhagwant Das met in the middle of the street with salutations and embraces. Two stalwart men shouldered the bridegroom into Shamiran's house, the little bell on the apex of his headgear tinkling through the gathering dusk. And after the reception rites were over all the guests were summoned to a great feast.

Into the night sky rockets rose with joyful crepitations, and red and green stars blossomed suddenly and floated gracefully to earth.

Just as the moment approached for Ramjit to cast his eyes upon Shamiran for the first time in his life, a current of excited murmuring began to flow from mouth to mouth. The Hon'ble Persaud Rampersad, elected member of the Legislative Council and East Indian guest of honour at the wedding, hurriedly drew Bhagwant Das aside and croaked the astounding news into his ear. Bhagwant Das, his tiny eyes like coals of fire, followed the politician with quick steps into an upstairs room, and there he saw for himself what he could scarcely believe.

The murmuring rose to a stormy sea of talk, and the old women knocked their heads together and felt just as if they had won a victory. For the bridegroom had fled, leaving behind him his wedding garments a tumbled heap in an upstairs room. Bhagwant Das roared, Moonia moaned, Ramnarine's dignity was outraged, but Shamiran did not understand what all the confusion was about.

Two days went by before they discovered Ramjit in a little room in Port of Spain. Not a word would he say to his irate father; but as soon as Moonia arrived he greeted her affectionately and presented Rampatia to her.

"Mai," said he, his eyes moist with joy, "You know Rampatia, who is from our village. I have loved her for a long time and we were married yesterday before the Court House clerk."

And Moonia saw that Rampatia was pretty, and her son happy, so she embraced them both; but Bhagwant Das swore a great oath at his son and turned his back upon him and strode out of the little room into the noisy street.

NOTES

1.   In "And Then the Hurricane Came" (*Pablo's Fandango*) the two East Indian fathers marry the beautiful Mulemeah to the ugly Sookram, and the ugly Sumintra to the handsome Mahadeo, with predictable – and disastrous – results.

Journalism

EDITORIAL NOTES

OF THIS ISSUE –

We launch our second issue as an *Occasional* Review (mark the word) of Literature and Affairs. It is the first in this island with these pretensions. The format alone is the result of long hours of thought and labour. We have sought to make the whole production as artistic without as within, and any success achieved in this direction is in no small measure due to the goodwill of our printers. To them the difficult and unusual task, if we may be forgiven the ambiguity, appeared to be a labour of love, and we who have had our own peculiar difficulties fully appreciate the spirit in which the work has been executed. The medallion,[1] which probably needs no introduction, is a temporary measure, pending a more symbolical design. We might, in fact, more completely look the gift horse in the mouth by saying that the land-locked harbour is not in the tradition we are seeking. Nor is the legend, in whatever way we might be disposed to translate it. Our motto, if one were necessary, would be something after the fashion of *ars longa vita brevis*,[2] which might quite accurately mean live and let live. With regard to the hope that is in us, we intend a quarterly. We should, indeed, have preferred to make a monthly call upon our friends, and even our enemies; but, alas! It looks like being our last. Understand us. We do not flee what has been curiously called "criticism". There is no closer critic of our work than ourselves. We have received, moreover, what praise has come our way with a degree of doubting equanimity; informed opinion and advice, with gladness; the unintelligible and sanctimonious gibbering of the "critics" with courtesy and even with kindness. An instance of the first must have been seen and read by everyone; of the second – well, that is our secret; but of the third we reproduce a sample below.* It reads:

> Letters protesting against the obscenities of the Magazine have been pouring into the *Guardian* office during the past week. One is from a Boy Scout who says: "Its disagreeable implications cast unwarrantable aspersions on the fair name of our beautiful Island." Another letter describes the volume as "nasty." The writer fears that other young writers will think it smart to be the same.

Splendid! And the only murmur which escaped us on reading this astonishing piece of writing was one borrowed from the Master:

> Out, out,
> Sweet Scout!

And if it be a travesty it is a travesty of Shakespeare and not of Miss Gertrude Stein.[3] Our purpose has not been to get into a temper with anybody, even if that would engulf us in the folly of "pouring" out words, however excellent in themselves, without any meaning in the context. We have no desire to lose our heads.

– AND THE FUTURE

Nor have we any desire to lose what little financial credit we have. Our problem is an economic one. We cannot conscientiously continue to draw upon our contributors without being able to offer something more than a mere and remote hope of reward; and pleasurable as the work is we are, not unwilling, but unable to pledge our all for its sake. As it is, we have been kept afloat so far by the generosity of the advertisers, to whom our thanks are due. But floating is colourless fun at best: we should like to be in the position to swim serenely or strike out boldly in the tide of life about us. To make this possible in the future, three things are necessary. First, the continued support of the advertising community; secondly, sufficient interest on the part of the public to subscribe to the periodical at the inevitably higher price of one shilling

---

*See the *Trinidad Guardian*, 22 December 1929.

and sixpence; and lastly, the co-operation of anyone aspiring to contribute to the growth of cultural life in the West Indies. Our aim is to afford our fellow men and women an opportunity of self-expression and expansion, and if the assistance required is forthcoming, to touch life at all available points. We do not propose standing still, and our programme for the not-far-distant future contains some surprises for our readers well worth watching; even if there are difficulties about it. We do not much mind difficulties: *la vie est facile pour les hiboux,*[4] the full perception of which we leave to the undoubted astuteness of our Boy Scout. We should like to enlarge the scope of the magazine and hope to publish from time to time critical essays on a variety of subjects of interest to our readers. Again, there is an abundant activity in the West Indies, a well conceived record of which would add to the literature of these islands, and we invite articles on, among other things, fishing, shooting, and yachting (which would include the going in motor-boats but for the noise they make) and nature studies. Everyone's experience in art, or literature, or life itself, is extremely important; the attempt should be to make it interesting. It will be seen that to achieve our aim none of the three elements mentioned above should be lacking; and the third necessarily depends upon the first two. By way of explanation we may say that of the profits of the first issue a considerable portion was spent in having a dinner to those concerned; while on the profits of this issue, much improved and more costly to produce as it has been, a considerable portion of the dinner will have to be forgone. Though that alone would leave us quite undismayed, we are unable to budge from the conviction that the work done by contributors should be reasonably paid. All this depends not so much on ourselves as on the public. We are able to think of only one other solution: that of endowment. But as there is not much profit in terms of dollars and cents to be made out of the work, an anxious capitalist will no doubt fail to recognize the pearl.

THE HARBOUR SCHEME

The Harbour Scheme is well on its way to fulfilment, if the attitude of the governments concerned is any indication; and, for none of the reasons advanced by either the Imperialists or the Minority, we are completely in favour of it. The difference between the lighterage and deep-water systems has not yet, to our knowledge at least, been fairly stated. It is this: the existing system is capitalist; that is to say, the profits from lighterage (which we, of course, real-ize are negligible) go into the pockets of just a few, and the vast majority of the people in no way benefits from what should be one of the public services. The deep-water scheme is communistic in principle; that is to say, the profits will go into the general fund. In speaking of profits with such optimism we follow, lamb-like, the predictions of the experts. Our faith in them is such that we very seriously commend to the attention of the Government a further scheme whereby the Harbour and Railway works may be merged. This, at least, would have the effect of enabling the Officer filling the new post of Director of Railways and Harbours to contemplate the more cheerfully his annual losses on the swings, being able to rely on the roundabouts. By the same token we should like to see the City Council take over the lighting and passenger transport of the town: but, alas, not yet!

EARLY CLOSING ORDINANCE

The Legislative Council has delayed long enough over the passing of the Early Closing Ordinance for (or perhaps against) the larger provision stores. Merchants, even Americanized merchants, are conservative people, so much so as to be almost Victorian, especially in this matter of their employees' leisure. The economically sounder view and – we are inclined to whisper it – the humaner view, is that all work and no play makes Jack a dull boy. The occupation of a provision clerk or salesman probably is and certainly ought to be most uncongenial. One must be oddly disposed, at any rate, to revel in it. It is therefore important that the good health and the good temper of the clerks should be respected and even fostered. We strongly advocate, for instance, the practice of allowing annual holidays all round, and even a porter should be able (he should indeed be obliged) to take at least one week off from work every year. He would of course receive his customary wage.

SOVIET RUSSIA

There has been some news of Russia lately in the local press, but unfortu-nately it has been heavily propagandized and as usual in such circumstances merely deals with superficials and not with root causes and motives. Recently we were reading Emil Ludwig's *Napoleon*[5] and it was astonishing for us to find references to and extracts from documents issued by the other powers against France during the régime of Napoleon that could be paralleled almost word for word by what is said to be news from Russia. Today we know the truth about France, and we also know that the German Armies in the late war did not sadistically mutilate, devour or murder the children of Belgium. We shall probably know the truth about Russia when the perspective becomes more panoramic. It is always thus: where the economic policy differs drastically from the other countries, in order to stifle the possibility of the spread of the new doctrine the other powers resort to exaggerated accusations of persecution against what they consider the delinquent country so that the passions of the masses may be aroused to blind their reason. But what most people do not know here is that a denial of these alleged atrocities has been issued by the head of the Russian Church. Even without that, as sane men we cannot conceive of any body of intelligent people, such as the Soviet leaders obviously are, suddenly reverting to savage and primitive type, as the Pope and Archbishop of Canterbury would have us believe. But why should his Holiness be so ready to condemn a lay Government for practices of persecution when incident after incident of none too lamb-like a nature has been recorded against the Church in history? Soviet Russia is attempting to put Socialism into practice. As to Socialism being analogous to atheism, as a writer in the *Port-of-Spain Gazette* suggested the other day, it is claimed by some that Christ was the greatest Socialist of all, and Mr Arthur Henderson is said to be a very staunch non-Conformist, and presumably Mr Brown is a church-goer. When religion has become steeped in superstition and almost idolatry the methods of eradication pursued by democracies in the past have always brought on them the charge of atheism. No: Soviet Russia is apparently attempting to overthrow the citadel of the strongest reactionary forces left in the country and from which it is reasonable to expect a *coup d'état* in favour of the old Czarist System; and for that no one can blame them.

THE CARNIVAL

The Carnival this year was significantly dull, and never has the customary period of repentance been more properly deserved. This Lenten season has justified itself. The trend of things is to commercialize into a laboured procession of glorified sandwichmen the troupes and bands and sideshows whose prime purpose should be to provide us with some sort of intellectual enter-tainment. A hobby horse, the Maypole, moko jumbies and nigger minstrels:[6] these are the sorts of things to be encouraged. There is in them opportunity for good dancing, clever songs and peculiarly local musical accompaniment. So too we should like to see more lorries whose scheme was purely decora-tive, or in some way symbolic. We are grateful to those who catered for us along one or another of these lines. But it is difficult to express admiration for some of the efforts seen in this year's show. The Carnival is not a trade show, though we fear it is tending so to become year by year. Mr Wrigley's chewing gum may be all very well in its way, but need we be subjected to it, at Carnival too, by the lorryful? Of the devastating dullness of the Cocomalt band, of the Celanese advertisements and of the songs that went therewith, the less said the better. In and out of the tents it was all of a piece with the picture we had of a certain gentleman who, combining business with pleasure, decorated his family and friends with caps bearing the name of a brand of tinned milk and stood them outside his front gate, to the admiration, it is supposed, of the passersby and the advancement of his particular product. Nor was the situation anywhere relieved by any indicative manifestation on the part of the trade participants. For what is the peculiar prank of a tin of Cocomalt? And is wriggling the mime most appropriate to chewing gum? We do not mind advertisements. Nor do we grudge the opportunity for advertising which the Carnival affords. But it is unsatisfactory to observe the gradual supplanting of a pure frolic by hybrid conceptions from Main Street. Our complaint is one founded in the fear of losing a public festival the essence of which is Satire and Burlesque: twin graces who, however easy of conception, are always dif-ficult of delivery.[*] All we ask of Mr Wrigley is to stick to his gum and leave Carnival alone in her labour: to the intent that when the tents are struck the long columns may go ringing down the road, making a little light of life and singing the last songs.

---

[*]We have deliberately refrained from considering the classical significance of Car-nival, with its curious manifestations. We have every regard for the feelings of our Boy Scout, as well as for our own, and a second censure from him would be more than we could bear.

SIR CLAUD HOLLIS

Speaking of Sir Claud Hollis, the then Governor-Designate of Trinidad,[7] at a dinner given in his honour by the West India Club in London on February 5th, Mr Charles F. Wood said among other things:

> Our Guest is one of those fine, public-spirited men of whom we are very proud, who, without any hope of substantial reward, are prepared to go to the far-flung outposts of Empire there to deal fairly and justly with the matters committed to their charge.

For two reasons it is undesirable that such fatuous remarks be made even at dinners given to Governors-Designate. The first is because they are untrue, and the second because they do more harm than good – if only because they are untrue. But perhaps Mr Wood does not consider a salary of five thousand five hundred pounds per annum "substantial reward" for carrying the white man's burden. It must eminently be in Mr Wood's knowledge that not six men in the island earn as much as that, and these men are considered very rich. Moreover, they run a certain amount of risk with their capital. And by the way, in these days of rapid and easy communication, can anyone define a "far-flung outpost of Empire"? On the other hand, presuming that Sir Claud Hollis has never been to Trinidad, we excuse him for thinking that he will be allowed to "share the life of the people in the island". Nonetheless, we take the opportunity of sincerely wishing Sir Claud a very happy and successful term of office.

Trinidad 1, no. 2 (Easter 1930)

NOTES

1. The "medallion" on the cover of *Trinidad* 1, no. 2, is the badge of the crown colony of Trinidad. It depicts the city of Port of Spain with Mount El Tucuche in the background and shipping in the harbour. The Latin motto at the base is a line from Virgil's *Aeneid* 4, 112, slightly altered to translate as: "He approves the mingling of peoples and their joining together by treaties."
2. Literally, "Art is long, life is short", a saying common to several Roman writers

including Horace and Seneca. It implies that life is never long enough for the artist to learn his craft sufficiently. "Live and let live", also a good motto for *Trinidad* (and Mendes), is not a translation of the Latin.

3. Mendes has in mind Lady Macbeth's "Out, damned spot! Out, I say!" (*Macbeth* 5.1.33). His reference to the American experimental writer Gertrude Stein (1874–1946) remains obscure.

4. Life is easy for owls. I have not been able to trace the sayer.

5. Published in 1915.

6. Mendes wrote several pieces about Trinidad's annual carnival (*Selected Writings*). After his return from New York in 1940 he and his wife Ellen judged carnival bands for twenty years.

7. Sir Alfred Claud Hollis was governor of Trinidad from 1930 to 1936.

A RETORT COURTEOUS[1]

To the Editor of the *Trinidad Guardian*

I REALLY CANNOT ALLOW DR TOTHILL'S criticizing "Trinidad"[2] to go by without the courtesy of a reply.

First, there are a few questions I should like to ask him: Where does he get his "metrical rules" from for the composition of an epigram? And, for that matter, are there any rules? Is not this talk about metre nowadays mere "baby-talk", so to speak? Dr Tothill says that the line: "It must have been funny and awfully nice" is not good English. Does he not know that inverted commas imply quotation? I can imagine his wanting me to write something like this: "It must have been facetious and refulgently amusing."

Perhaps he does not know that the colloquialism, which is something entirely different from bad English, has always had its place in English verse. Let him read this from Mr J.C. Squire, a modern poet:

> God heard the embattled angels sing and shout:
> "God straffe England" and "God save the King",
> God this, God that and God the other thing.
> "Good God," said God, "I've got my work cut out!"[3]

Now it appears to me that the final colloquialism of the above quatrain is not, according to Dr Tothill, good English. But isn't that beside the point, completely beside the point? Isn't it the idea that matters in an epigram of that genre?

Again, does Dr Tothill really mean that all my epigrams are obscene? If an epigram is obscene, why should it have a context to make it appear not obscene? (I draw that inference from what he says.) And surely Dr Tothill, because I know him to be widely read, is perfectly aware of this fact: that no really revolutionary book (revolutionary, that is, in thought and teaching) good or bad from the literary standpoint, was ever popular in the lifetime of its author? You may be as artistic as it is possible for you to be in trying to convince people who are opposed to divorce that divorce should be a desirable thing for them as well as for everybody else, but will you not succeed only in exasperating them the more?

And I do not know that an obscene book is made "palatable" for the generality of people by the fact of its being a work of art. Dr Tothill will I daresay remember what happened when Boccacio's *Decameron* appeared in the fourteenth century: he will also remember what happened when James Joyce's *Ulysses* appeared in the twentieth century.[4]

And it might interest him to know that I had a letter from Mr E.J. O'Brien recently telling me that he was listing, from the first issue of "Trinidad", as being the best for the year 1930, those very stories[5] which were condemned as vulgar and obscene by most people in this island. So there you are!

It is impossible for me to agree with him about "René de Malmâtre".[6] First, no serious writer has ever shown or will ever show consideration for the prejudices of his public. Why should he? Secondly, I fail to see why "blasphemy has to be extremely humorous" to be presentable. (Dr Tothill seems to me to be obsessed by the silly notion of how a thing shall look in the eyes of the public. It is as though he said: "Dress me up in a suit of evening clothes and I am a perfectly respectable, perfectly conventional gentleman" – which is absurd.)

Blasphemy, qua blasphemy, is presentable to all sorts of people. Mr Benson chose to be satirical about it in his story, and because of that alone I think that even those blasphemed should be able to read him with pleasure and profit. I am sure that St Anthony, if I know anything about him at all, would have enjoyed those digs in the sides given him by Mr Benson. Finally, the last two lines of Mr Benson's story should satisfy Dr Tothill completely: it is a perfectly moral epigram (moral because true) having as its immoral "context" all that has gone before it.

Furthermore, I cannot understand why Dr Tothill should want us to respect people's prejudices when he is perfectly clear about "Trinidad" "voicing the opinions of a small but cultured coterie, who are followers of the literary and artistic revolt against the generally accepted canons" – it is a pity he didn't spell the word with two ns – "of the pre-war period. In other words, it is a revolt against discipline." I take it that he means a revolt against both literary and moral discipline.

Now Dr Tothill in his article is obviously attempting to write serious criticism, and this can be said for him: he has a point of view and so an attitude towards the magazine. His point of view is this: pre-war literary and moral conventions were right; post-war literary and moral conventions are wrong. Very well; but shouldn't Dr Tothill know that it is quite fatuous to say that a thing is wrong without saying why it is wrong? But this is only by the way. My point is that, having recognized the spirit of the magazine, he should not have attempted to advise us to write for the purpose of pleasing him. Dr Tothill is Dr Tothill; "Trinidad" is "Trinidad:" they are completely strange to each other.

He says further: "If opinions that are unpalatable to the community are to be offered for our consumption, then they must be artistically presented, and must not offend in matters of good taste." Now I beg to submit that this sentence as it stands means precisely nothing. It is the sort of slip-shod writing of which Dr Tothill should not be guilty.

Exactly because I realize that "the reading public has a perfect right to choose its own literature", I am withdrawing from the field of local magazine adventures. I am not asking people to buy "Trinidad"; I am simply saying that I was mistaken in thinking that there was a sufficiently large public in the island to support the sort of magazine that "Trinidad" is. Had I, in the teeth of this circumstance, continued with the periodical, I would have sympathized with Dr Tothill's complaint; as it is, I find it just childishly petulant.

A friend of mine recently pointed out to me that there is not a single story in this issue of "Trinidad" based on the theme of love. Again I must ejaculate: there you are!

Trinidad Guardian, 11 May 1930

NOTES

1.   Cf. Touchstone in Shakespeare's *As You Like It*, 5.4.71.
2.   W.V. Tothill, "More About Trinidad", *Trinidad Guardian* 9 May 1930.
3.   From *Epigrams* by J.C. Squire (1916).
4.   The writings of Boccaccio were among the objects publicly burned by followers of the Dominican priest Girolamo Savonarola in 1497. *Ulysses* (1922) was banned and burned in several countries. (The book went on trial for obscenity in the United States in 1933, was pronounced a work of literature and cleared of the charge.)
5.   The stories concerned were C.L.R. James's "Triumph" and Mendes's "Her Chinaman's Way".
6.   A humorous story by E.G. Benson about a French count who, after a life of vice, reforms and enters Holy Orders. In this he has the help of his uncle, now in heaven, and various archangels and saints. The story is narrated by an abbé and the irreproachable last two lines read: "Facts," said l'Abbé as his fat round face disappeared in a cloud of tobacco smoke, "are indispensable to any legend".

A glance at Mendes's "Commentary" (republished in *Selected Writings*) will show why Dr Tothill's charges of obscenity and blasphemy acted on Mendes like a red rag to a bull.

THEY ARE ARTISTES

ALTHOUGH SOME OF US HAVE NO technical knowledge of music and poetry and painting, there is no gainsaying the fact that we are all endowed with a spiritual percipience that lights up for us the beauty spots in the works of the painters, the poets and the composers of music. We say: we like this, or we don't like that, and there is difference of opinion upon this and that amongst us, but there is no doubt that we know when we like a thing and we know when we don't like it. There can be no fixed standards by which an individual's capacity for appreciation of the arts may be measured. Works there are which are recognized by all as landmarks on the way to the development of one's fullest vision of beauty: the Beethoven *Opus 110* for piano, Tolstoy's *Anna Karenina*, Giorgione's *The Tempest* – in all of these there is to be found that touch that makes the whole world kin. Let it not be forgotten, however, that the weight of time hangs heavily over these creations and the weight of traditional opinion; which is to say, we have a background to these that gives us the clue to what our own mysterious reactions should be in hearing or reading or seeing them. With works that we hear, as in music, for the first time, works that we have no knowledge of, it is different. We falter at first, we make a wrong step, and where there is that subtle something in the piece that evokes within us a sympathetic response, we climb boldly and shout out from the Toucouche towers[1] how wonderful it is and how perfect. I am thinking of a book (it will go unnamed) which I read some years ago, and when I had finished reading it I thought it so beautiful that I fell to telling my friends about it: and when friend after friend had read it and said to me: "You are wrong; I don't like the book; it is not good," I began to search myself to see if I could find the reason for my going astray in judgement; but I could not find it, and as I could not find it I said to myself, with a little hurt in my pride that I was solitary in my opinion, that everybody else was wrong and I alone right. Time has lent perspective to the view, and these days I see clearly that I was wrong and everybody else was right; and, what is more, I know now where I went wrong. So that, especially where technical knowledge is lacking, as in my case, whatever I might say about Tuesday night's recital must necessarily be personal, coloured by my idiosyncrasies of mind, tinged by my spiritual particularities, phrased by the little knowledge I have picked up, as a beggar has pennies, here and there.

Unfortunately, with a music recital the matter does not rest there. A man is moved to write a book out of the activity of his imagination or the press and surge of his experiences, it matters not which. The gift, when the book is written, is a direct gift to the reader. The painter paints, and his gift too suffers the touch of no intermediary. The most unsophisticated person can be brought face to face with the original. Not so with music, unless the composers themselves be alive and capable of rendering them. But even composers die, and what then?

Between the composer and the listener, a foreign person is introduced: the player, the interpreter; and if the interpreter be great in spirit then there will be superimposed upon the particular piece he is playing shades and touches of his own personality, shades and touches that might put the piece through so great a metamorphosis that we can hardly recognize in it what we had, by long association, come to know so well. And I think that that is the reason why the writers and the painters are better known to the generality of mankind than the composers. Let me explain my meaning.

Take a given number of intelligent people and let them, first, listen to a chosen piece of music a dozen times as played by a dozen different musicians; then let those same people visit a particular picture twelve days in the month. I am sure that the proportion of them understanding the composer's intention will be less than the proportion understanding the painter's intention, and the reason is obvious. It is so difficult, for instance, to judge of a Chopin Prelude as played by, say Cortot and de Pachmann.[2] For myself, I do not think that Cortot plays Chopin as Chopin wanted to be played. Cortot has not that consumptive touch which de Pachmann has. But that, of course, is merely speculative. Chopin, we are told, played his own compositions with so light a touch as to preclude the backseats of his audience hearing very much. So where are we? And is being able to read the score an advantage in sensing the spirit of any particular composition? I do not know, though I should hope so to a certain extent. But that is a different consideration: like the reader reading a novel, like the gazer looking at a picture.

Now what of Tuesday night's programme? It does me no harm to confess that there were only four pieces with which I had a nodding acquaintance: Mozart's *Turkish March*, Mascagni's *Cavalleria Rusticana*, the *Minuetto* of Beethoven and Sarasate's *Spanish Variations*; and all these pieces, as with the others of the programme, I am sure, were arrangements for the mandolin and guitar. Here, further, has been brought into play an alien influence which can do nothing but provoke a distorted sensing of the music's colour, for let it not be forgotten that when a composer chooses the violin or the piano or both to fashion a pattern of escape for his mood, he is doing exactly what the painter is doing when he decides that blue or red or both shall predominate in his picture, or what the writer is doing when he subtilizes language for the sake of his theme (George Moore in *Héloïse and Abelard*, for instance.)[3]

Let me say at once that all these difficulties Los Alpinos overcame, and indeed, lent the rare combination of mandolin and guitar an artistic significance which one would not have thought possible. As was to be expected, in the Granados and Sarasate pieces they were best. The indigenous sensuousness of the Spanish composers found a local habitation in the instruments of the musicians; and where, as particularly in Mozart's *Turkish March*, there was a tendency on the part of the mandolin to tintinnabulate, in the Spanish numbers that irritating characteristic, because of the quality of the music, no doubt, and the spiritual affinity between music and musician, was completely alchemized and became, instead, pleasant and exhilarating at the same time. Beethoven's *Minuetto*, to my way of thinking, was not a wise choice and might have been, with advantage, replaced with something of Albéniz. In spite of the romantic shiver of the music, the instruments appeared to be quite inadequate. I closed my eyes and felt the musicians striving after a will-o'-the-wisp that kept eluding them at every turning. They never caught up with it, but the chase was so sincere and the cause of failure so obvious, that perhaps, after all, the effort was justified. Not strangely, Schubert's *Musical Moment No. 3*,[4] which I had never heard before, found an affiliation with mandolin and guitar, but – and I was not surprised – Los Alpinos did not give us Schubert. To use a picture: we were given a squat phlegmatic Teuton wearing a Valentino tango hat, and that made it extremely interesting, for it demonstrated how cunning a national trait can be with art-forms alien to it. Who Marques[5] is, I do not know, but my introduction to him by way of his *Preludio* was certainly exciting. The phrasing of the mandolinist in this piece was superb. So far as the untrained ear is capable, I caught not a single sound-flaw. Particularly pleasing was the Indian melody given as an encore. I understand that Los Alpinos, when in Peru, heard this melody sung by the Incas and promptly scored it. On Tuesday night it gave them opportunity, as no other piece did, of showing the audience what transforming qualities a sense of rhythm can have. Where Los Alpinos showed their virtuosity was in the remarkable balance between the two instruments. Seldom did either instrument attempt to exaggerate its prerogative of sound, so that the harmony between them was as the harmony we sometimes find between man and woman.

I do not hesitate to say that Los Alpinos are artists such as we have very very rarely had here. Their forerunners were: Sykora and perhaps Madame Patti Brown,[6] all simple, sensuous and passionate.

I have left myself little space for writing about Mariucha's singing and dancing, but I am sure she will forgive me my discourtesy to the grey-honoured dictum that women should be given precedence of treatment at all times when I tell her that I belong to that misfortunate class of individuals which is apathetic, or perhaps I should say insensitive, to dancing and the singing of folk songs. This, however, I did not miss: her infectious vivacity. The audience gave unmistakable evidence of having caught the infection. They clapped their hands in unison, they stamped their feet, and occasionally a thin whistling sound, from some wag in the dollar seats, impinged itself upon the choppy air like a bullet flying past the ear.

Trinidad Guardian, 25 September 1930

NOTES

1. Mount El Tucuche.
2. Alfred Cortot (1877–1962), Swiss pianist and conductor; Vladimir de Pachmann (1848–1933), Russian pianist.
3. The Anglo-Irish writer George Moore (1852–1933) came under the influence of the Celtic Twilight movement in art and literature. Mendes may be suggesting that *Héloïse and Abelard* (1921), a story of doomed lovers, suffers from overwriting.
4. A "musical moment" was a title used especially in the nineteenth century for a short performance piece. Franz Schubert's *6 Moments musicaux* were completed in 1827.
5. Possibly the Mexican composer Arturo Márquez (1882–1948).
6. Bogumil Sykora was a cellist who gave a recital in Trinidad ("Music" by H.McD. Carpenter, *Beacon* 1, 11: 42–44). The black soprano Madame Patti Brown (1870–1950), born in Georgia, gave recitals especially in the 1920s, and toured extensively in the United States, the Caribbean and South America.

THE SIGNIFICANCE OF MR VASSILIEFF

MORE THAN TWO MONTHS HAVE GONE by since Mr Daniel Vassilieff gave an exhibition of his oil paintings at the Royal Victoria Institute. The catalogue of his forthcoming exhibition, which starts today and which will last for a week, shows a list of about 150 pictures.

During the past two months Mr Vassilieff has visited La Guayra, Caracas and Barbados.

The imposing list of canvases for his new exhibition tells the tale of hard and prolific work. I have heard it said by a number of people who should know better that because Mr Vassilieff works rapidly his pictures cannot be good.

Such a remark is born of ignorance.

Rapidity of execution is never a safe reason for which to condemn creative work. True enough, it more often is than not; but sometimes it happens not to be.

Cézanne at one time was in the habit of doing six and even seven canvases a day, and Voltaire wrote his *Candide* in less than a week.

Furthermore, Mr Vassilieff's canvases are small. There is never anything elaborate about them and they are for the most part done in the Impressionistic manner.

Naturally, with so many canvases to show for two months' work, there will be just two or three gems, a dozen or so good pictures and the rest are more than likely to be merely mediocre; but the artist who in a twelvemonth can produce a dozen or so gems, no matter on how small a scale, is to be taken seriously, and very seriously at that.

But the truth is that Mr Vassilieff is not really a quick worker. Since he has been in Trinidad he has done no still life and no portrait. He brought with him from more southern latitudes a few still lifes, two of which were undoubtedly magnificent pictures: a jug and a book.

These two pictures were the result of many months' work; and indeed, all of his still-life and portrait work is done laboriously.

He cannot do a portrait in under sixty sittings: a still life might take him anywhere between three and twelve months, and I have known him struggle for four hours with a garden scene that had in it all the concentrated power of a still life.

His land- and seascapes are apparently done quickly. Had I time I would make an attempt at proving that what looks like quick work is not really so: it may be quick execution but nothing else. For Vassilieff, as I shall hope to show in a moment, is not after the scene as such, but the scene as a projection of himself in terms of tropical colour, tropical form and tropical movement.

This makes of speed in execution a virtue. Let me explain.

Mr Vassilieff paints quickly in the same way that Matisse, Van Gogh and Cézanne painted quickly.

The Impressionist technique differs from the Classical and Romantic in that it seeks to differentiate between the detail as a detail (the Pre-Raphaelite school for instance) and the detail in relation to other details.

Impressionism, in the first place, is the result of simultaneous vision that sees a scene as a whole as opposed to consecutive vision that sees nature piece by piece.

That is to say that the first glance at a scene is always the most vital for the Impressionist because at that moment no detail has had time to sink into his sight.

The Impressionist does not want to see the details in a landscape, and the process of evading them is the act of creation.

Therefore, working rapidly is part and parcel of the Impressionists' technique.

Impressionism, of course, does not stop there. There is, for instance, the development of the new palette which enunciates the science of complementary colours, but Vassilieff does not appear to have made use of this so far.

It is difficult to classify Mr Vassilieff, and I think it is this difficulty which makes him so significant.

A friend of mine recently remarked to me that Vassilieff is not a great painter and I reminded him that his remark was merely an evasive one.

It is the most obvious remark to make when one has no artillery with which to defend one's position.

I know quite well that Vassilieff is not a great painter.

On the other hand, I am just as sure that he is an artist.

He knows how to create beauty.

He has a remarkable eye for form and particularly colour: and where he succeeds in fusing these two, the result is always beautiful and good to look upon.

Paul Gauguin, who at one time was in these parts,[1] worked on his tropical salvation in his own peculiarly original fashion.

Vassilieff has been in the tropics only for a few months and it is amazing to observe how absolutely true the tones of his colours are.

His greens, browns and sky tones are impeccable; and occasionally there creeps into a hill or cloud a suspicion of blue that is very exciting.

He has also caught tropical movement in a very certain manner. A wisp of cloud will convey this sense of movement in an otherwise perfectly still canvas.

At other times, as in the canvas of barrack-rooms owned by Mr Algernon Wharton the whole picture sweeps away from the onlooker in a sort of hurricane movement.

This picture, by the way, is certainly a work of art. There is perfect fusion of colour and form in it and it furthermore gives evidence of the vitality that moves the artist's spirit.

Opposed to this there is the garden scene I have already mentioned. The composition is perfect and the spiritual content quiet and delicate.

I believe this to be the most charming of his landscapes.

Outside of Gauguin's few pictures done in Martinique, I do not think these islands have been painted by any important artists.

Mr Hugh Stollmeyer is still young and his best work is yet to come.

Mr Vassilieff also is young and is exploiting a new field.

It seems to me that he will gain an international reputation sooner or later for his tropical canvases.

He has the artist's vision and infinite capacity for work; and though his reputation will undoubtedly come later than sooner his burning urge will recognize no defeat, but will rather drive him on to fuller and finer accomplishment.

Trinidad Guardian, 20 October 1932

NOTE

1.   Gauguin stayed for some time in Martinique in 1887.

ART TAKES SHAPE AND FORM IN TRINIDAD
AT THE GARRET GALLERIES EXHIBITION

I HAVE BEEN ASKED TO WRITE something about the Art Exhibition now being held at the Garret Galleries in the Home Industries' building. I do so gladly because I find it easy to write about something that is extraordinarily interesting, extraordinarily exciting and extraordinarily significant.

I find the exhibition interesting because most of the work shown has for its material local types and local scenes.

I find it exciting because of its diversity. I find it significant because it unmistakably shows that the amorphous consciousness of the island is beginning to take artistic shape and form.

Not by bread alone do we live, but by the spirit too: and try as I might to honour those institutions that have specifically set themselves the task of instilling this precept into the daily practice of people, I am convinced that it is art and art alone, which knows anything of that truth which Pilate sought to understand.

Artists – for Shelley did not mean poets alone – are the unacknowledged legislators of the world;[1] and I would add, teachers also in the moral sense of living and getting and spending.

What does the artist care for social obligations and all the finery in which our civilization is clothed?

He sees into the naked body and finds it good and finds it diseased.

He probes beneath the surface of the mind's apparent placidity and discovers there the conflict of ages and the struggle for triumph. And what he sees he puts into a pattern and lo, the good is more beautiful than ever and the bad looks forth with new eyes.

A miracle is wrought: a flower has been grown from rocky ground and starved tree – and those that have eyes to see are the brothers, on a lower plane, of the artist himself.

Now what of those who form this small independent group? I do know where to begin, because Hugh Stollmeyer is the most significant of them all.

His is a wisdom alive – because it is young. Oftentimes he fails in his execution, but always the spiritual content is there; and when form and content merge together in one pure visual pattern, as in most of his abstract landscapes, the result is always arresting and satisfying.

Just how he uses [*sic*] this form of expression, that form and the other. He is like the visionary who would seek God by touching life at all points.

You see him tentatively step into this strange land and that, and you almost suffer with him the richness of his joy – or sorrow, if you like.

He does not always return with the same kind of treasure, but it never lacks value because of its close relationship with human experience.

His *Mother* is a magnificent picture. It might almost be called the Madonna for all its primitive purity and savage tenderness.

The pattern which he weaves out of the hairs at the back of the head so that the head might almost be said to be haloed gives the picture a sacred intensity which lifts it from the world of reality to the world of the imagination.

Here it is not difficult to see that bright flash of fire which differentiates the artist from the craftsman.

Hugh Stollmeyer has hitched his waggon to a star: he should go far. Let him work and he will get there: to the Land of Nowhere and the Land of Everywhere.

I am inclined to fall in love with Ivy Achoy for the delicacy and sureness of her brush. She is a finer craftsman than Hugh Stollmeyer; on the other hand, she has not in any of her things that touch that makes the whole world kin.

All of her exhibits are done in the Impressionistic manner: daubs for faces, daubs for bodies; but withal, the interrelation of her colours, the disposition of the bodies in a group, the composition in a still life, the vivid buoyancy of her light – all proclaim the ascendancy of the artist over her material. In my view, her most delightful thing is the still life called *Chalice Lilies*.

There is, if I may say so after having seen his work only in reproduction, something of Paul Nash[2] in it; I mean, of course, the vague deliberateness that one so often finds in Paul Nash's still-life work. But has Miss Achoy very much farther to go? I wonder!

Hugh Stollmeyer works in oil and watercolours, Ivy Achoy in watercolours and so does Stephen Haweis.[3]

But what differences there are between them all in general. Most of Mr Haweis's work is purely decorative and the amazing quality of it is that it is decorative not only in line and pattern, but also in colour.

I agree entirely with the *Guardian*'s Art Correspondent when he says that "Haweis has missed the violence, the exotic quality of the tropics."

I suggest, however, that what Haweis has lost of the tropics in colour he has gained of them in line, and, closely looked at, it will be seen that he deliberately subordinates colour to line.

It is as if he had said: "I shall take care of line; let colour take care of itself" – and colour has in some strange fashion looked after itself most successfully.

The tropicalness of his *Forest Scene* is entirely brought out in line, with colour playing a secondary, though sympathetic part. It lacks the burning play of the tropics' multitudinous colours, but the tapestry effect of the line amply compensates for such an absence.

Both Henri Philippe and James Patton[4] exhibit one picture each. The former's naïve; but the latter's still life, sombre in colour and distorted in perspective, is an admirable example of simplicity in composition.

I have left Mrs Pashley[5] last because hers is an altogether different kind of work.

Mrs Pashley's medium is the Batik, Java's strange and beautiful indigenous art. Here everything seems to me to depend upon design; and yet Mrs Pashley has succeeded in portraying the human face in a lively human way.

How charming those black boys and girls look on the silken surface. How charming and how alive! Mrs Pashley's masterpiece in this métier is her *Crop*.

It is an august grouping of men and women reaping. It is simple and pure and magnificent in composition and design. Its balance is perfect.

Its lines flow about and around the broad cloth in lovely rhythm. It is the second movement of the *Appassionata Sonata*[6] translated into terms of line and composition.

I have seen some genuine Javanese panel Batiks at Dr Harland's[7] house; Mrs Pashley's, with an entirely different mise-en-scène and in another tradition altogether, are just as good. Can I say more?

Trinidad Guardian, 15 January 1933

NOTES

1. P.B. Shelley, *A Defence of Poetry* (1821).
2. Paul Nash (1889–1946) was a British artist. He was official war artist during the First and Second World Wars.
3. The artists mentioned here were *Beacon* contributors.
4. James (Jim) Patton was the artist friend with whom Mendes lived for a time in New York City (*Autobiography*, 91).
5. Mrs Alice Pashley was a founding member of the Trinidad Society of Independents in 1929, and of the Trinidad and Tobago Art Society in 1943.
6. Beethoven, "Sonata no. 23 in F-minor, op. 57".
7. Dr Sydney Harland contributed to the *Beacon*'s debate on racial intelligence.

LETTER TO DR DAVID PITT[1]

19 Stanmore Avenue
Port of Spain
March 30th 44

Dear Dr Pitt:

I am writing this because I feel you'll be interested.

My introduction to the West Indian National Party was made at a recent mass meeting at the Prince's Building held under the auspices of the Party. At that meeting Marryshow, Adams,[2] Gomes and yourself spoke and I gathered from the matter and manner of your respective speeches that the orientation of the Party was radical if not indeed revolutionary. On the strength of that assumption I joined the Party.

Last night I attended my first meeting. The subject of the evening revolved around a talk on the political status of the civil servant delivered by the Chairman of the Port of Spain branch, Mr H.O.B. Wooding.[3] Imagine my surprise when I discovered that, instead of bold leadership coming from the chairman of a political party on the vital question of the civil servant's present and future political rights and privileges, there emerged instead solely an attempt at *interpreting* Government's regulations! Not a word about their rightness or wrongness, not a word about the Party's attitude towards them except that because they were there they were to be accepted in the speaker's translation of them – and this after a confession on Mr Wooding's part that the Colonial Secretary's[4] letter to him on the subject was as vague and evasive as it possibly could be!

After all, it seems to me that a political party, founded upon the aspirations embodied in the constitution of the West Indian National Party, is there primarily to fight against unjust and reactionary laws and regulations wherever they may be found in our island, and particularly where they affect the members of that party. And surely it is the function of a chairman faithfully to reflect the ideology of the party he represents and by so doing lead and direct rather than lamely acquiesce in a corpus of rules that is so obviously out of joint with the times in which we live.

In the counsels and deliberations of a leftish organization like the WIN [West Indian National] Party, to confuse the reform approach towards problems with the legalistic can be fatal, particularly where the party is a young one. And if the type of leadership demonstrated last evening, a leadership that was in direct opposition to the aims and purposes of the Party, is perpetuated then I for one can see nothing but defeat for our organization in the end. As one speaker so aptly put it last evening: "Our Win Party will become our Lose Party."

It is heartening to record that the discussion that followed was far in advance of Mr Wooding's halting words and ideas. The members present showed themselves fully aware of what ought to be done effectively to combat an outworn set of regulations, the very vagueness of which reflects their dishonest nature. But of what use is such awareness when its official spokesman is either ignorant of the kind of enemy he is up against or recognizes the enemy and chooses a path calculated to afford him the best of two worlds? The alternative might be all right for Mr Wooding; for the WIN Party it is courting suicide.

A final word. As I find it impossible to speak in public because of an almost neurotic self-consciousness, my impressions of Tuesday night's meeting have taken the present form.

Fraternally,
Alfred H. Mendes.

NOTES

1. Dr David Pitt was the leader of the West Indian National Party.
2. Important politicians. Theophilus Albert Marryshow was from Grenada. I assume Adams to be Grantley Adams, later Sir Grantley Adams, the Barbadian federal politician, statesman and later national hero.
3. Hugh Wooding, later Sir Hugh Wooding, was a barrister. He later became mayor of Port of Spain, chief justice, and privy councillor. He became chancellor of the University of the West Indies in 1971, and gave his name to the Hugh Wooding Law School in Trinidad.
4. The colonial secretary for Trinidad in 1944 was A.B. Wright.

MR A.H. MENDES RESIGNS

To the Editor of the *Trinidad Guardian*

IN DECIDING TO SUPPORT MR W.E. Julien in the recent Grenada elections,[1] the Executive of the West Indian National Party acted in direct opposition to the party's aims and purposes as embodied in the programme and constitution.

I say this because I consider Mr Julien to be a dyed-in-the-wool reactionary.

I therefore regard the Executive's support of Mr Julien as a betrayal of the party's aims and purposes.

As this leaves me at basic variance with the active policy of the Executive, I am left with no alternative but to resign my membership.

A.H. Mendes
Port of Spain

Trinidad Guardian, 15 June 1944

NOTE

1. At this time Grenada's government was a modified form of Crown colony government. Native Grenadians were permitted to elect five of the fifteen members of the Legislative Council.

TRINIDAD'S FIRST SCULPTOR

THE FIRST EXHIBITION OF SCULPTURE EVER held in the island is now to be seen at the Royal Victoria Institute. It happens to be a one-man show and it is exhilarating to report that the pieces portray a talent that places Mr George H. Herbert, the exhibitor, on an equal footing with any of our mature artists in the fields of writing, painting, music, and the dance. What James and Mittelholzer have done in fiction, Stollmeyer, Alladin, Basso, Cameron in painting, Atilla and the Lord Executor[1] in folk song, Clarke and Thomasos[2] in verse, and McBurnie in the dance – Herbert now does in sculpture. I declare him their peer in every respect.

Mr Herbert appears to be a full-blooded Negro in his early thirties. Because he has had no academic teaching, nothing has intervened to alienate his work from the sources of its inspiration. True, there are some things in the exhibition that are trite, but the good pieces – and their proportion is surprisingly high – are all stamped with the quality of indigenousness. I do not for a moment suggest that this is solely because Mr Herbert has not been "trained"; but I do contend that, given the fact of a man's possessing a genuine creative urge, particularly in behind-God's-back places whose populations are a hodge-podge of races, it helps the gift to grow naturally and healthily when it is left to bask in its own sun and dig in its own soil. A young people, taking their first timid steps into the realm of artistic creation, can be warped and twisted beyond all recognition in such essential things as spirit and scene by alien influences; and it is this danger that our local artists have constantly to guard against. Let them be themselves, let them recognize and accept their heritage of dougla, calypso, poui and bongo, and I'll be ready to give them the benefit of any doubt in the treatment of the things that are theirs. In other words, for such people there is hope; for the others, none. To be a snob in any artistic form is to be damned at once.

I have said that Mr Herbert appears to be a full-blooded Negro and I have said this for the purpose of making a brief observation. Examine for a moment the names mentioned in the first paragraph of this article: James, Mittelholzer, Clarke, Thomasos, Stollmeyer, Alladin, Basso, Cameron, McBurnie. Of them, one belongs to a European by descent, one to an East Indian,[3] also by descent; all the others are either Negro or partly Negro. The inescapable conclusion is that the sooner we stop talking about race superiority and race inferiority, the sooner shall we put unscientific nonsense behind us and pave the way for better relations in the human family. Moreover, and let us make no mistake about it: the work being produced by all these native sons of ours can take its place with pride and dignity beside that of men who belong to the metropolitan centres of the "civilized" world.

Now Mr Herbert has chosen – or perhaps he has had no say in the matter – to express himself in a plastic art form, to me the most difficult medium with which to communicate whatever may be lodged in the spirit and mind of individual men. Music enters the understanding in a variety of ways: it has colour, rhythm, pattern, and its disembodied form assails all the senses at once. Writing is an accumulation of words on paper, each word possessing a multitude of nuances and associations; and in good writing all the words are so related to each other as to crystallize into a three-dimensional meaning: something with bone, blood, flesh and sinew, so to speak. Painting too has qualities that aid immediate perception: colour relationships, perspective, design: you see the synthesis in terms that are intimate with human experience. Not so sculpture – for me at least. I can best intimate my meaning by putting it this way: whereas writing, music and painting gain their aesthetic effects by giving, sculpture does so by an act of taking away. The writer gives words; the painter gives lines, forms, colour; the music composer gives notes. On the other hand the sculptor, when he works in his favourite media, wood, stone, or marble, performs an incessant act of subtraction The process of shaping his block of wood, or marble, or stone into a thing that sublimates the spirit of the onlooker depends entirely on what he *leaves* of the wood, stone or marble – not upon what he *adds* to it. Addition, subtraction: I cannot stop now to analyse the psychological effect of these two opposites upon the human being, but I have an idea, and I offer it *en passant*, that the former technique creates works of art that are easier to stir aesthetically than those created by the latter. I shall leave it at that.

And now to the items of sculpture themselves. There are thirty-seven in all, from which I select nine as being outstanding: *Water Carrier, the Gentleman, Mother and Child, Labour at Rest, Carnival Steel Band Group, Birds of a Feather, the Sacrifice, The Fisherman*, and *The Burden*. Two of these, *The Sacrifice* and *Mother and Child*, are as rich and thrilling as anything I have seen in wood in London, Paris or New York. All nine, with the exception of *The Burden*, are in wood, native woods. Herbert surfaces the completed work with linseed oil and a light application of wax and this combination gives a bright polish that heightens chiaroscuro, an essential ingredient in the presentation of sculpture.

Allow me to make the following four groupings of my nine selections:

Abstract – *Water Carrier, Birds of a Feather*

Pure Form – *The Sacrifice, Mother and Child*

Sociological – *Labour at Rest, The Fisherman, The Burden, Carnival Steel Band*

Satirical – *The Gentleman*

Water Carrier is a hollowed-out length of dark poui; and although Herbert in his catalogue does not refer to it as an abstract, its lines and the manner in which they are related to each other are so freed from all casual and adventitious interest that its significance as a means is lost and instead its significance is felt as an end in itself. This is only another way of saying that the thing in itself, or what the philosophers up till recently called "the ultimate reality", provokes the emotion.

I have placed the grouping of Pure Form next the Abstract because the strictly limited reservoir of knowledge and understanding of the plastic arts from which I draw makes it difficult for me to distinguish the real difference between the one and the other. I can see, of course, that whereas *The Sacrifice* and *Mother and Child* are objects that bear a close resemblance to the things they represent, *Water Carrier* and *Birds of a Feather* do no such thing. I am nonetheless convinced that in both group cases it is the significant form that exalts me to ecstasy. The emotion that permitted the creator to imbue the amorphous wood with significant form is communicated to me and I am stirred consequently to aesthetic emotion.

On second thought, I am not so sure that it isn't form alone that makes a sculptured object a work of art.

Mother and Child, in mahogany, is liquid with lines that flow along rounded crests of arms and legs intertwined in a pattern of pure loveliness. As it should be, the features of the woman have not been carved out; and the two figures, fused by a miracle of revelation and craftsmanship, are a new expression of an old story.

The Sacrifice, in balata, is a startling study in contrasts: on the solid back of what appears to be an elephant, and is when viewed from a certain perspective, reclines the form of a woman as delicate in its delineation as a cocoon. What amazes is the manner in which Mr Herbert has succeeded in spreading this delicateness, this cocoon-like quality, over the whole piece.

I cannot end without a word about *The Gentleman* as it reveals an unexpected side of Mr Herbert. The piece is an excellent satire on the Anglo-Saxon gentleman with just enough bitterness in it to relieve the urgency to burst out into laughter. The arms are folded upwards across the chest, the hands resting lightly on the coat lapels in a gesture of complete respectability. Someone beside me remarked on the resemblance to Sir John Shaw.[4] Maybe there is a physical resemblance; but what I have heard or read about our present Governor convinces me that there can be nothing of an obsolete and certainly decadent type in one so active and so obviously concerned as himself with the plight of people who live in slums and poverty.

Published in shortened form, *Trinidad Guardian*, 19 October 1947

NOTES

1. Calypsonians. Atilla the Hun was Raymond Quevedo, and the Lord Executor was Felix Garcia.

2. Alfred McDonald Clarke and Clytus Arnold Thomasos, who wrote as Norman Collingwood, were both *Beacon* writers. Mendes's critical assessments are

typical of his generosity towards fellow artists (with the notable exception of Richard Wright).

3. Hugh Stollmeyer, whose family was originally from Germany, and M.P. Alladin respectively.

4. Sir John Shaw was governor of Trinidad from 1947 to 1950.

WHITEHALL GROUP MAKE HISTORY WITH THEIR WEST INDIAN PLAYS

MANY YEARS AGO GERALD WIGHT WROTE a play[1] and produced it in one of our Port of Spain [movie?] theatres. As far as I know, it was the first to be written by a local man and the first of its kind to be acted on the Trinidad [stage?].

Although the play revealed considerable talent it was unfortunately as alien in theme and content to our islands as a [Greek?] drama. That was understandable for Gerald Wight, like myself and some others, was schooled in England. During the first impressionable years of our lives we were away from [our] native island – only to discover on returning from abroad how difficult it was to re-orient ourselves into the home scene.

There followed upon the Gerald Wight play a long decade of inactivity in writing local drama. Then came three Trinidadians with pens that were too florid and a knowledge of the stage that was too flaccid: Arthur Roberts, D.W. Rogers and Norbert St Louis.[2]

This, however, can be said of them: the matter and manner of their Thespian essays were Trinidadian to a fault. That their plays were naïve, artificial, and passé – and sometimes pompous – must be forgiven when we remember that they performed the [ground?] work in clearing a path to the role of the local scene in West Indian playwriting. I for one honour them for this.

On Friday evening last the Whitehall Players put on three curtain-raisers at the Government Training College, two of them local in setting and authorship. Allow me to say at once that in my view they marked a surprising step forward in the creative development of our people.

I say this because both playwrights revealed a flair for the theatre that is rarely found in an insular community like ours, for the very simple reason that the drama's audience is limited by the nature of its presentation; the drama is invariably a late manifestation in the history of any people's creative expression. Because it can afford to cater only to the more intelligent and sophisticated elements of a community, it needs intelligence; it needs savoir faire.

Moreover, the problem of presenting local plays in our island is complicated by the fact of our being a racially heterogeneous mix. The play should be a mirror of life; the conflict of ethnic groups in the Caribbean is so significant an aspect of West Indian living that it must intrude into most of our attempts at art expression, and particularly the novel, the short story, and the drama.

Fortunately for Errol Hill and the Whitehallers, the two curtain-raisers written by members of the group were faced with no such [intrusions?].

For make no mistake about it, I'm willing to stake my pigmy reputation on the prophecy that "Brittle and the City Fathers" by Errol Hill and "How Then Tomorrow" by Errol John, both young men, will be regarded by future generations as the first two successful plays written by Trinidadians and produced and acted on the local stage by Trinidadians.[3]

The first is a satire on our one democratic institution, the City Council, the second a fantasy with a message as new as it is old. Both show a remarkable grasp of the techniques of playwriting; the dialogue is crisp and convincing, the situations turned [*sic*] to fine points in their respective patterns, the characterization rounded and full-blooded.

Hill uses the local dialect to clever advantage while John, eschewing dialect and a terrestrial locale, yet manages to convey something of the essence of the West Indian temperament. Both deserve the hospitality of metropolitan boards.

I am amazed at the histrionic talent of the Whitehall Players. For instance, in what large city could you possibly witness more polished performances than were given by Cyril Browne as Brittle and Cecil Gray as Robert Baldwin?

I should have preferred to see Gray wearing a better-tailored suit, but his acting was in such impeccably good taste, his movements about the stage so natural, his diction so unaffected that I for one forgot the comic little coat sitting above his buttocks.

Browne's role was a difficult one: it required restraint and sensitivity in counterpoint to the Mayor's bluster and braggadocio. Only once did he seem to me to pitch his voice in too high a key – the one flaw in a first-rate piece of acting.

Before I take up my quarrel with Errol John I should like to give Hill, for what they are worth, three tips: watch the tempo of the play's movement. "Brittle and the City Fathers" started off after the fashion of runners in the last few miles of a marathon race. The pace should have been brisk.

Secondly, he must impress upon two or three of his players the virtue of homeliness in speech. Here Osborne Ashby was the main offender. In all art, the moment it is obvious that an effect is being deliberately sought, the effect is lost. And thirdly, be concerned over clothes. In this respect I liked the conceptions of Simon Peter and Morbleu.

I cannot be anything but frank with people whose creative ability I respect and admire. If the promise contained in "How Then Tomorrow" is fulfilled, it is more than likely that Errol John will write plays of social and technical significance. Moreover, he is perhaps the member of the group with the biggest potential as an actor.

But quarrel I must with him over his interpretation of a character he himself created.

As I understand the Joe of his play, there is no moral room for self-pity on his part. The Joes of our world are not rebels because of their genes; they are rebels because of a politico-economic system that fosters and encourages man's inhumanity to man. Such Joes, in the first, middle and final analysis, have been sinned against, and the guilt is a collective one summed up in the Higginsons, knighted and otherwise, of our dispensation.

Errol John's voice, breaking like a Pagliaccio[4] in the throes of losing his inamorata, is out of joint with the theme of his play. Instead, casual defiance should have been the tonal quality given his voice and manner in the dialogue with Simon Peter.

After all, his hell, as he himself observed, had been lived on earth; and standing face to face with Simon Peter, the one moral weapon left to him was quiet defiance. The rebel does not beg; he accepts the consequences of his brothers' evil-doing as reflected in punishment upon himself with dignity and a disregard for pain that holds no further meaning for him.

Trinidad Guardian, 5 September 1948

NOTES

1. Gerald Wight was a businessman and a well-known figure in Trinidad in the early twentieth century. I have not managed to trace his play.
2. Arthur Roberts and DeWilton Rogers were both schoolmasters. Despite Mendes's reservations, their plays seem to have been very popular at the time (Stone, *Theatre*, 22).

    Norbert St Louis wrote a play, "Kathleen" (unpublished), which was performed in 1945 (Stone, *Theatre*, 218).
3. Errol Hill remembered Mendes's judgement in later years, though he had forgotten the exact wording (Stone, *Theatre*, 31n9).
4. A clown. Mendes is probably thinking of the cuckolded Canio in Leoncavallo's opera *Pagliacci*, who weeps as he puts on his clown's make-up.

BLACK DOT QUINTETTE PRAISED

DURING THE WEEK JUST GONE I attended two shows, "Calaloo of 1948" and the Black Dot Quintette. The first included two one-act plays, some dances, and a short operetta, all purporting to be local creations; the second was a vocal recital with a young pianist thrown in for good measure. "Calaloo of 1948," produced and directed by Gabriel Francis,[1] aptly illustrated what happens to our people when they try to hang their hats higher than they can reach: in the attempt they stand on stools that topple over. The second more than aptly illustrated what good and lovely things may come from the man who, having talent, recognizes its limitations and stays within them.

"Calaloo of 1948" failed dismally. It is obvious that Mr Francis possesses an urge to do something: he should try and find out what that something is before publicly committing himself.

One Wednesday evening last at the Royal Victoria Institute, the Black Dot Quintette was a bird of a different feather. I had not heard of the quintette before and did not even know what medium they used. Need I say that I went to the Institute with some misgivings?

My first little shock of surprise came while reading the introduction to the programme. "The enjoyment we got from singing together served as the stimulus to work, and each song learned urged us on to the next with the result that our material was soon exhausted" – could any idea have been more clearly and simply expressed?

As I read on, I became more and more impressed until I said to my wife sitting beside me: "This quintette is good." "But you've never heard them," she objected. "This quintette is good," I repeated with the obstinacy of a man whose hunch is being questioned by his wife.

My next little shock of surprise accompanied the raising of the curtain for the first item on the programme. Against a background of green palms, red splashes of ixora[2] stirred the aesthetic eye. On a pink-washed board, supported on trestles, the programme group number was posted in black Roman figures. A grand piano dominated the décor. I have seldom seen such good taste expressed in so few touches – or perhaps good taste is always best expressed in few touches.

As the quintette walked on to the front of the stage, arranged themselves in two rows with the three tallest in the rear, rested their clasped hands in front of them, and bowed to the audience, I whispered to my wife: "This quintette is good." She did not reply.

What followed completely vindicated my hunch. From the moment the five young men, all clad in dark suits, their five faces like crotchets or dark dots above the footlights, slipped into their opening bars you felt you were listening to something fine and true. And when, halfway through the first song, "Who Is Sylvia?",[3] my wife grasped my hand in her excitement, I knew she was willing to concede me victory.

Here then is a choral quintette so perfectly balanced, so whole in their separateness, so integrated as to become, in creative moments, a single instrument for song. For me, and particularly in their lieder, the tonal quality of their sound-ensemble was that of stringed chamber music. It amazed me that human voices, restrained in pitch, reduced to volume as intimately related to each other as the lines in a Cézanne landscape, the harmonies synthesized in patterns of perfect proportions, could so bewitch me that at times I had to remind myself that the music was not being made by a string quartet.

Once in a while Lynch's soft tenor took off on its own for a few measures to be answered later by Oxley's robust bass, and this contrapuntal treatment of songs that were originally written for single voices heightened the effects of the harmonies.

"The unscrupulous critic has sometimes remarked," observes the introduction to the programme, "that we know nothing but Negro Spirituals." Well, although I have said otherwise, I sing no other type of song as well. I think this is understandable: for the performing artist to give of his best to the work being performed he must be culturally, racially and temperamentally identified with it. In the Negro Spiritual, only two other vocal artists have moved me as deeply as I was moved on Wednesday evening: Paul Robeson and Marian Anderson. Can I say more?

Except to warn both Lynch and Oxley never again to attempt solo singing. Insofar as their art is concerned, they are only parts of a whole; torn from the whole, they become unrecognizable fragments.

To put it the other way, the quintette's oneness is so part and parcel of its art that even the introduction of instrumental accompaniment, not to speak of accompaniment that threatened to ruin some of the quintette's renditions on Wednesday evening, is both alien and destructive. In effect, I am saying that Joseph, Oxley, Loman, Casimir and Lynch are doomed artistically to remain a Siamese quintette for the rest of their lives.

I hail young Joseph Goddard. He will go places with his piano if he makes it his companion morn, noon and night, day in and day out, for all the years ahead of him.

Trinidad Guardian, 3 October 1948

NOTES

1. Gabriel Francis wrote a play, *Gone Forever* (unpublished), which was performed in 1945 (Stone, *Theatre*, 206).
2. A showy bush with tightly packed flower heads of tiny red, pink, yellow or white blossoms.
3. A song from Shakespeare's *Two Gentlemen of Verona*, set to music by Schubert. Ellen Mendes had herself been a professional singer and dancer when a young woman.

CRITIC DEFENDS HIS OPINION

To the Editor of the *Trinidad Guardian*

I AGREE WITH MISS MCCRACKEN WHEN she suggests that the critic's expressed opinions do not often indicate the extent of the audience's appreciation of a performance. On the other hand, I must remind Miss McCracken that an audience's reactions to a show are irrelevant to the validity or otherwise of the critic's judgement. Judging in this context is mainly a matter of taste, and whenever I exercise my function as critic it is my taste, fortified by the experience of a lifelong interest in all forms of artistic expression, that makes the decision. I willingly admit that my taste can err – and has often erred.

Miss McCracken informs us that Ken Oxley is one of her pupils. I nevertheless remain convinced that Mr Oxley, if I am to judge by what I saw and heard on September 29, should not attempt to sing solo.

With an ensemble like the Black Dot Quintette, trained voices in the individual sense do not concern me. I am concerned with the voices trained as a whole, as a quintette. That the five may have trained themselves doesn't in the least matter; what matters is that they recognized their potential as a group by singing together for pleasure, and in this way succeeded in fashioning an instrument that communicates their own joy to listeners. This they could not have learned to do any better by going abroad "to school" and all that they have yet to learn – and they have much – they can learn right here, by themselves. The academic influence can often be fatal.

In his eagerness to defend Mr Francis and "Calaloo of 1948" Mr Le Maitre fires his blunderbuss from so many angles, and so erratically, that I think he should first learn how to take aim before pressing any trigger. What difference is there between a review based on a dress rehearsal and a review based on the formal presentation, particularly when it is possible for the actors, as Mr Le Maitre himself says, "to excel at rehearsals and fail completely at the show"? When I wrote about our people hanging their hats higher than they can reach, I meant exactly what I said: that we should never try to do what we are not equipped to do. As for "the resounding applause" mentioned by Mr Le Maitre, I refer him to the first paragraph of this letter. Moreover, youth, courage and ambition do not alone make an artist. And surely Mr Le Maitre must know what my own feelings are about the people's liberty, for heaven knows I have expressed them often enough.

Finally, I must thank him for the compliment he pays me when he compares my enthusiasm over the Black Dot Quintette's recital to that of "a child finding his stocking filled at Christmas time".

Alfred H. Mendes
Port of Spain

Trinidad Guardian, 9 October 1948

HENRY HALL'S ENGLISH PLAY
HAS DEFINITE CREOLE FLAVOUR

SOME TIME IN JUNE LAST "YOUNG BLOOD", a comedy in three acts by Henry W. Hall, Principal of the Government Training College for Teachers, was presented in the GTC concert hall by the College Literary and Dramatic Club, and reviewed by Canon Ramkeesoon in his "Evening News" column. With much of the Canon's review I find myself in such complete agreement that I have decided to approach the play from the angle of Henry Hall, the players, and the Teachers' Training College.

In "Young Blood" and its repeat performance last Friday evening, there were many significant things. First, it is written by an Englishman who has been living in our midst for the past seventeen years. Secondly, although the cast is all English, and upper middle class at that, the players were a mixture of Negro, Chinese and East Indian.

Thirdly, all the physical work necessary to the production was performed by the college students and their Principal. And fourthly, it was obvious to me that both Principal and students accepted the activities of their dramatic club as forming part of the college curriculum.

I have known Mr Hall for only a short time, but I have come to the conclusion that he is that rare type of Englishman who has succeeded in so adjusting himself to our island and its way of life as to be himself one of us, a Trinidadian. Never does he stand on a height. Indeed, on common ground with us, he recognizes weaknesses and strengths alike and accepts them as the mixed heritage shared by all peoples of the earth in more or less evenly balanced proportions.

Where I would have hesitated, before attempting to put upon the boards racially miscast players, he went right ahead as if it were the most natural thing in the world, remarking with a twinkle in his eyes: "My students say this is an English play with a creole flavour" – and by heavens the students were right.

As for the players, I must confess that they intoxicated me with the joy they obviously felt in playing together. Now it is an article of my credo that no group of people, doing something in concert for the pleasure they get out of it, can fail to do that thing well.

"Young Blood," as I read it in published form, did not strike me as being a likely vehicle for local talent, but by the time the Government Training College players had got into their stride with West Indian gesture, mannerism, and accent, the piece had lost its English colour and caste and had become the raw creole comedy of a Port of Spain middle-aged rake feeling young all over again because he had fallen in love with a Sangre Grande[1] bronzed beauty in her late teens.

You may imagine my surprise on learning from Mr Hall that a batch of students had walked up to his house just off Queen's Park East, gathered up the furniture in his living room – heavy Morris chairs, a large sofa, a solid desk, a table, and so on – and transported the stuff in arms and on heads through the streets to the GTC hall for stage décor. Can you blame me for feeling that principal and students work together like one happy family?

Certainly it seems to be that Messrs Marshall, Bevan and Molotov[2] can learn a lot from Henry Hall and his students.

Trinidad Guardian, 17 October 1948

NOTES

1.   In north-east Trinidad.
2.   Important American, British and Russian political figures in the mid-twentieth century. Marshall is presumably George C. Marshall (1880–1959) after whom, under President Harry Truman, the Marshall Plan of 1948, to aid the post-war economic recovery of Europe, was named.

The Welshman Aneurin "Nye" Bevan (1897–1960) was a member of the British Labour Party. He was minister of health 1945–1951, and is generally credited with being the architect of the National Health Service.

Vyacheslav Molotov (1890–1986) was a Soviet politician, a protégé of Joseph Stalin. From 1939 to 1949 he was minister of foreign affairs.

FIVE MOST SIGNIFICANT ARTISTS ABSENT
FROM SHOW AT ROYAL VICTORIA INSTITUTE

AS YOU ENTER THE UPPER HALL of the Royal Victoria Institute housing the eleventh exhibition of the Trinidad Art Society which concludes today, you will see facing you on the far panel a canvas covered in pink and brown, with a splotch of green for relief. It depicts the interior of a room, is numbered 83, and is painted by a young girl named Althea McNish. By my own standards I pronounce it the best picture in the show.

Indeed, I will go so far as to say that it is, in its medium, as pure a work of art as has been made by any Trinidadian at any time. Except for Leo Basso, I know of no one in this island more gifted as a painter than Althea McNish.

Let me say at once that the number of created, as opposed to painted canvases in this exhibition is extremely small; this is usually the case with an exhibition fostering and featuring the work of new talent. To be taken into account is the absence from this year's show of Basso, Alladin, Cameron, Codallo, and Boscoe Holder, five of our most significant artists. Boscoe's brother, Geoffrey, is there, but he appears to be bound to a highly stylized formula that tends to cramp his development.

Of the 160-odd oils, watercolours, drawings, pastels, gouaches, and pieces of sculpture, I can find no more than about a dozen possessing the quality that transcends craftsmanship. In one watercolour, numbered 118 and painted by Ramon Garcia, a prosperous North American artist, the technique is superb, the picture uninspiring.

On the other hand, an oil numbered 36 and painted by G.O.L. Daly, who started painting late in life, is poor in technique and strangely exhilarating as a picture.

I am trying to say that it is possible to create a work of art with a technique that is far from the standards of conventional perfection. A statement in terms of line and colour can be important, but never as important as the aesthetic meaning it conveys.

This is the point at which I part company from those who insist that "schooling" is essential to the growth of creative spirit. I contend that the man with the afflatus – surely the *sine qua non* of the artist – makes his own rules, his own idiom of utterance, simply because he is different from all the rest of us.

Take for instance some of the Post-Impressionists: who taught Van Gogh his technique? What could Matisse possibly have learned from the academicians, what Cézanne? And mark how utterly dissimilar from each other are their respective vocabularies. Or take some of the rebels: Modigliani, Picasso, Vlaminck. Was it not Vlaminck who said: "I flee from the monotony and severity of the art galleries"? – meaning, of course, that he would have no truck with academic schools of painting.

The very expression, academic school, is a sign of the spurious to the creative person.

To talk about teaching technique to the man possessed by the urge to create, and the gift for making that urge come true, is in my view a contradiction in terms. This is why Diego Rivera,[1] on being asked some years ago by his government to take charge of a school for instructing gifted children in the art of painting, did so by sending his pupils out into the fields with pigment, canvas and brush and by telling them simply to paint.

Do not misunderstand me. With schools in the societal sense I have no quarrel. I believe that when men and women gather together to engage in a common creative pursuit, the joy in work is heightened, the spirit of emulation spurred. This is where the Trinidad Art Society has been and is serving a useful purpose.

Moreover, no matter what he may say in false humility, the artist needs a vehicle for carrying his work to the public. The Cézanne who painted half-a-dozen masterpieces a day and left them to rot in the hedges without the slightest regard for the glory they could bring him is indeed a rare bird.

My concern as I approach an exhibition of painting is to ferret out the created canvases from the literal translations. Recently I shocked a friend of mine by remarking that a portrait should resemble more the painter than the subject. Frankly, I am not interested in any form of expression that ends up by being the Victorian idea of an accomplishment. I seek instead that rare quality that sublimates colour and line by lighting them up with the artist's imagination.

Not necessarily must a canvas have the cognitive element, though I must confess to the flaw in me that makes it difficult for me to perceive pure form in an abstraction. Where, however, elements in a work of art can be related to familiar objects, be those ever so distorted, I am instantaneously moved by its pure form.

I come finally to my selection of the best exhibits:

Oils – Numbers 83, 85, and the uncatalogued "The Washers" by Althea McNish. Numbers 26, 28, 29, 30 by Carlisle Chang. A promising young painter whose pictures are full of lyrical movement.

Watercolours – Numbers 126, 127 by Althea McNish. Both the same subject and both gems. Number 125 by Ursula Joseph. A primitive. Note how the rhythm of the wash conforms to the grain of the wood.

Gouache – Number 154 by Louis Agostini. Note how the space is filled with greens, blacks and whites. An abstraction in essence.

Drawings – Number 156 by Kathleen Ogier. Vibrant lines. Economy of means. A powerful symbol.

Sculpture – Number 1 by Karl Broodhagen. One of the best things in the exhibition.

Trinidad Guardian, 14 November 1948

NOTE

1.   The Mexican artist Diego Rivera (1886–1957).

ERIC CAMERON'S WATERCOLOURS
POSSESS A REFLECTIVE GLOW

ERIC CAMERON MAKES HIS LIVING AS a surveyor in the engineering branch of the Port Services Department and expresses himself creatively through the medium of canvas and brush. Long before I ever knew that he painted, I came upon a wash-drawing he had made of the airport Government at one time proposed to build on the Laventille reclaimed land.

It marked my first intimation of his artistic urge, and ever since then I have watched his growth with an interest deepened by two reasons: the realization that he is perhaps the finest watercolourist this island has cradled, and the kindling of a friendship that has given me knowledge of as rare and fascinating a personality as I have met in my fifty years on earth.

Eric is now thirty-six, and has been painting since his teens. One of his earliest canvases, an oil, hangs in the drawing-room of his home on Kitchener Street. For me it typifies the manner in which most of us West Indians who have attempted to make things of beauty have started our careers: ignoring the scene and essence of our home, we have tried to portray what we have assumed to be the [missing word] and lore of faraway peoples.

Indeed, it has seemed to us in our fledgling years that our own trees and birds, people and customs, hills and valleys were not the stuff of which art could be made and so we have committed the unpardonable sin of imitating the style of the alien, and using the substance of unknown countries.

Speaking for myself I have some respect for the talent that comes to grips with the soil and spirit of its own folk even though the performance is graceless. On the other hand, of the talent that clothes the imitation even impeccably, I am contemptuous. Such an act can never be an act of faith but only of treachery – and every work of art is an act of faith if nothing else.

But Cameron's adolescent imitative phase did not last long for soon he was going out into the fields and making watercolours of scenes that must have been familiar to him from childhood.

Although done in the unconventional technique of applying the pigment opaquely all over the paper, and with the representational element heavily delineated, these first pictures held a warmth of colour-tone and surface-texture that revealed the intimate relationship between artist and subject matter. This alone was significant, for I believe that no work of art has ever been created where this affinity has not existed.

It is some years now since Eric Cameron has discovered that a prime essential of the watercolour is that is should glow as if reflected from a bright mirror. The light wash of colour, the untouched spaces and interstices, the mosaic of daubs, the blend from the right perspective into the recognizable features of the land- or seascape – these are some of the devices you will find in his most recent work.

Eric is still a young man, but he has already produced at least a dozen pictures that will inspire joy for as long as they last. I am curious to see what turn his idiom will next take.

Trinidad Guardian, 17 November 1948

ARTIST RETAINS STIRRING QUALITIES: ALLADIN, BACK FROM ENGLAND, SHOWS PIECES PAINTED SINCE HIS RETURN

ALLADIN IS BACK WITH US AFTER a stay in England with a British Council scholarship. He attended the Birmingham School of Art for one year and, as the result of an extension to his study leave, he was able to put in two months with the Chelsea Polytechnic School of Art in London. He liked England, he liked the English people; but, as is not uncommon with equatorial dwellers visiting northern latitudes in the winter months, he did not like the cold. This, however, did not so dampen his temperamental warmth as to preclude his losing his heart here and there.

Under the auspices of the Trinidad Art Society, Alladin is now showing fifty of his pictures in the Whitehall exhibition room, twenty-two of them oils, eight watercolours, eight pastels, four pen sketches, and the remainder in what he calls powder tempera.[1] For obvious reasons I hasten to add that with only one or two exceptions all the exhibits were created since his return from England.

From the moment I heard that this gifted Trinidadian was planning to give an exhibition of his most recent work, I was agog with curiosity and excitement.

Those of my readers who are familiar with my views are aware that I hold a theory which is unpopular with a large number of my fellow men. My theory is that in the case of a person possessed with the creative urge and blessed with an amplitude of vision and imagination, academic training in "schools" whose teachers know nothing of the scene and conditions from which the pupil comes can often distort the freshness of the talent and sometimes destroy the talent altogether.

I wish, however, to make it clear that my theory's relationship to academic training is not intended to be driven to absurd conclusions. For instance, how silly it would be of me to suggest that instructing the potential artist in the technique of mixing and applying his paints, of manipulating his brush and knife, of the effects of pigments upon different kinds of surfaces, of the values in perspective of the various colours, and so on, can be of anything but vast value to him!

The correct use of instruments for making this or that has been learned always the hard way: the heritage of experience has been added to from generation to generation and so what we know today of any particular technique is the result of the knowledge accumulated from the past.

For me the danger in attempting to instruct in the art of painting lies in the tendency of most teachers to impose upon the pupil manners and modes of expression held sacrosanct by them.

This danger has been so well seen and understood in our time that a system of teaching popularly known as "free" is now being used in most metropolitan centres. Indeed, it has even reached our shores for Alladin tells me that he has himself adopted it for his class at the Government Training College!

Now in what way has Alladin illustrated or failed to illustrate the soundness of my theory? All I will say at the moment is that in the pictures now being exhibited there is not a single trace of his having lost any of the qualities which first stirred us.

His "nativeness", his use of colour, his figure-compositions, his sociological content – these are all there and presented in the manner we associate with him. This is only another way of saying that Alladin's case fails to prove my theory – and I honour him for it.

Trinidad Guardian, 11 September 1949

NOTE

1.   The catalogue for the exhibition shows that there were five pen-and-ink sketches, and one item, *Figures and Heads*, under the category *Various Media*, in addition to the items listed by Mendes.

ACTING PORT SERVICES GENERAL MANAGER EULOGIZES "C.P."

QUITE RECENTLY I WAS ENGAGED IN negotiations with the Shipping Association over increases in the tariff rates resulting from the *ex gratia* allowance awarded to the workers. The argument was bitter and at the end of one particularly mordant exchange Mr Hunter, the Secretary of the Shipping Association, his blue eyes burning and his pink face pinker than ever, turned to me and said, "By Heavens! You know, Mendes, that you are very nearly as good a bargainer as Mr Alexander." I was extremely flattered by this.

As you know, we have met here this afternoon to bid farewell to C.P. Alexander as an employee of the Department. I have, over the past few years, wondered at odd moments what the two initials "C.P." stood for. I had never seen them written out in full in the newspapers and I had actually begun to grow suspicious for it seemed to me that Alex, as he is familiarly known to us all, was deliberately hiding something. Perhaps, I said to myself, the letters stood for two such names as "Clarence Percy" and what true Union leader bearing such sissyish names would not want to hold them in concealment from not only his admirers, but even more so, his detractors. I recently made enquiries and was relieved to learn that Alex's two names are "Cecil Phillip", as manly and masculine Christian names as any leader of men would want to have.

Perhaps it is best that I should give a brief sketch of the last two or three decades of Alex's life before saying anything further. I believe that it was in 1927 that Alex entered public life for the first time by being associated with Captain Cipriani in his famous Labour Party.[1] In those years, as you know better than I probably, and as our Commissioner of Labour will tell you a little later perhaps, there were no trade unions.

Sometime in the early 1930s the Longshoremen's Branch of the Labour Party was formed and it was this section of the Captain's party that looked after the interests of the waterfront workers. During all these years Alex was working with the Railway, but early in the 1930s he came over as a stevedore with the old Steamers' Warehouse Association and it was during this first phase of his relationship with the waterfront that was to become his whole life that he stole away upon tramp ships to pay brief visits to Mexico. We know that he has since paid many visits to Mexico, visits when he had already attained a position of eminence in his field, and I am left wondering if during one of these earlier trips to the land of Chimborazo, Cotopaxi he had not discovered some black-eyed wench who stole his heart away.[2]

In 1937, a year of turbulence for the island when Butler[3] ran wild and the island itself nearly ran after Butler, the Seamen and Waterfront Workers Trade Union came into being. Alex was still on the sidelines, or I should say on the outside, looking in; and perhaps even then he saw himself as the leader of this body in the not-too-distant future.

During that decade our Government took a momentous decision and constructed a deep-water wharf scheme, at the completion of which Government decided to take over the old Steamers' Warehouses from private enterprise and weld them into one department under State control. Mr Parry,[4] the first General Manager of the new concern, arrived in 1939. Mr Raphael Leotaud had been in charge of the business that was being replaced by the new Government set-up and it was at this particular time that Alex first began to make his weight felt. I will relate you a story that is in my view quite significant and you will see why in a moment.

There was in those days, and for that matter he is still with us – you may see him at any time in shed No. 1 if you do not yet know him, and if you have had any contact with our wharves he will be very well known to you – there was at that time a longshoreman by the name of Papito Toussaint. Papito had run foul of Mr Leotaud some months before and Mr Leotaud had fired him. Yes, quite as recently as 1939 Managers had the power to discharge their employees out of hand. Papito, for some reason which I have never been able to fathom, approached the young Alex and put his case before him. He had been out of work for about twelve months and had he not paid enough of the penalty for whatever misdemeanor he had committed? Alex listened and decided that here was something he could put his teeth into. He sought an interview with Mr Parry and laid the matter before him. Mr Parry, wise old owl that he was, called in Mr Leotaud and explained what Mr Alexander had come in to see him about. You will remember that I told you that the change-over from private ownership to Government was about taking place and Mr Leotaud, like numberless other employees of the old set-up, was shaking in his shoes wondering if he would be retained under Government control as an officer in the Port area. Alex, of course, knew of all this, and was fully aware of Mr Leotaud's fears. After Mr Parry explained the matter to Mr Leotaud there was silence for a while when Alex, using his histrionic instinct, said quietly: "Well, Mr Parry, I do not see, Sir, why you should disturb yourself about this matter. After all, it is Mr Leotaud's business and it is Mr Leotaud who will have to control Papito in the future for I personally have no doubt at all that Government will continue to use Mr Leotaud's valuable experience for many years to come, Sir. I suggest you leave this to Mr Leotaud to decide, Sir." Mr Parry, winking inwardly, assented with avidity. Well, the very next morning, bright and early Alex received a sweet note, you may even call it a love note, which read: "Dear Alexander, I have thought over the Papito case and I have instructed that he be reinstated with immediate effect. Sgd. R. Leotaud."

This was to mark the path along which Alex was to travel in the future in his negotiations with employers and I shall have a little more to say about this in a while. In 1945 Alex was elected the President General of the Seamen's and Waterfront Workers Trade Union. He had come into the new Wharves set-up as Foreman in 1939, the year of the birth of the new Department, and in less than six years had risen to top rank in the Union. He was now, in other words, the undisputed leader of the longshoremen and stevedores and lightermen. He has just left us to give the whole of his time to the affairs of his Union. He has left us as President General of the Union, as a member of the Port Advisory Board, as a member of the New International Confederation of Free Trade Unions, and as an executive officer of ORIT,[5] and last but not least he now leaves us as General Wharves Foreman, the highest rank to which a worker can rise. In other words, he has climbed the ladder of his class (and I use the word in its purely scientific meaning) right up to the top.

Any further step that he may take will topple him over from being a member of the working class to being a member of the *petite bourgeoisie* and knowing Alex as I do, I feel that that forms no part of his plans for the future. This briefly is Alex's story to date.

I come now to what I consider to be the most important part of what little I have to say this afternoon. I ask the question – why is it that Alex has risen as he has risen? Here is a man who was obviously born in poverty; a man by all the rules of the game condemned to anonymity from the day of his birth, and yet he has risen over these immeasurable difficulties, difficulties that men, with few exceptions, fall before in self-confessed defeat. He has overcome all these hurdles and is now an acknowledged leader of the waterfront workers, acknowledged by the workers themselves and accepted by the employers as being one of the most astute and worthy men they have to deal with in their bargainings across tables.

I ask, why has this happened to C.P. Alexander? I have known Alex now for some three or four years. As soon as Mr Parry felt that there was a reason for believing that I would one day fill a high-ranking post in the department, he began to brief me about all those leading figures whom he knew I would have to deal with in the course of my duties. Amongst them loomed largely our friend Alex, and the old man left me in no doubt that he held Alex in affectionate regard. I know I speak for both Mr Culhane and Mr D'Arcy when I say that we too hold Alex in affectionate regard.

Marine Guide, October–November–December 1951

NOTES

1. Captain Arthur Andrew Cipriani (1875–1945) was a city councillor and mayor of Port of Spain. He was known as "the champion of the barefoot man" because of his compassion and care for Trinidad's poor.
2. From W.J. Turner's poem "Romance" (1916). The volcanoes Chimborazo and Cotopaxi are actually in Ecuador, in the Andes mountain chain. (Mendes is doubtless thinking of "Shining Popocatapetl"!)
3. Tubal Uriah "Buzz" Butler, a charismatic and popular labour leader. Mendes was in New York in 1937 during this period of civil unrest.

4. Harry Parry, an Englishman, later recommended Mendes for the post of general manager of the Port Services Department (*Autobiography*, 137–39).
5. Organización Regional Interamericana de Trabajadores.

TRINIDAD ART SOCIETY EXHIBITION: TWO CROMWELLS

FOUR YEARS HAVE GONE BY SINCE I last reviewed a Trinidad Art Society exhibition. I have been moved to return to the task because of two pictures now on view at the Royal Victoria Institute – and both are the work of Mr Joseph Cromwell.

Before I say what I think of them – and why – it is necessary briefly to re-state my creed in matters of this sort.

Put in the simplest terms, a painting is a work of art only when it awakens an aesthetic emotion in the onlooker. But what must a picture have in order to awaken this emotion?

Let me try to answer the question in this way: you and I are looking at a piece of Chinese pottery of the Sung dynasty,[1] a jar, say. Because we are both gifted with the sense of apprehending the quality that distinguishes a work of art from a thing of beauty like a tree or a flower, we are lifted above the stream of life and into a realm that knows no affinity with terrestrial experience.

Moreover – and this is of great significance – a jar is not an object in the sense in which a tree or a butterfly is an object. The tree and butterfly are living things that came into being in the early dawn of time; the jar a utensil evolved by man for the easier satisfaction of his physical comforts and needs. It is obvious that somewhere along the path of man's efforts at making a jar he came upon the astounding discovery that if moulded in certain shapes and forms he could be moved by it to a state of exaltation beyond any emotion he had known before. This is why it has been said that pottery is pure art:

there was nothing in earth, sky or sea which man could use as a model for creating his jar.

Now let us suppose that we are looking at a picture in which there is a tree, a cloud, and a butterfly. As a child I may have been fond of catching butterflies and the painter may have so fashioned the specimen on the canvas as to recapture for me the early rapture of those butterfly-hunting expeditions. You, on the other hand, may have kissed your first love under a tree overhung by a golden cloud, and gazing at the painting recalls that blissful memory and you are stirred in a warm human way. In other words, you and I are referring the forms of the picture back to the world from which we came and, if it is a work of art, if it possesses significant form freed from imitative intention in the manner of the Sung jar, we are accepting the picture as we would a photograph. We are missing the one thing that gives it the distinction of being a work of art – its dynamic form; and although our appreciation may be genuine and jolly, it is not an aesthetic emotion.

Against the background of the above remarks, I now wish to consider Cromwell's two pictures: one he calls "Game of Marbles", the other "Unbalanced Landscape".

Now why have these pictures, painted by a twenty-four-year-old man who has never left these shores and, as far as I know, never "studied art", stirred me aesthetically?

Take "Game of Marbles". It is a small canvas done in what at first glance appears to be a flat pattern of three horizontal rectangles – pink-orange foreground, dark-green middleground, and purple-blue background. Once focused, however, the horizontal planes, upper and lower delicately balanced in area by the bisecting middle plane of green, are seen to be three-dimensional because of the manner in which the colours recede from warm pink-orange to the cool green and the cooler purple-blue.

Had the development of the painting been arrested at that stage there would have been no aesthetic consummation to an exciting possibility. The horizontals and their receding colours are harmoniously balanced, the cognitive elements in the horizontals felicitously subdued to the colour tones – and that would have been all. But mark how the artist's instinct, stumbling into sublimation, has startlingly added the solid black verticals of legs, arms, tree trunks and door-openings, the white blouses on the boys and, above all, and as the hub from which all the related forms radiate, the ring in which the marbles are disposed. These add zest and surprise and vividness to the forms.

I have used words like legs, tree trunks, marbles, to describe what I want to say, but they should not have been used at all for this is not a picture of objects as the mind conceives them in terms of natural types, but a picture of things. Its title desecrates the sensibilities.

The other picture, "Unbalanced Landscape", is quite different in that its forms are mainly triangular, its colours yellow and green, and its texture impasto:[2] the paint seems to be almost modelled on the canvas. Let us take a look at it.

You will observe how the four triangles of yellow road, left-bottom green field, right-bottom grey-green hill, and top-centre green hill, converge and meet at a point almost in the centre of the canvas, and how the triangle motif is repeated in the sky with the lines of the trees and the hill. There is in it just a touch of Cézanne for it possesses something of his dynamic realism and certainly his masses and tensions. The sky, resonant in colour quality, is pulled forward to the picture-plane by the same resonant quality of colour in the road: half-close your eyes and two masses vibrate[3] with light.

Here too there is a hub around which all the masses are aesthetically organized and from which the lines flow from plane to plane. I suppose Cromwell called this landscape unbalanced because of its compromises with linear perspective: actually this is one of the picture's plastic virtues.

Published in the *Trinidad Guardian*, 7 November 1954 under the heading "Vivid Form and a Touch of Cézanne".

NOTES

1. 960–1279 CE.
2. Laying the paint thickly on the canvas.
3. Brother Fergus Griffin used this line as the title for his attack on Mendes: "Squint . . . and the Masses Vibrate."

LETTER TO THE EDITOR OF THE
TRINIDAD GUARDIAN

48 Goodwood Park,
Port of Spain.
15th November, 1954

The Editor, *"Trinidad Guardian"*,

Sir,

What justification is there for Bro. Griffin to say in your Sunday issue that there has been a "general onslaught on the public in an effort to educate the masses and dragoon them into seeing art through the discerning eye of the judges"? After all, the judges were not self-elected; they were invited. Once having accepted the invitation, surely it was their solemn duty to judge the canvases in accordance with their own individual tastes and standards.

I wish to assure Bro. Griffin that the task of selecting and beribboning was sincerely and honestly approached, and that there was a diversity of standards and tastes amongst the panel of judges.

Moreover, my review expressed my own opinions – with which obviously Bro. Griffin does not agree. I cannot quarrel with him for disagreeing with me, but I can certainly raise my eyebrows in astonishment when he writes: "The vast majority of the people" attending the annual exhibitions "deeply resent this sort of treatment". What on earth does the Brother mean by "this sort of treatment"? – an honest expression of views?

In stating my ideas I was attempting to "enlighten" no one: having offered in far too small a compass of words – a compass imposed upon me by the exigencies of the newspaper's space – the hypothesis that seems to me to be most satisfying, I tried to apply it to two pictures in the exhibition.

Let Bro. Griffin by all means argue with me; on the other hand, this does not give him licence to impute, not only to me in particular, but to the Art Society in general, motives and attitudes that are nowhere visible in my review.

I have never "set myself up as the arbiter of taste in this Colony". On art I hold strong convictions and it should be my democratic right to express them without being exposed to blows below the belt.

I suggest that Bro. Griffin should guard against permitting his disagreement with anyone to dull his sense of fair play and affect his good manners when he finds himself in controversy with one of his fellow men. The tone of his article was in execrable taste.

As for its matter – such as there is of it – I shall give him my reply in the columns of this newspaper sometime later this week.

Yours truly,
Alfred H. Mendes.

Published in the *Trinidad Guardian,* 17 November 1954

MY REPLY TO BROTHER GRIFFIN

WHEN I WAS LAST IN LONDON I attended a Royal Academy art exhibition. It was a revelation. Never shall I forget those rows and rows of dull and insipid canvases: an accumulation of mediocrity dressed up in the most meticulous and perfect craftsmanship you have ever seen in your life. The critics, with few exceptions, stretched and yawned through their reviews during that week and the usual jokes about Academy exhibits were cracked in the press. And then silence – followed by the long night of oblivion for every single one of those immaculately painted quackeries.

When I lived in the States the story of an experiment conducted by the famous Mexican artist Diego Rivera was published far and wide. Selecting a number of gifted Mexican children ranging between the ages of five and fifteen, he provided them with brushes, paints, and canvases, gave them some lessons in their use, and turned them out into the fields and woods to make pictures as they pleased. In a year or so, Rivera was able to collect about sixty canvases which he brought to New York and exhibited in a fashionable gallery. I visited the show three times. Brother Griffin may not care to accept my judgement so he must believe me when I say that art critics of the highest reputation agreed that a large proportion of the pictures, although executed in naïve and sometimes crude craftsmanship, were works of art.

A few years ago in Los Angeles an artist friend of mine took me to see an exhibition of Haitian paintings. Fifteen artists were represented, amongst them the three famous B's – Benoit, Bazile and Bigaud – and, of course, Hector Hyppolite, the inspired priest of Vodun who died in 1948, and Philomène

Obin, the documentary primitive.[1] Indeed, all the pictures were primitives and their craftsmanship unpolished and simple – but what vital and stirring forms, and relations of forms, they contained! I do not have to remind my readers of the immense impression these unsophisticated painters have made and are still making upon the American connoisseurs of art.

I have related these three stories because I think they illustrate an important point in my creed: that just as clothes do not make the man, so does craftsmanship not make a work of art.

It would be silly of me to suggest that it is unnecessary for the young painter to learn how to use his tools and materials. Moreover, hard and unremitting toil usually goes hand in hand with the creative urge; but an infinite capacity for taking pains,[2] lodged in one who has not the afflatus, the instinct for form, will never give birth to anything but pretty inanities or perfectly executed objects for suggesting emotion and imparting information. A work of art is always an object of emotion, an end in itself and never a means to an end.

Brother Griffin seems to be confusing technique with craftsmanship. Is not technique the idiom, the characteristic manner of a painter? This is where I feel that the artist must work out his own salvation for it is he and he alone who can forge a style, a manner best suited to his matter. And let there be no mistake about it: technique is to a picture what style is to writing. "Le style, c'est l'homme" – as Pascal says.[3]

I now return to the crux of what appears to be the difference of opinion between Brother Griffin and me. I say appears, because apart from his references to craftsmanship and drawing, and that incredibly fatuous observation: "the first thing we look for in a painting is craftsmanship without which a work is devoid of all merit", the only indication we have of what he demands in a work of art is contained in the quotation from Eric Newton's "European Painting and Sculpture",[4] a definition which Newton himself admits is one of many with which he agrees. In fact, although Newton was under no compulsion to define art in a book which is avowedly a history of art, he offers a number of other definitions in the paragraph immediately preceding the one from which the Brother draws his quotation. For instance, he confesses that "if an artist wants to construct a purely formal pattern of line and colour or mass or sound, I will say 'How beautiful!'" Now this is exactly what I claim to be the *sine qua non* of a visual work of art: a purely formal pattern of line and colour; or, to use Clive Bell's phrase, significant form. And it is significant form which arouses aesthetic emotions in the spectator. This contention of mine provoked the Brother to accuse me of superciliousness; I suspect, however, that those who are incapable of feeling aesthetic emotions always question the good faith of those who say they do.

I have never contended that a representational picture (Cromwell's pictures are all representational in the Post-Impressionist meaning of the word) cannot be a work of art. What I have always claimed is that it is significant form, and significant form alone, which confers upon it the distinction of being a work of art and not the fact that the man, or the tree, or the cloud is impeccably portrayed on the canvas and that these cognitive objects awaken emotions in us related to our common everyday experience of them.

Mr Clive Bell, whose book "Art", published in 1914, has had such a profound influence on those who are interested in the subject, says this: "Most people who care much about art find that of the work which moves them most the greater part is what scholars call Primitive . . . As a rule primitive art is good . . . for, as a rule, it is also free from descriptive qualities. In primitive art you will find no accurate representation; you will find only significant form. Yet no other art moves us so profoundly . . . in every case we observe three common characteristics – absence of representation, absence of technical swagger, sublimely impressive form . . . Very often, I fear, the misrepresentation of the primitives must be attributed to what the critics call wilful distortion. Be that as it may, the point is that, either from want of skill or want of will (mark well the phrase 'want of skill') primitives neither create illusions nor make display of extravagant accomplishment, but concentrate their energies on the one thing needful – the creation of form. Thus have they created the finest works of art that we possess."

Finally, Brother Griffin's suggestion that there should be established "some permanent set of values which might be applied to the choosing of paintings at the annual exhibitions" strikes me as being preposterous. Who is to decide on this "permanent set of values"? – Brother Griffin himself, or Colin Laird, or I perhaps, or all three of us in addition to the other members of the panel of judges? It is obvious that both Mr Laird and I will have no truck with the Brother's standards; and I can assure them both that they would find it impossible to fashion a code from the diversity of views and tastes they will find amongst my judging confrères.

Published in the *Trinidad Guardian*, 25 November 1954 under the heading "Critic Says Work of Art is AN END IN ITSELF, NEVER A MEANS TO AN END".

NOTES

1. Rigaud Benoit (1911–1986); Castera Bazile (1923–1966); Wilson Bigaud (1931–2010); Hector Hyppolite (1894–1948); Philomène Obin (1892–1966).
2. Said by the Scottish philosopher David Hume (1711–1776).
3. This aphorism, in its original form "Le style est l'homme même", was pronounced by Georges-Louis Leclerc, comte de Buffon, in an address to l'Académie Française in 1753, "Discours sur le Style".
4. Published by Penguin Books, 1941.

EDITORIAL: CHRISTMAS

OUR FAVOURITE SEASON IS ONCE AGAIN at hand. Christmas – the very word is like a bell which rings in memories of other Christmases spent when we were children. Indeed, the child's whole life is a looking forward to each twenty-fifth day of December. The Season is like a spell that charms with its lovely symbols: Santa Claus, the Christmas tree, twinkling coloured lights, spangles glittering in the deepening dusk, the pillowcase or the stocking (we preferred the pillowcase because of its size) bulging with toys, the carols in the late evening of Christmas Eve and the early morning of Christmas Day – these things last with us until life's journey is ended. When the years are heavy upon us and the spirit has been torn and tossed about by time and tide, Christmas takes us back to the innocent and happy years and we are once again happy, once again innocent. This is Christ's most precious legacy to those of us who are nearing the last sleep.

Nature, too, seems to join in the jubilation by dressing herself up in bright colours wherever the poinsettia and bougainvillea are cultivated. We sometimes think that these bushes should be to us at Christmas time what the mistletoe is to our northern friends. The burning brightness of the poinsettias' great red clusters of leaves seen in the dawning or fading light is a thing of joy. And think of the months the blooms last! – if blooms they may be called. The green leaves begin to turn in November; by Christmas week they are bursting with colour which does not begin to fade and die before April. We can think of no blossoming more loyal to its role of brightening people's lives.

For ourselves, we pick off stems of these leaves, dip them in boiling water and arrange them in patterns on our dining table, our dressing table, and our doors for the Season: in this way they will last for weeks and at the end be as fresh-looking as when first picked. For years we have been doing this and today they have a meaning for us, a meaning that is intimately associated with the Season. Indeed, without these crimson leaves in our house Christmas would not wholly be Christmas for us: they have become the flaming symbol of the day Christ was born.

As for the bougainvillea – we can think of nothing in Nature more breath-catching than the purple variety in bloom. These we have seen standing side by side with the poinsettia – and both are Christmas celebrants. The crimson against the purple, or vice versa, brings to mind the colour combination so favoured by the Roman Emperors – one of whom crucified the Son of God and none of whom, despite the ostentatious panoply of power they were all so proud to display, could touch the hem of the Christ-skirt in their influence for good over the world of men and women. This too – the bougainvillea – helps to bring into our homes the spirit of Christmas and for many of us who were born in the warm Caribbean islands the bougainvillea has come to have a Yuletide significance. It is good that this should be so for it gives us "a local habitation and a name"[1] when our customs are associated with things indigenous: it gives us a special identity and feeling of belonging in the community in the midst of which we were born, grew up, and attained maturity.

This, then, is our kind of Christmas, a Christmas that is not white with snow, the trees denuded of their greenery and the air tingling and shivering with cold. The manger of Christ's Bethlehem was wrapped in warm air and no white coverlet of snow proclaimed an advent of man's Saviour. The ancient carol sings only of the holiness and silence of the night[2] – and the author must have known what he was talking about. And so it seems to us that the traditional white Christmas which arouses in so many of us the tenderest of emotions is not as true to the reality as our own warmth, our own picture of green trees and burning blooms. But let these things pass, these outward trappings of an inward verity – important though they be.

For those of us who are past the prime of life, Christmas recaptures our childhood dreams and joys. It is said that men and women renew themselves in their children; we add that this is never more so than when the miraculous dawn finds us on hands and knees assisting our ecstatic children [to] open the parcels left behind by the benign white-bearded grandfather, Santa Claus. It is then that the ageing heart quickens, the slowing pulses beat faster, the blood throbs with the rhythm of youth. It is then, squatting on the floor about the glimmering tree, the first bird-calls echoing from the yellow poui in the garden, the children uttering little shrieks of delight, it is then that we are children once again – children with our children. In life, can there be any richer transfiguration than this? Is this moment of return to innocence not worthwhile waiting for every twelve months? Let him who will deny the affirmative to these rhetorical questions conceal his betrayal in shame.

Above all, Christmas is what it is because of Christ. "Bring back Christ into Christmas" has been our island slogan for the past few years. Unfortunately, slogans are so glib that we have grown into the habit of accepting them at their face value. The pace of our modern age is too speedy, we say, to allow us to think, to meditate upon the eternal truths of life. Helter-skelter we are moving towards a time when capsuling and packaging everything we do will be the order of the new day: no time for the leisurely meal, the dawdling journey, the lingering conversation, the protracted engagement. It is a pity.

Christmas without Christ is the white without the yolk. The very essence of the Season is the Christian ethic, something which over the past two thousand years has seeped down into the generations of men and created a civilization that has transformed the act of living together into a semblance of brotherhood and understanding. From that miracle of fifth-century BC[3] Athens we learned the art of democracy, and much else besides. By the Romans we have been guided into an acceptance of law and order. But Christ, who came to us in between them both – the Athenians and the Romans – gave us the gifts of faith, hope and charity; and without these things the other two could never have satisfied the aims and aspirations of man. Let us, therefore, during this Season always carry with us Faith in the teachings of the Sermon on the Mount, Hope for a better world in the future, and Charity for all things living on earth – and of these Charity should take pride of place at every turn.

But any effort at putting into practice a cardinal virtue for a specific period of time is like going to church on Sundays and forgetting during the weekdays all about the priest's or parson's Sunday exhortations. The exercise of virtue in our lives is indivisible – just as liberty is. We cannot compartmentalize the practice of virtue (Periclean Athens called it "aretê" – excellence) by assigning it only to certain days and times. It is of course necessary and good that the Christmas Season should recur at regular intervals of time: men and women, by the very nature of their minds and hearts, require repeated reminders of the things of the spirit if they are not to live by bread alone. And without Charity in our thoughts and actions every minute of our lives, as without mercy, no gentle dew will fall from heaven[4] to mollify anger, drown pride, and dissolve the curse of man's inhumanity to man – and bless those that give and those that receive.

These are key words in the context of the Christmas Season – give and receive. Thucydides,[5] perhaps the greatest of all historians, relates the story of a powerful Thracian tribe, the Odrysians, whose privilege it was only to receive gifts – as opposed to the Persians of Xerxes who only gave. As between these two ancient pagan powers, the prototypes of others in the centuries that followed, we should certainly say that the Persians of 450 years before Christ foreshadowed the Saviour's teachings much more nearly than the Odrysians – for receiving without giving (and we are not speaking in the literal sense of the words) is a denial of the Christian creed. Indeed, the giving and receiving of gifts during this holy and happy time is, as all else at Christmas, a symbol of what man's duty is to his fellow man throughout his span of life on earth. And if we look at the custom with our spirit and not our mind, we shall immediately see that the custom is not one of receiving at all, for the receiving half is only the reaction to the giving half. First and foremost we give: what follows is irrelevant to Christ's teachings. It is on this note that we wish all of our readers a happy Christmas.

Trinidad Singer, Christmas 1965

NOTES

1. Shakespeare, *Midsummer Night's Dream*, 5.1.17.
2. Perhaps "Silent Night" by Gruber and Mohr, 1818.
3. The period 460–429 BCE, when Athens was governed by Pericles.
4. Cf. Portia, "The quality of mercy is not strain'd". Shakespeare, *Merchant of Venice*, 4.1.181–82.

5. Greek historian of the fifth century BCE. According to Thucydides, the Odrysians, whose territory included parts of modern Greece, Bulgaria and Turkey, did give gifts, as incentives to getting things done. Gift-giving also seems to have been characteristic of Xerxes, king of the Persians from 486 to 465 BCE.

EDITORIAL: LIFE, WORK AND SUCCESS

SUCCESS IS A SCIENCE. LIKE ANY other science it has its axioms which can be broken down into principles of action, and which can be learned.

A great many people don't realize this; they go through life hoping. But, as Lord Beaverbrook[1] once said: "Don't trust to Luck." Luck is like the sirens of Scylla and Charybdis,[2] temptresses that took, and still take, men to their doom.

It has been said that the day is divided into three equal parts: eight hours for sleep, eight hours for work; and eight for enjoyment. But let work be a pleasure and you then have eight hours for sleep and sixteen for enjoyment.

Perhaps you smile – a cynical smile. Perhaps you say to yourself: what nonsense is this. But let us think a little, let us try to analyse the nature of work. Without work we cannot improve our conditions of life. Had our forefathers, going way back to Neanderthal man, sat on their haunches and done nothing with the hostile world in which they found themselves, we would long since have become extinct as a human family. Indeed, the immediate ancestors of Man may never have evolved into Man: in short, the human family would have remained unborn.

Looking back upon our experience of earth-life, does this thought bother you very much? Has life on earth been worthwhile? We think the answers to these questions will go a long way towards defining what work really is.

We can only speak for ourselves. Without attempting to delve into the mystery of the source of life, we can face the reality by saying that life is, and has always been – as far as our Earth goes. In every stone, in every brook, in every tree, in every beast, in every insect, in every fish, in every man – there is life. Therefore, life must have been coeval with Creation – eternal backward as well as forward, if we may use a clumsy phrase. So that life is obviously a force which is part and parcel of all matter – has been from the beginning – that had no beginning, and shall be to the end – that shall have no end.

If our reasoning has any meaning at all, then surely the earth that has been offered us as a place for experimenting with multiform life is an exciting, an exhilarating stage for human beings in the evolution of their minds and spirits. In other words, a worthwhile phase – apart altogether from the aesthetic and emotional thrills we derive from the natural beauties of cloud and field and hill.

So far so good. But look at life from the back, from the front, from above, from below, and we see this *élan vital*, as Henri Bergson[3] called it, in an irrepressible state of unending flux. The movement never ceases; the mutations go on and on. Mountains are upheaved from submerged land, from flatland with the infinitely ponderous rhythm of Time itself. Cold gives way to heat – and then to cold again. Dinosaurus dies. The prehistoric primates come – an aeon creeps by and they change into man. What more restless than life?

This is precisely why life is life – it is restless until it dies; and then it rests, for death is stillness, absolute stillness. It is the restlessness of life that perpetuates life, that has driven men from generation to generation into taking what they have found on earth and changing it for the better – sometimes for the worse, but for every three steps, two are forward and only one is backward. The restlessness that forges the changes, this is the quality in life that makes work what it is: another restlessness that is not another at all, but life itself. Restlessness – life: they are synonyms. Rest – death: these too are synonyms. Restlessness – work: for just as life is restlessness, so is life work; and work, restlessness.

You may think we have come to the end of the road but we haven't. Let us return to the opening sentence of this editorial: "Success is a science." We are a long way – or so at first glance it seems – from that flat statement and if we are to prove our case to the hilt we must tie this statement to all that we have said about work and life and restlessness. Do you see any relationship between the two: success and life?

We confess that we do. We confess that we see a relationship that is organic, functional, for the very nature of the restlessness of life presupposes a striving after perfection – or success – which, of course, is never reached. There cannot be perfection, there can only be a ceaseless striving after perfection. There can never be perfection because perfection is God and Man cannot be God. The success that Man achieves is thrust upon him by the restlessness of life, by work; and work, no matter what form or direction it takes, springs from the creative urge with which all men are born.

And now we have arrived at a very important thing indeed. What is the creative urge? So far, we have been talking about the restlessness of life and work, in other words the forces that lie outside of Man. The creative urge is that compulsion inside of Man, that piece of the restlessness of life that is lodged in each of us – in a very few cases, large pieces (these are the geniuses), in the vast majority of cases, small pieces. This is the demon, the fury inside of Man that drives him, willy-nilly, into work. Ask Michelangelo what his creative urge did for him. Ask Beethoven, Shakespeare, ask Einstein and Galileo, ask Kant and Henry Ford, ask Picasso what their creative urge did for them and we'll wager with one voice that they will reply: "It made us touch life at its highest point." Is this not another way of saying: "It made us supremely happy"?

So, to return to your cynical smile in the fourth paragraph of this editorial, wipe it off your face. We were dead serious when we talked of eight hours of sleep and sixteen of enjoyment. In work we are creating: a great number of us keep our civilization moving forward to those points where massive advances occur. To create is to enjoy life, the full content of life, its overflowing cup, and it can never be anything but work that gives us that feeling of being most alive.

The point of all this is that idleness is misery, despair, desolation of the spirit – remember that Goethe, the famous German poet,[4] calls despair "the second soul of the unhappy" – whereas work is exhilaration, aliveness, happiness. In work we come nearest to God and in our nearness to God we stand upon the tip-toe of life.

But now it is time to get down to the brass tacks of everyday living and to use the argument we have advanced in our editorial. We start by saying that every year we must set ourselves a target. We must say to ourselves: "By the end of this year I shall have achieved such-and-such a promotion" or "I will have increased my earnings by so much." Don't make your target too far-fetched or extravagant. Study yourself and see if you can assess the size of the creative urge with which you are endowed – and then set your goal. Keep it reasonable – and then achieve it. If you have never tried this before, try it now. You'll be amazed at the intense satisfaction, the profound happiness you will derive from the experiment. The happiness, the exaltation will be akin to what the painter, the music-maker, the scientist, the industrialist gets from his work.

After all, promotion never takes the dedicated man by surprise. He is ready for it. He is master of his job and master of his ambition. His eye is on the step above. He is prepared for opportunities, indeed, sometimes he even makes them himself – or he takes them when they come along.

Consider the men at the top. All of them started with the universal instinct to create – which is only another way of saying that they started with nothing more than any of us. We can hear what you are thinking: education, background, pull. But where have our world's great men really come from? Look into our history books, read the stories that have been written about the men who carried our civilization forward from peak to peak, the men who exemplified the restlessness of life to the utter extreme: from what beginnings did they emerge?

For heaven's sake, let us stop blaming everybody but ourselves for our "bad luck". Let us put self-pity behind us as Christ put the Devil: "Get thee behind me, Satan." The world owes no human being a living; it is we who must do for ourselves what the world cannot do for us. The restlessness of life propels us forward and upward: resist and death takes over.

Trinidad Singer 3, no. 9 (1966)

NOTES

1. William Maxwell Aitken, first Baron Beaverbrook (1879–1964). He owned the London newspapers the *Daily Express*, *Sunday Express* and *Evening Standard*.
2. Of these mythical monsters, though all were cannibals, only the Sirens were temptresses, sweet-voiced singers, part-women, part-birds and with the claws

of leopards, who lured sailors to their deaths with song. Scylla was a woman with three heads who perched on a rock and picked sailors off the decks of their ships with her snake-like heads, and Charybdis was believed to be a monster who lived at the bottom of a whirlpool and sucked voyagers down to their doom.

3. The French philosopher (1859–1941). The phrase, which means "vital impulse", occurs in *L'Évolution Créatrice* (*Creative Evolution*), 1907.

4. The Romantic writer Johann Wolfgang von Goethe (1749–1832).

Letters

TWO LETTERS FROM GEORGE PADMORE
TO ALFRED H. MENDES

Regent Palace Hotel
December 1950
Friday 5.30 p.m.

Dear Alfred,

Sorry to have missed you. I presume that you took the kid[1] to a show. I called at Clifford Hotel and was told to come here. I went to your room 798 but got no reply. Enquired if you had left a note for me saying when you would be back, but found nothing. Well, farewell and bon voyage. I hope you and the kid have a safe and pleasant voyage. Take care of Dorothy[2] when she comes out. If she finds her feet, I have advised her to stay away from dying Europe until the storm is over. The crisis years will be 1953–1954. This will give me time to get away. I feel the urgent need to get back to help the "barefoot masses". That is a job to be done and I see none of the careerist middle-class politicians "going to the people". I am leaving you a pamphlet on the W. Indies which I published after the riots in 1936–1937 to enlighten the British public on W.I. affairs. Sir Stafford Cripps[3] [is] an old friend of mine and the printers. He is very interested in the W. Indies and helped Manley[4] found the P.N.P. The other pamphlet will throw light on Africa. Watch developments on the Gold Coast[5] next year. Thanks for the "naughty" book. D and myself read it last night but it taught us nothing new. However, it was entertaining. The tie is to enable you to present yourself on arrival as a "city gentleman". Hope the wife approves of my taste. The photos will remind you of one of your great admirers. Do keep the fire burning. Our country badly needs more Alfred Mendes's [*sic*]. One day we shall meet again. Until then, God speed you on your way.

Affectionately yours,
George Padmore

Love to Carlton, Gomes, Quintin, and give a kiss to Doris.[6]

22 Cranleigh House
Cranleigh Street
London N.W.1.
22 March 1951

[Dear Alfred,]

I must offer you my apologies for not replying before. Since Dorothy's departure I find myself overwhelmed with work, for so much of the domestic arrangements which we shared for 15 years have [*sic*] now fallen on my shoulders. Added to which, I have been exceedingly busy helping to direct the recent Gold Coast elections, as I am the London representative of the Convention People's Party.[7] You might of [*sic*] heard of our sweeping victory. I do hope it will be an inspiration to our local politicians. I shall try and keep in touch with you, but I am expecting to fly out to the Gold Coast with some Labour M.P.s soon and don't know when I shall be back. There is so much to do and so little time! The international situation is threatening, but the general atmosphere here is a burning desire for PEACE. There has been a remarkable anti-American feeling developing here among the intellectuals and the LEFT. Did I send you Professor G.D.H. Cole's letter in the New Statesman and Nation? If not, Dorothy has a copy and she can let you read it. Do you ever see her? She has already got a fundamental grasp of the local situation and writes me enthusiastically of the people and their potentialities. I had the pleasure of meeting Beryl McBurnie.[8] The most interesting woman

I have ever met from the W. Indies. For I know only too well the cramp [*sic*] mid-Victorian atmosphere in which most of our young women still live. It must have required great moral courage on her part to inaugurate the "Little Carib". I heard that you did much to inspire her. It is the best cultural effort that London has ever seen from the Caribbean. As regards your observations of Peter's[9] books. We enjoyed your comments, but Peter like myself, cannot agree with you as regards his superiority as an artist over Richard Wright.[10] As we are all good friends, we were able to approach your evaluation objectively. Peter has great promise but surely he lacks the depth and delineative abilities of Dick. "Native Son" is a profound psychological work; which if Dick writes nothing else again will have established for him a permanent place in the literature of the first half of the century. Like Dostoevsky's novels, "Native Son" is a powerful social document and indictment on a social system – Americanism. Or is it the American way of life? I am so old fashion [*sic*] I never seem able to keep up with the current euphemisms. Well, I must close now. How is your son? I heard from Carlton that he sustained some injury.[11] I do hope that the lad is better. I look forward to meeting you again either here or in P-of-S. where we can have a meal in one of your exotic restaurants and talk over art, literature and life. We are passing through one of the great crises in human society and we dare not predict a future. It's interesting to reread the letters of Cicero, and compare today with the crisis the old Roman faced with the disintegration of the Republic. To understand the present one must turn back to the past. Who will be the Gibbon[12] of the 20th century?

With my best wishes and respects to your wife.

Your compatriot

G.P.

NOTES

1. "The kid" was Irene Mendes, later Schirmacher, daughter of Mendes's eldest son Alfred John "Alf" and his wife Cathy. She was then three and a half months short of her fifth birthday. She remembers spending one night at the Regent Palace Hotel before taking the boat for Trinidad, arriving in Port of Spain (she thinks) on Christmas Day, 1950.

2. Dorothy Pizer, Padmore's partner and co-worker.

3. Sir Richard Stafford Cripps (1889–1952) was a politician in the British Labour Party.

4. The Jamaican lawyer, politician and national hero Norman Washington Manley (1893–1969) founded the People's National Party in Jamaica in 1938.

5. Modern Ghana in West Africa.

6. Carlton Comma was a librarian and member of the *Beacon* group of writers and intellectuals. Albert Gomes, the *Beacon's* editor, was a writer and politician. Quintin O'Connor was a union leader, activist and politician. I have not been able to identify Doris.

7. The Convention People's Party was founded in 1949 in the then Gold Coast by Dr Kwame Nkrumah to help pressure Britain into granting the country its independence.

8. In 1950 Beryl McBurnie was awarded a scholarship by the British Council for a familiarization tour of Europe and a course in physical training methods. She took it up in September of that year. During this period she met Alfred Mendes and Eric Murray in Spain and George Padmore in London.

9. The South African writer Peter Abrahams (1919–).

10. See introduction, xxxiv.

11. Peter Mendes, then aged twelve, had a pocketful of torpedoes (illegal firecrackers) which exploded while he was playing football. He was badly burned on the upper thigh. He was told by the doctor that had penicillin not been invented and available – he was on it for four weeks – he would most probably have lost his leg. (Tosca Mendes, with some assistance from Peter).

12. Edward Gibbon (1737–1794), the British historian and man of letters, and author of *The History of the Decline and Fall of the Roman Empire*.

GLOSSARY OF TRINIDADIAN WORDS AND PHRASES

barrack-room. Room in a barrack-yard

barrack-yard. Tenement consisting of two rows of wooden buildings facing each other across a communal yard space used for cooking and washing clothes

behind God's back. Somewhere remote, far from towns and people

Boca. Mouth (Spanish); the island of Trinidad is separated from the mainland of South America by channels, the Bocas del Dragón (Dragon's Mouths) in the north, and the Bocas de la Sierpe (Serpent's Mouths) in the south

bongo. A dance of African origin performed to drumming especially by men, at wakes in honour of the dead

callaloo. Soup or vegetable dish made from dasheen leaves and coconut milk, which may include okras, dumplings and salt beef, and especially crab; the term is used by extension to mean a mixture of different ingredients

calypso. A popular satirical song aimed at recognizable people or situations, and providing social commentary

cane squeezer. A small hand mill used to extract the juices from sugar cane

conch-shell. The large, decorative shell of the marine conch which, when cut at the closed end, is used as a musical instrument to summon people to a gathering, or to sound a warning

dougla. Person of mixed African and Indian descent

down the islands. A cluster of small islands in the Dragon's Mouths, some with holiday homes built on them. A favourite area of Trinidadians for boating and picnicking

eddoe. An edible tuber. Unlike the tannia (q.v.) its leaves are not edible

flambeau. Torch made of wood wrapped in a cloth soaked in pitchoil and set alight (French)

galvanize. A corrugated metal sheet coated with zinc to prevent corrosion, widely used in the Caribbean for roofing and fencing

kerosene tin. Tin which originally contained kerosene, used across the Caribbean for storage and cooking

keskidee. Bird of the family of Tyrant Flycatchers, named for its cry of "Qu'est-ce qu'il dit?" (French: "What is he saying?")

manicou. Opossum, a nocturnal marsupial rodent, brown with pointed snout, big ears, and long prehensile tail; hunted for its meat

moko jumby/jumbie. Male carnival character dressed in rags, who dances on stilts.

mountain dew. Illegally distilled rum

musti. Person of mixed race, usually with one black and one white parent

papelon. Dark brown sugar shaped into a cone or cut into squares and wrapped in banana leaves

Pitch Walk. An asphalted path on the perimeter of the Queen's Park Savannah; a favourite walking area for the inhabitants of Port of Spain

pitchoil lamp. Lamp with a hollow base, usually made of glass, filled with kerosene, and lit by a wick soaked in kerosene

poui. A decorative shade tree which flowers annually in the dry season with masses of yellow or pink blossoms

praise. Prayers

prickly yam. Yellow yam, a root vegetable with prickly stems

provision(s). Usually eddoes, yams, dasheen and other starchy tubers

Savannah. The Queen's Park Savannah in Port of Spain, Trinidad, a large park of about 232 acres known as "the lungs of Port of Spain"

spree. Party (noun and verb)

tannia. Edible tuber with large, arrow-shaped green leaves, also edible, on long stalks

tattoo. Armadillo, a small mammal with protective shield plates on its body; hunted for its meat (also spelled *tatou*)

BIBLIOGRAPHY

WORKS BY ALFRED H. MENDES

The Autobiography of Alfred H. Mendes. Edited by Michèle Levy. Kingston: University of the West Indies Press, 2002.

Black Fauns. London: Gerald Duckworth, 1935. Reprint, Millwood, NY: Kraus Reprints, 1970; London and Port of Spain: New Beacon Books, 1984.

The Man Who Ran Away and Other Stories of Trinidad in the 1920s and 1930s. Edited by Michèle Levy. Kingston: University of the West Indies Press, 2006.

Pablo's Fandango and Other Stories. Edited by Michèle Levy. London: Addison, Wesley and Longman, 1997.

Pitch Lake. London: Gerald Duckworth, 1934. Reprint, Millwood, NY: Kraus Reprints, 1970; London and Port of Spain: New Beacon Books, 1980.

The Poet's Quest. London: Heath Cranton, 1927.

Selected Writings of Alfred H. Mendes. Edited by Michèle Levy. Kingston: University of the West Indies Press, 2013.

Spare Moments. Port of Spain: Spack Printing Office, 1924.

Three Poems. Port of Spain: N.p., 1924.

The Wages of Sin and Other Poems. Port of Spain: Yuille's Printerie, 1925.

SECONDARY SOURCES

Allsopp, Richard. *Dictionary of Caribbean Usage.* Oxford: Oxford University Press, 1996. Reprint, Kingston: University of the West Indies Press, 2003.

Anthony, Michael. *The Making of Port-of-Spain,* vol. 1, *The History of Port-of-Spain, 1757–1939.* Cascade, Trinidad: Paria, 2007.

———. *The Making of Port-of-Spain,* vol. 2, *Port-of-Spain in a World at War, 1939–1945.* Cascade, Trinidad: Paria, 2008.

Baptiste, Rhona. *Trini Talk: A Dictionary of Words and Proverbs of Trinidad and Tobago*. Port of Spain: Caribbean Information Systems and Services, 1994.

Besson, Gérard, and Bridget Brereton, eds. *The Book of Trinidad*. Port of Spain: Paria, 1992.

Brereton, Bridget. *A History of Modern Trinidad, 1783–1962*. Oxford: Heinemann International, 1989.

de Boissière, Ralph. *Life on the Edge: The Autobiography of Ralph de Boissière*, ed. Kenneth Ramchand. Caroni, Trinidad: Lexicon, 2010.

Look Lai, Walton. *The Chinese in the West Indies, 1806–1995. A Documentary History*. Kingston: University of the West Indies Press, 1998.

Mendes, John. *Cote ce, Cote la: Trinidad and Tobago Dictionary*. Arima, Trinidad: N.p., 1986.

Sander, Reinhard W., ed. *From Trinidad with Love: An Anthology of Early West Indian Writing*. London: Hodder and Stoughton; New York: Holmes and Meier, 1978.

———. *The Trinidad Awakening: West Indian Literature of the 1930s*. Westport, CT: Greenwood, 1988.

———. "The Turbulent Thirties in Trinidad. An Interview with Alfred H. Mendes. Port of Spain, 6 October, 1972". University of Texas at Austin, Texas.

Stone, Judy S.J. *Theatre*. Studies in West Indian Literature, ed. Kenneth Ramchand. London: Macmillan, 1994.

Winer, Lise. *Dictionary of the English Creole of Trinidad and Tobago*. Montreal: McGill–Queen's University Press, 2009.

INDEX

ACKNOWLEDGEMENTS

I continue to be grateful to all at the University of the West Indies Press for their cheerfulness, helpfulness and informed, tactful guidance of my writings to the finished products. Very special thanks to Linda Speth, who has made it all happen.

Another constant is my typist, Jennifer Thompson, who has endured pressure of deadlines, radical changes, last-minute additions of vitally important material somehow overlooked – all the usual problems attendant on the preparation of a manuscript – and has coped with endless patience, tolerance and efficiency. Couldn't have managed without you, Jen!

Alfred Mendes's family have always supported my work enthusiastically. Their generous assistance in supplying details of Mendes's life, usually in response to frantic email messages, has enabled me to shape a picture of the man as well as the writer, both for myself and for his readers.

My greatest debt is to Alfred H. Mendes himself. His sister-in-law Ruth Mendes once remarked to me: "I loved Alfy! He was *fun!*" I have had my own fun in working with Mendes's writing for over twenty years now. I would have loved to have known the man.

www.ingramcontent.com/pod-product-compliance
Lightning Source LLC
Chambersburg PA
CBHW021648110726
47902CB00007B/1878